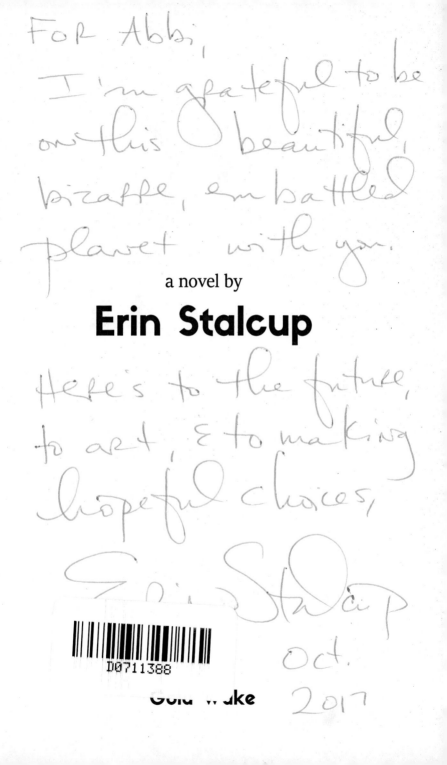

For Abbi,
I'm grateful to be
on this beautiful,
bizarre, embattled
planet with you.

a novel by

Erin Stalcup

Here's to the future,
to art, & to making
hopeful choices,

Erin Stalcup
Oct.
2017

Gold Wake

EVERY

LIV

ING

SPECIES

Contents

Saturday, September 9th, 2023

Sunday, September 10th, 2023

for Mom and Dad, the very best parents

Arte Poética
Si no quieres quedarte a mirar la tormenta
Yo la miro por ti.
                    —Juan Antonio González-Iglesias

Ars Poetica
If you don't want to stay and watch the storm
I will watch it for you.
                    —Translated Curtis Bauer

I.

"WE'RE DOOMED! What's the Appropriate Response?"

Arrow Sullivan read the headline of the paperless newspaper to her mother and father amongst scattered take out containers flecked with tostada and relleno. All that Styrofoam was made from mycelium. They'd eaten dinner on the deck like they did most summer nights, but this was the first time since their five acres of forest had been scorched. "Supporters of The Aviary say it will be the first living museum, the only place in the world where people can see every species of bird known to humankind. Critics say that this is the first admittance that all the world's species cannot be saved, and a haven for the few serves as an emblem of eminent extinction for the rest." Arrow had a quiet voice, but she enunciated well. She'd felt hollow since the fire, but now the air was cool and bright with the ozone tang of coming rain, her mouth was warmed by spice, and she told herself to relax. She looked up at azure sky and iridescent-edged clouds through too-long purple bangs. Her mother was always reaching to sweep hair out of Arrow's eyes. As a child Arrow found this judgmental, a tidying, but now she knew her mother just liked a chance to touch her grown child's face. Arrow had told the stylist she wanted heliotrope hair, and Arrow was always turning toward the sun, even as the ultraviolet burnt her skin, even as she wore hats and salves against it she basked and baked in the rays, wide cheeks warming even as people warned her to turn away; and Arrow was always waiting for rain.

"I'm glad you had an appetite," said Siobhan, Arrow's mom. Arrow was ravenous. Her father hadn't finished his plate. Then, "I think you two should still go," Siobhan said. "You can't do anything more about this." She gestured in front of them: blackened trunks of ponderosa pines and burnt undergrowth. "It might be good to get away."

The setting sun made the ponderosas shimmer, their needles glinting along the edges. In early summer the wind was constant, a daily aggravation in this part of the world, but their swaying made the trees seem alive. The sun heated their trunks until they released a sweet scent, like dough; nature produced the vanilla bean but it was surprising for a stoic, armored plant to smell like sustenance. Yet its spines tasted acrid if you bit them, a mouth full of herbal tang, the way a plant in the high desert should taste, Arrow always thought. You couldn't touch two trees at once on their land and it was easy to walk amongst them, feel with them. They grew slowly, but seemed sentient. Patient. And they looked the same, now, just—darkened. The fire hadn't ascended the trunks to the branches. *Charred, not burned*, Arrow said again and again to herself. Their cores were okay.

Sullivans had lived on these five acres for three generations. Arrow's grandfather bought and built on the land in the 1960s, and she carried the arrowhead chipped from volcanic glass that he'd found while laying the foundation, evidence that others had lived here before. She and her father, Grant, had worked for years to protect the land from fire, their acres in the middle of the largest ponderosa pine forest in the world. Throughout the drought in Arizona they soaked their soil with purchased water along the dripline, the circumference under the longest limbs of each tree, where the roots grew to their thinnest point, best able to drink rain dripping from branches. And they thinned their forest back to the historical average, eighty per acre, trees far enough apart that a crown fire couldn't start, fire couldn't climb and jump from treetop to treetop. Fire used to come through the forest and clean it, kill the small, weak trees, leave only the largest trees behind. But non-Native people decided fire was destructive, only, and fought it, so the forest thickened to the point that a blaze could annihilate it all. Because of their work this fire passed through quickly, singed but didn't kill their trees. Arrow looked out at the obsidian-barked pines, the ash layer over their cinder dirt, stones made by a volcano a millennium ago, and she told herself this was exactly what was supposed to happen.

They'd driven around to see how their neighbors fared. The acres south and west of them were destroyed, the treetops burnt so just a matter of time before they fell. The Lewises lost their house. The fire had dropped at the perimeter of their property. Their acres would soon stand alone, separated from the rest of the forest.

In truth, Arrow needed a distraction.

"But it would be a shock all over again to see it when we return," Grant said. He and Arrow were both taking it hard, this best-case scenario.

Her mother was the optimist. "Maybe," Siobhan said. "But the monsoons will be here soon, and they might wash away some soot. A lot can change in eight weeks. You have time to decide, but I think you should do it." Her mom loved the land, its stark splendor, but she wasn't as tied to it as they were. She'd moved here from Boston. "You have the tickets. You've always wanted to see New York. And the contest—a chance to see every kind of bird on earth! And it's your birthday present." Arrow was turning twenty-one.

Arrow had been to Boston, but vacation for her and her family had mostly been camping trips in the states that bordered Arizona. Her mother's family's East Coast snobbery turned her into a West Coast snob. Her cousins summered in Bar Harbor or The Hamptons or Cape Cod and Arrow didn't remember which was which and would respond, "I'll backpack in Bryce for two weeks," or, "I'm swamping all summer," then patiently explain hoodoos and her job doing grunt labor for paying tourists during trips down the Colorado River, looking up at The Canyon's striations. She'd describe how different the rapids were now that the river's level was so much lower. Arrow felt ownership of her region. She would love to backpack through Europe and Asia like her cousins did, but her parents made less money than her aunts and uncles, and Arrow had to work in the summer to buy books and pay rent. Arrow went to college in Flagstaff, her hometown, because she'd gotten scholarships. She'd seen Las Vegas's version of New York and Paris and Cairo and Bellagio, and now that London was being evacuated she'd heard they were building a replica in Vegas, but Arrow knew she'd never seen anything like New York City.

She wanted to go. She wanted to see it.

At the northern tip of Manhattan, the sixty-six acres of Fort Tryon Park had been transformed into The Aviary. Climate zones were built to house twelve of every living species of bird on earth—Polar, Desert, Coastal, and three kinds of forest: Deciduous, Coniferous, Rain. To launch this museum, Cabela's and Canon teamed up to host the Birds of the World Timed Birding Contest. One thousand pairs of birders would be the first to see The Aviary and would compete: three days to identify as many species as possible; on the fourth day ten million dollars would be awarded to the first place pair. Each of the 250 sovereign nations had sponsored a team; the United States sponsored fifty indigenous teams; there were fifty indigenous teams representing the rest of the globe; the ACLU sponsored fifty Visibility Teams made up of underrepresented individuals; Amnesty International sponsored one hundred Peace Teams combining members from nations that had experienced recent or historical conflict; and there were five hundred pairs of paying customers.

This is what the birds would see if they ventured beyond the climate where they were most comfortable, though they didn't have language to say it: a glare of barren white, a swath of verdant green, scarlet desert sand, a lucent lake, a sea. Alpine lichen abutted arctic ice, cacti stood adjacent to grassland, and all three kinds of forest flanked each other—leafed, needled, jungle—just like on the planet, but compressed. No walls separated environments, so contestants would walk under a canopy of branches and arrive in the tropics, moisture streaming from unseen machines in the sky. Nearby, mechanisms masked as stones circulated frigid air in the late New York summer, kept ice intact for a small space, and contraptions released snow every hour on the hour. Chilled air drifted away at the edges, transitioned to a woodland of spruces, firs, and pines. Farther along, contestants could stand between a miniature ocean and a freshwater lake, see two shores at once. Sand led to the arid zone, where an apparatus baked the liquid out of the air. The tightest knit of chain-link surrounded the park, an optical-fiber canopy stretched overhead.

Inwood Hill Park had been converted to a campground for contestants: 196 acres of original forest north of The Aviary, the only place in the city you could still see trees that had been alive for over a century. Many New Yorkers thought the parks were what was left of prehistoric forest, and skyscrapers had grown around what had been preserved, but in fact most of Manhattan Island had been flat as a field. Fort Tryon Park had been rocky and thin-soiled until nearly one hundred years before when Frederick Law Olmsted brought in fertile dirt, planted oaks, moved boulders, scooped out promenades. Olmsted positioned every stone in Central Park, situated each tree, dug and filled the lake, then duplicated his work in Fort Tryon. The architects for the Canon and Cabela's Birds of the World Timed Birding Contest pulled out Olmsted's maples, replaced them with palms and piñons.

The masses were gathering, preparing to compete to see who could witness the most beauty, bringing their cravings and fancies and fears, drawn as if the colored lines of subway tracks on maps stretched across the globe to wrap people and pull them close—and New York City was planning a party to greet the beginning of the end of the world.

American Ballet Theatre would perform a double bill of Swan Lake and Firebird. The Metropolitan Opera would present *Die Vogel*. The Museum of Natural History would have an exhibit called "Extinction": one wing holding paintings, photos, and stuffed specimens of every extinct bird, so contestants could come as close as possible to seeing every species that ever existed; a wing featuring taxidermy of other extinct animals; a wing of artifacts and relics of extinct peoples and languages; and of course dinosaurs. Revive & Restore sponsored an exhibit called "De-Extinct," where you could see live species that had been returned, but weren't quite yet ready for release into the wild. The Cloisters showcased medieval conceptions of birds, tapestries, and illuminated manuscripts. Art galleries hosted Brandon Ballengee's erasures of Audubon's prints, Frederick Murphy's and Alicia Kanade's photographs of viruses that could decimate the human population, and photographs from *National Geographic* entitled "What Still Remains." Banksy's retirement project would be to graffiti a bird a day in an obscure location during the month of September so some could search outside of the park, for free, and the resuscitated piano bar Rose's Turn would host an all-bird-name drag show, emceed by Tequila Mockingbird. Most bars would feature bird-themed cocktail specials; some restaurants would feature fowl-free menus for the duration, while others would run ostrich and squab and quail and pheasant and turkey specials beyond the regular chicken. "Come see the spectacle!" the papers all proclaimed. "Celebrate obliteration in all five boroughs."

London fashion designer Alastair Askgold was there to study plumage for his next collection. Local Dominican/Cuban American film director Ivan Ríos was there to teach a course in apocalypse cinema and promote his new movie, *Passenger*, about de-extinct zombie Passenger Pigeons. Icelandic climatologist Thorbjorn Hjálmarsson and Baltic climatologist Dalia von Uexküll were a team; two Vatican priests in vestments; two female members of the International Brotherhood of Electrical

Workers; two female physicists; Thankful Alton, the descendent of a witch with the same name who was tried in New England fifteen generations ago, and the descendent of the minister who tried her, Michael Moody; two transgender men; two transgender women; a genderless team; a contestant from The Republic of Ireland paired with a contestant from Northern Ireland, Israel and Palestine, Serbia and Bosnia and Herzegovina, Sudan and South Sudan, North Korea and South Korea, Russia and Georgia, Russia and Syria, China and Tibet, the United States and North Korea, the United States and Vietnam, the United States and Afghanistan, the United States and Iraq, the United States and Iran; an interracial couple from South Africa; two gay Saudi men who'd been offered sanctuary in Sweden; animal activists seeking to infiltrate and release the birds; experts with Life Lists 8,057 birds long; a woman who lives in a walled subdivision in São Paolo and a woman from the favela of Cidade de Deus; a team of climate-change deniers; Sami from Sweden; Maasai from Africa; Maya from Belize; fifty US tribal teams—Coeur d'Alene, Nez Perce, Lenape, Abenaki, Kānaka Maoli, Inupiaq, Aleut, Kiowa, Osage, Massachusett, Narragansett, Lakota Sioux, Dakota Sioux, Salish, Mohawk, Tillamook, Tohono O'odham, Iroquois, Quechan, Caddo, Catawba, Cayuga, Chippewa, Chickasaw, Chumash, Chinook, Cheyenne, Cherokee, Crow, Creek, Comanche, Apache, Arapahoe, Powhatan, Penobscot, Pequot, Pawnee, Absentee-Shawnee, Duckwater Shoshone, Paiute, Ute, Blackfeet, Hopi, Diné, Hualapai, Havasupai, Ho-Chunk, Kickapoo, Acoma, Zia—less than five percent of the tribes that exist; two Appalachian miners who removed the top of their own mountain; citizens of Nagorno-Karabakh

Republic; citizens of Pridnestrovian Moldavian Republic; Republic of Abkhazia; Kosovo; Taiwan; Gibraltar; Greenland; Brunei; Seychelles; a team from the underwater nation of Kiribati, a country with no land, but citizens. Arrow and Grant Sullivan were there to see it. Academi was hired as mercenary security, in case problems arose.

Thursday, September 7th, 2023

The Day Before Canon and Cabela's
Birds of the World
Timed Birding Contest

II.
Solomon

Called rats with wings because why? They don't bite. They don't spread disease. Dis-ease people feel because they might get shat on from the sky, okay. But pigeons poop while perching, not while flying. Those rats that brought the plague, pigeons are nothing like that. They each have a personality, a style, a way of bopping through the world. Some fast. Some slow. I'm not sure if they're happy or not. You can't tell from looking at me. I'm slow. I used to be fast. I feed them, yes, sometimes before and sometimes after I feed myself. Am I happy? None of these reporters ask me that. They ask me nothing. I'm not there. Not where the action is. The fancy birds. The police, they asked me to move. They were polite. Dark sunglasses. They know me. They tried not to embarrass me, yes. When they said the city wanted to present as clean an image as possible of New York, they said, "Not that you're dirty, Sol, just, you know, you keep yourself up real well, but people without a home make the city looked flawed. Here's fifty bucks. Sleep elsewhere for a week." Not enough money to pay for a place, they know that, but I wouldn't want to be inside anyway. Sleeping outside when it's hot is what rich folk used to do. On porches. I pay attention to the city in a way those within walls never do. The way different insects sing in September rather than in May. How cars slip in January. Yes, I make do even in winter. We have our ways. It's not hard at all in the summertime here. No, I do not beg. I am a small businessman. For decades, since before recycling was hip, since before it was an expectation, starting back when we thought it might save us, I've collected Washington Heights' bottles and gotten paid to do it. It used to be the only way those things got remade or reused was if someone took them to the facility. All those soda and beer and fizzy-water drinkers pay five, then seven, cents per, and I get their deposits back! Now trucks will pick up all recyclables—put them in clear bags so waste workers can see what's inside, for a while, now every residence has a green bin and a black one for compost. But the people on my block, we keep the old economy. They put their bottles in brown paper bags and I know they're for me to take. Started small—Ms. Ramirez said to me, "Solomon, I don't have time to run my bottles to the center, would you want to do it for me?" Said it so some neighbors could hear, and said, when I brought her back her two dollars and change, "No, you keep it, you did the work." I gave her back her bag, and she started setting it in the garbage area and more and more appeared and then other buildings too. Never did drink. No drugs. There's no easy flaw here to see. I'm here, talking to myself because no one talks to me. And it felt that way even when I had a house and a job and looked like you. Most of you. Felt like no one was ever talking to me. So I let it all slip away, piece by piece. I make enough to get by. I eat just fine. Plenty for the pigeons, too. Good food, seeds and fruit and what they really need, not bread and fries others give them. I buy books and talk to the dead. I don't ask you why you are the way you are. The rats didn't bring the plague, anyway, it was the fleas on their backs. Who do we blame for who rides on whom? I live off of other people's waste. I drink milk out of returnable cartons. I return. The newspaper tells me some people in India live in garbage dumps, eat and wear and live inside what others throw away. I don't have one of those paperless devices, those iPills people read and see everything on now, see everything through. Those flexible, foldable tablets. I feel like they keep paper newspapers going just for me. The newspaper is flexible and foldable. I buy everything I have. Warm coats at the Goodwill. I carry the same briefcase I always did. I didn't steal a shopping cart, I bought a laundry cart at the bodega. When it's warm, I take baths at the beach. It's easy to get away from people in this city. People aren't ashamed of me in shops. I look raggedy, but I am not dirty. I don't camp where other homeless people converge. They aren't any more compassionate or thoughtful or insightful than anyone else. Aren't any worse, either. I have the same hard time talking to them. There's a colony in most parks up here. Isham and Gorman and Bennett and J. Hood Wright, whoever he was. They never name parks after women. I had a riverfront view until they asked me to move, said people from all over the world were coming to camp in my park like I do every day. I stay away from people too because I like to feed the pigeons, and most people don't like that. Get annoyed when a flock gathers. The gust and feathers in their own food. They're afraid of getting pooped on, that's all it is. Pigeon poop can eat away stone. It can also fertilize gardens. They say because I feed them there are more of them, but I think I'm just feeding what's already there. They could eat without me, sure. They're smart. We produce plenty of waste in this city. But if I can make it easier for them to get full, why not? They're good at survival. But why not make things easier. I like their company. Their nice voices. To keep them away people use spikes, nets, sticky gels, coiled wire barriers, ultrasonic noisemakers, holographic frighteners, fake owls, electrified strips. They put the birds in houses and steal eggs and replace them with fake eggs so they make no more babies. I suppose people would like less of me too. Feral descendants of a once-domesticated species. You can make pigeons fancy, but you have to get involved to change them. If you let them be, they all pretty much look the same. But there are differences. Some more copper pink, some more light, some very patterned. I like pigeons more than people, yes. I live on the periphery of this city. Pigeons live everywhere. People raise them on their roofs. They've asked me to move farther to the edge and I have, for the time being.

III.
Ivan Ríos
and Alastair Askgold

The theater was packed with his students: eighteen-year-old freshmen just starting at NYU, taking a summer class with a semi-famous professor to get ahead, middle-aged New Yorkers who took classes for fun. A soft launch in his classroom, before the world premiere at Radio City Music Hall tomorrow night. The film was unchangeable now, but seeing the reaction of a group who wanted the best for him would prepare Ivan to see the reactions of the critics. He was the kind of artist that made narrow work: if one person got it, he was content. Or a few. Famous in certain circles, big in the Bronx but not yet in the center—somewhat famous as an academic, but not yet as an artist—the thing he wanted most. But it was also the final day of class, and he needed to wrap up his students' learning even as he unveiled his own creation.

He stood on the stage in front of the pewter screen, walked and gestured while he spoke, his classroom persona turned on: glasses, slim-fit blazer over a t-shirt and jeans, leather Chelsea boots. He wondered what the London fashion designer he'd just met thought of what he was wearing—his randomly assigned partner for the birding contest, the man who'd tagged along to see his film—but Ivan didn't let the thought linger. It was time to teach. "My goal in this course has been to show highlights from the evolution of the cinema of catastrophe. We began with monster movies—those ancient classics that look so campy to our eyes, so fun—Frankenstein's monster; Gojira and all the American adaptations; aliens; robots and machines. Then vampires, that three-decade craze from Anne Rice in the '90s to *Twilight* and *True Blood* in the teens. That transitioned us into disease films: *12 Monkeys* and *Outbreak* and *Contagion* and last year's *Infection*, and that's when things started getting modern and real and scary, right? The first indication of an actual threat, not a monster, something that could truly winnow the human race." Nods in the audience. Amazing to Ivan, still, how much people wanted to be frightened. And, how much they mostly wanted false threats, how resistant most were to admitting the actual doom and ruin ahead.

"Disease films transitioned us into zombie films, a longer-lasting craze even than vampires. From voodoo to viruses: *White Zombie* and *The Serpent and the Rainbow* up to *World War Z*. But you know my favorite days. The days that leave the zombie trope behind while still nodding to it. First, Music Video Day." Students laughed at the reverie face Ivan made. "*Trouble Every Day*, that creepy music by the Tindersticks." One student actually shuddered. "Mogwai totally enhanced *Les Revenants*, yeah?" Nods of assent. "And even though people were pissed *Zone One* didn't have an all-New-York soundtrack, Anastasia Saints killed it, didn't they?" Enthusiastic agreement. While Ivan hoped he'd made space as a teacher for people to disagree with him, he did think he was right about most things concerning apocalypse art.

He'd be saying most of this stuff anyway, but he was aware of going on a little long, aware of the one person in the audience who hadn't taken his class, the one person left to impress. Alastair Askgold. "You know I still think *28 Days Later* is the best zombie flick because it uses destruction to think about gender and race. And, well, none of us could take our eyes off Cillian Murphy." More laughs. Nothing was off-limits to talk about in an analysis of film in Dr. Ríos's classroom. "And I love how that series leaves behind zombies and disease to take on climate change. Unlike *28 Weeks Later*—which pretends like it isn't going to be a zombie movie, but is—*28 Months Later* is not a zombie movie. An aftermath movie. The first post-apocalyptic film of its kind: the apocalypse is over. We made it. How do we live now? An antidote was found, heterochromia iridis makes people immune. But that island containing England, Scotland, and Wales was abandoned. Too much tragedy. Which feels prescient now, yeah, as those islands get taken over by water, not zombies? Selena and Jim have lovely babies, and we see how race is still an issue, but less. We've got better things to worry about. And then in *28 Years Later*, full-on resource-war horror. People are still killing people. In *28 Decades Later*, we've colonized space. We watch the plants and animals that still live down below, but we can't be there anymore. The earth has gone on without us. There's still *28 Centuries* and *28 Millennia Later* to make, and I hope one of you will be the one to do it." More laughter, nervous and proud, and Ivan added, "I mean that. This is the best part of teaching, for me—telling you all to best me. Overthrow me. Get better than me." He meant it. He went on.

"*The Happening* and *The Day After Tomorrow* were terrible films, that's not how it's been going down at all, is it? But they allowed filmmakers to start exploring the idea that there is no monster; the monster is us—and yeah, that's the theme of all horror, all of it, but it finally showed up here, in apocalypse cinema, to tell us that the devouring we should be terrified of is our consumption of resources, not zombies cannibalizing faces. So we spent a day watching the international community admitting, through film, the doomsday that is real. That Japanese film, *Genbaku*, A-Bomb, where nuclear contamination makes butoh-dancing zombies. They survive, but aren't exactly human anymore. I've never seen a more horrifying movie. Danish director Lars von Trier's *Melancholia*, my all-time favorite apocalypse film, which is really about depression, a common catastrophe. The Icelandic film, *Ísjaki*, Iceberg, where zombies are the only ones who survive climate change (and of course Sigur Rós did the music for that one). People are starting to make art about calamity, and I think it's really exciting. I want you to take two things away from this class. The first is that film comes from film: new cinema is made from old reels. There is a lineage, even if it's not linear. And, art can help us cope with reality. As we begin to admit our current environmental peril, I'm excited to see the responses to come. Documentaries are useful, but at this point, we don't need more information. And, my students, I am so honored that I get to show my first film to you, first."

The applause felt real. He saw smiles as the room darkened. He thought he had the best job.

And he hoped his students couldn't see how terrified he was—not of the response to his first film, he did want the critics to like it, he wanted to be famous, but he'd done the best he could—but of the fact that he had no idea what to make next. He was empty. He'd said everything he had to say about destruction and ruin. *If we get scarce, then maybe we'll get better.* He had no more ideas. He'd never before been without a project, and it left him feeling—bereft. Scared nothing would ever come to fill the sudden absence, the gap in him shaped like this film.

He felt a tingle as he sat next to Alastair, wondered if it was obnoxious to assume a fashion designer was gay, or at least slept with men.

Alastair said, "I'm excited to see this," then, "Good luck," then, "I mean, merde." And Ivan was grateful this stranger seemed to know what was at stake.

The opening shot was a black screen with pigeon-blue letters: *Passenger.* Then:

"There will always be pigeons in books and in museums, but these are effigies and images, dead to all hardships and to all delights. Book-pigeons cannot dive out of a cloud to make the deer run for cover, or clap their wings in thunderous applause of mast-laden woods. Book-pigeons cannot breakfast of new-mown wheat in Minnesota, and dine on blueberries in Canada. They know no urge of seasons; they feel no kiss of sun, no lash of wind and weather. They live forever by not living at all." —Aldo Leopold

Fade to scientists tinkering, clicking computer screens, pouring things into test tubes, siphoning fluids with needles, injecting things into petri dishes. It's sped up just enough that they look robotic and awkward. Ivan had gotten his two favorite bands from when he was a teenager to do the soundtrack—Radiohead and Tool—a feat that still made him giddy, and Thom and Maynard's quietly moaning, soaring voices were perfect for this scene. Everything is calm, but not quite. One woman stands out because she is the only woman, the only black person. White lab coats. A voiceover uses technical language, not dumbed down for the layperson. A geneticist would be able to tell the explanation is correct, while most moviegoers would understand the process enough to simultaneously feel it was possible and magical. Somatic cell nuclear transfer. Reconstructed genome. Blueprint. Synthesized DNA. Embryo. Chimeras chimeras chimeras.

A scene where two scientists trade facts over dinner. Steak, potatoes, wine.

"Passenger Pigeons were the most populous vertebrate in North America."

"They were forty percent of the continent's bird population."

"Their population exceeded that of every other bird on earth."

"Five billion to zero in a few decades."

"In 1860, a naturalist saw a single flock that he estimated to contain 3.7 billion birds."

"A single nesting ground occupied 850 square miles; thirty-seven Manhattans."

"Flocks blotted out the sun."

"*Ectopistes migratorius.* Wandering wanderer."

"People thought if they buried pigeon bodies in their gardens it made their blossoms brighter."

"I have a recipe for pigeon pie."

"On September 1st, 1914, Martha died. She outlived George by four years. Whether depressed or just old, she barely moved."

"*Science* magazine published an article claiming that the birds had all fled to the Arizona desert. Others said they went to the Chilean pine forests. Or somewhere east of

Puget Sound. Or to Australia."

"Some said every Passenger Pigeon joined a single megaflock and disappeared into the Bermuda Triangle."

"We couldn't believe we killed them all."

"If we create a monster, will we be able to kill it off?"

"Sure. We've done it before."

It's an absurd scene, simultaneously ridiculous and realistic.

And then, a completely innocuous pigeon. A beauty, shown close, the sublimity of seeing a creature not seen for over a century. Here it is. It's real. Rosy breast, speckled wings, pale steel back. Ivan hired the best computer graphics guy from his master's program, a friend who did the effects for cheap, and they looked fantastic. The impossible made possible. So pretty, and nothing in the angle or the music indicates that anything eerie is happening, just delight in looking, a long gaze at an old, new thing—but the opening was so unnerving that it still lingers. And those red eyes.

Cut. Next shot, dozens of pigeons. Still in a lab, so still uncanny, but flying, tending to eggs. Acting normal.

Next shot—hundreds in the wild.

They all build their nests on the same day. Each female lays one egg, all on the same day. All the babies are born thirteen days later; close-up on the hatchlings. They are tended to for fourteen days, then the parents all abandon them, all on the same day.

The scientists applaud, because they are behaving just like Passenger Pigeons. The music is joyful, but a bit reserved.

"Did the original ones have red eyes?" a man in a lab coat asks another, cautiously.

"Yes."

Then shots of flying pigeons. Things are starting to get ominous. Eerie. Flocks rise and land in funnels, like tornados. Their disturbance of dirt seems like an eruption, ash or smoke from a volcano. As they fly, their dung falls like snow.

A scientist looks up from a book, reads, "'For one species to mourn the death of another is a new thing under the sun. Had the funeral been ours, the pigeons would hardly have mourned us.' Aldo Leopold."

There are repercussions. Disrupt nature, and it will disrupt you.

They are us.

First they swarm an orchard, eat every apple. Next, more ravenous, they eat a winery down to the vines, every grape and leaf. They are doing it again. But then they start on people, pecking faces. They act like a horde. They act like weather. A close-up—a pigeon pukes the flesh it's just eaten to eat something else it prefers, an infant's eyeball.

Full-on grotesquerie.

They come down the chimney. They come through window glass.

Tool shows they've still got hardcore chops, Radiohead's electronica is unnerving and insistent, the music a controlled counterpoint to the chaos on screen.

Agnes, the only female scientist, the only black scientist, and her friend Lydia, a pale, brunette beauty, are getting ready for book club. The swarm darkens the sky. Skulls bang against glass. Lydia looks around the room for a fast way to commit suicide, goes to the bathroom for pills and pulls out a bottle of wine, but that will take too long. "Do you have a gun?" she asks.

Agnes thinks the gun is for the birds. "The first time they were killed with guns, hands, whips. A stool pigeon was tied to the ground, and they'd all land, thinking a roosting spot had been found, then get caught in nets."

"Are you saying we should do that again?"

"I think this is the consequence of that. I think we have to somehow undo that."

"They remember?" Lydia asks.

Agnes shrugs. "Intergenerational trauma?"

Then Lydia asks, "How do we undo it?"

"Share resources?" Agnes has been thinking about this, has come up with a plan.

The women take the food they have, first what they prepared for book club that night, what they were going to eat themselves, with their smart friends, feta and herb pasta salad with garbanzo, lemony Caesar, garlic bread, and a homemade blueberry pie. They reach a bowl or dish out the window and let beaks eat from their arms, grimacing against the image of their veins being ripped out. Agnes looks at Lydia and laughs, pours a bowl full of Barolo and five pigeons lap at it, but they don't seem to really enjoy. Everything else they devour. "Keep going?" Lydia asks and Agnes nods. Boxes of cereal, blocks of cheddar, sushi nori, bananas, tempeh, tortillas, bratwurst, homemade kimchee, zucchini, all get removed from packaging then handed out the window. The women can't tell if the same birds keep returning, but they get the sense that each is different and they have to feed each member of this flock. They start opening cans, all the ones in the back of the pantry reserved for food drives or natural disasters, tuna and artichoke hearts and tomato soup and black beans and okra, they open each and hand it out and a bird carries it away, beak clamped tight on the rim.

It's silly and sinister, both.

After every bit of food is gone from the house, Lydia closes the window. They split two bottles of wine, the only sustenance left, the only thing the pigeons didn't want, and sleep, curled around each other for comfort.

In the morning everything seems tranquil. The sun wakes them through glass, and there is no sound. They look out the window, and all the birds are still there, but they aren't frenzied, aren't hysterical. Steadily watching them.

They wonder how the neighbors fared. The glare of sunlight shows the glass wasn't broken, at least not on this side.

Agnes says, "We can survive three weeks without food. But what exactly would we be waiting for?"

Lydia agrees. "Either our offering worked, or it didn't. If it worked, we should tell people before they build an arsenal."

The women walk out of the farmhouse slowly, their spines erect, and the birds don't ruffle.

Cut. A montage of people offering food to the birds. One family sets out a plate of chow mein. Another, piles of Indian vegetables like paint on a palette. Tacos. Lasagna.

It's not really a happy ending. The moody final track isn't joyful, and all the smiles are strained. The faces of the birds are expressionless, but they don't attack. One bird snaps off a head of broccoli from a garden but doesn't eat every bush. The final image is a tree full of birds, only bits visible through the leaves, red eyes occasionally catching the light.

"Ew," someone said, which was the emotion Ivan was going for. This was over, and not over. They would always be watched. What was done cannot ever be undone.

As the credits silently rolled, everyone clapped and every student came up to Ivan after and told him what they thought was great, and they were clever about comparing it to other films they'd seen together. He was proud of them and of himself. Rosario, a student who'd visited his office hours the week before, said it made her hopeful. He was touched. When she'd come to his office, she'd explained that she knew the movies were just movies, she didn't believe any of them were real or possible, but there were just so many of them. So much disaster. It scared her that everyone was so scared. So Ivan told her the truth, that he thought about this a lot. He didn't patronize or condescend. He said private disaster happened to everyone. A spouse is murdered. Someone loved dies a slow, watched death. Rape. Injury. Sickness. And shared disaster—famine, fire, flood. Hurricanes. Drone strikes. Sure, we'd invented planes powered by algae, and nuclear fusion heated our showers, but people still starved to death and didn't have clean water.

"I know!" she said, exasperated, as if that were exactly why she'd come and he wasn't making her feel better yet.

He explained that disasters were becoming more shared, because of increased occurrence and connectedness. Media. And he tried to explain to this pretty, distressed person that what he hoped would soon happen would be that for the first time in human history we would admit, truly, that suffering was unavoidable. And then two things might happen. We might actually, truly try to relieve the suffering of others. Some efforts would be frivolous and some would pay off. And, we'd finally, truly start to appreciate now.

"But that's just Buddhism, right?" she asked.

"Sure. But people have been able to avoid those truths for a really long time." He held up his arm in the dappled sunlight and turned it, the rays and shade changing the color of his skin. Rosario held up her hand and spread her fingers, and the slight webbing turned pink. They both looked out his office window, to the tree doing just that to the sun, and both stared in wonder at leaves every shade of green in their layers against the light, shot-through lime, glistening emerald, the ones on the edge a robust chartreuse. A pigeon pecked and plodded three stories below them, a regular pigeon, a feral New York City rock dove, the kind that lasted, and Ivan felt he'd said all he knew how to say, so added, "I love pigeons."

Rosario looked down and said, "Yeah. I know you do. Thanks, Dr. Ríos."

He said, "You're welcome," and watched Rosario stand and walk from sunlight into fluorescence.

"Your film is a horror film in the tradition of zombie cinema, I get that," Rosario said to him as the closing credits still scrolled. "An obvious tribute to Hitchcock. Totally. But, you don't need to know Hitchcock to get this; it's just a bonus if you do. That movie terrified me, but yours, it made me feel less afraid. Like maybe some of us will come up with solutions."

He said he was so glad. That was exactly what he was going for.

Alastair was waiting for him when he finished, leaning against a wall, looking casually stylish. "That was great," he said. "Really. I loved how it was about the world, and not."

"Thanks, man. Yeah, that was exactly what I was going for. Let's hope the critics see it and agree."

"They might not. It was pretty weird."

"True. Very."

"You got big names to do the music. This is your first film?" *How famous are you?*, Alastair seemed to be asking.

"Well, neither band has made an album in a while. I think they're huge. The kids nowadays think they're dinosaurs. I asked them because why the hell not? They said they'd never worked together, were big fans of each other. They're doing it for the other band more than for me. But, they said they dug the script." Ivan realized he was talking too much again.

They'd met that morning. Ivan Ríos hadn't had a partner, but he wanted to see the contest. He didn't know anyone who would marvel as much as he would at birds, so he trusted fate to find him someone random who was suitable. He paid the admission fee and called it "research," even though his latest film was complete and about to be released.

Filmmakers of color were still rare, so he'd hoped they'd pair him with another, call them a Visibility Team, refund his money. The entry fee was substantial. But they were only making what was trendy to be visible visible. People with disabilities, trannies—people that had been there all along but that no one wanted to see until now. An apology for all the years. Ivan wasn't sure a parade of difference was the best way to promote equality, but yeah, he would have taken the free ticket. And maybe a naming of the world could work against the erasures that had happened throughout history. His heritage—too simple for the terms Hispanic or Latinx—didn't offer any obvious pairing for peace; Dominican and Cuban was enough conflict inside of him. Pair him with a Haitian? But they had no beef with Cuba. He was from Washington Heights, born and raised. The neighborhood was still Dominican, between Harlem and the South Bronx, it still hadn't gentrified fully, but he figured that was because it was the next place most likely to be underwater. His mom and dad made sure he'd seen both islands he was from, and while he considered himself a New Yorker, this island home, he drank Cuba Libres with Brugal as a sign of solidarity with his parents' nations.

All he'd known about his partner was a name, and when he'd met Alastair Askgold that morning at the registration desk, the stranger was both dapper and disheveled. His pants and shirt were wrinkled, but of the finest quality fabric, and he held his contest-sanctioned Gore-Tex jacket with a Union Jack embroidered on the back draped over an arm. He handed Ivan a bamboo-paper cup of coffee and fished cream and sugar out of his pocket. "I didn't know how you took it."

"Both, thanks," Ivan said. "Where are you from?"

"London."

"Displaced?"

"Not yet. Likely soon. You?"

"Here. The Heights." They established that neither was a birder, could identify maybe ten types each, and both were there for research. Clearly why Google's algorithm paired them up. Alastair was a fashion designer, he'd said. Ivan wondered about that—costumes at the end of the world—but people told him cinema was no longer necessary and he disagreed. Alastair had said, "Women still care about how they look. My father was a gambler and a vagabond. My mother raised me. I've always loved women.

She was a glove maker, in a factory, brought home scraps. My grandmother was a milliner, back when feathers were still fashionable in London, not yet tragic. She always had bits and baubles for me to play with. I got famous doing what they already did. I'm interested in fashion after feathers. Metal feathers, fabric feathers."

Ivan wondered how famous he was. He found Alastair fascinating, and sexy, and was glad when he was interested in coming to the soft opening of his film. He wanted to be interesting to strangers. And foreigners. Now, in the empty auditorium, they had to decide what next.

"Thanks for giving me the sneak peek," Alastair said. "I hope the world loves it tomorrow. I'm too awake to sleep, though we have to be up at dawn. There's a crucial cricket match on about now. Ireland versus England. I could watch it in my room of course, but is there a bar you like?"

So Ivan took Alastair to an Irish Pub in Washington Heights.

The bar was all done up for the contest, borrowed taxidermied birds mounted on the walls. A branch with every bright thing perched in color order: red Cardinal, orange Oriole, yellow Finch, Bluebird, green parrot, Indigo Bunting, Purple Martin. A black raven and white dove balanced on a branch below. They didn't look alive. They looked preserved. Ivan wanted to touch them the way he wanted to lay his hands on paintings in art galleries. Another wall was full of hybrids. A rabbit with raven wings. A mouse with sparrow feet. A snake with macaw wings and falcon talons. An eagle with a unicorn horn. A sparrow with zebra-patterned feathers.

Alastair was almost the only non-local. Ivan watched

him watch people from his neighborhood—girls in Adidas bling, girls in t-shirts with tons of jewelry, tight leggings, studded leather jackets, girls in dresses and high shoes, pretty, pretty boys in tight shirts, impeccably shaped thin lines of facial hair. Girls and boys in vests with no shirts underneath.

They projected the match from Alastair's iPill onto the wall of their booth and ordered a Boddington's and a Brugal Cuba Libre. Alastair paid and said to keep the tab open. They served Cuba Libres here the way Ivan liked—a glass nearly full of rum and ice and lime, just enough room at the top for the waitress to pour in a little Coke from a small glass bottle. So the first few sips were strong, made Ivan tipsy quick. But he got to keep adding in Coke as he drank it down, so the cocktail lasted. There was always something to do with his hands, a sip to take to punctuate whatever he was saying.

"I love how any Irish bar in every neighborhood of New York has the appropriate beers on tap," Alastair said. "They may have Sex on the Beach as a special, but they will pour a proper pint."

"Some things never change."

"So what's the best one?" Alastair asked. "Of all the films you've ever seen?"

Ivan loved to talk about this shit. "*Genbaku.* A-Bomb. The screenwriter's grandmother was not killed by the atomic bombing of Hiroshima, but a pocket watch was embedded in her leg and couldn't be removed. She had been a dancer, had to quit, still danced at home but with a hitch in her step. The writer, Suzume Takahashi, loved the way her grandmother couldn't keep perfect 8/8 time anymore, imposed her own rhythm over the music, couldn't conform to the metronome because of the timepiece in her body. But her grandmother was a very sad person. Suzume grew up thinking every country had had a bomb, thought that had been done to each place. Then she realized no, only her home. All the people she knew had known people who'd died, people who were forever altered. She started studying butoh, a dance form basically invented in response to the atomic attacks. Her film starts in Japan with all the characters performing Kabuki and Noh. But then there's a bomb. The survivors are poisoned. Radiation has warped them. They can only move like butoh. And then the film shows it has happened everywhere. People in rags, bodies pale with ash, dancing across the snowy Alps, the burning red desert, through forests. Moving without rhythm or syncopation, utterly without comprehension of time. It's ghastly. Plotless and beautiful. I wish I'd made it. Best zombie movie ever."

Alastair said, "Sounds intense," and Ivan had to no idea if Alastair liked intensity. Then, "You've been asked that before." Ivan couldn't tell if he was impressed or suspicious.

"Yeah. People always want to know. Who's your favorite designer?" Tit for tat, Ivan thought.

"That changes every season. Whoever is doing work least like me. The person I need to either embrace or reject to do my next work—that's the temporary favorite. So Shelly Sherlock right now. She's doing these sinister Little Red Riding Hood capes out of real wolf fur. The skin of rare, endangered animals. I can't decide yet if it's brilliant or totally fecked. Or, rather, how much of each." Alastair shrugged, quaffed, then turned his attention to the match, so Ivan did too. He wondered how talkative this man was.

The television announcer ran through the tournament to that point: Canada versus Jamaica, Australia versus Wales, Kenya versus The Bahamas, Bermuda versus Barbados, Antigua and Barbuda versus Trinidad and Tobago, New Zealand versus Zimbabwe, Northern Ireland versus Scotland, Sri Lanka versus South Africa, the West Indies versus Pakistan, India versus Bangladesh. All the former British colonies pitted against each other, and London underwater. The highlight reel showed the owners of the Indian team watching in a box, wearing cream suits with Windsor-knotted dark ties, sipping black tea with milk, eating brown soda scones with hand-churned butter. A bartender in a tuxedo at the edge of the frame served up perfect pours of Guinness. The seated owners yelled in Hindi and English at their players on the other side of glass. Bangladesh won.

"I don't get it," Ivan said. "We watch baseball and soccer."

"Football," Alastair said. Then, "It's hard to explain."

The match started. Ivan listened to the announcers, words he didn't understand sounding delicious in his ears. Took four wickets. Paceman. Spinner. Very good bowlers. Thirty-three not out. A fifty-ball hundred: the fastest in World Cup history. Close to 1400 runs scored. Drinks: Ireland 160/5 in 37 overs. Bowled out for 58, fourth lowest in tournament history. Two runs stylishly driven, fuller length delivery outside off, O'Brien drives it past cover, great commitment there by Collingwood at sweeper cover prevents a boundary at 126.95 kilometers per hour. Joyce drives a well-tossed up delivery. Mooney is really expressing himself out there, Broad will rue that drop for some days to come. Short ball outside, Mooney stands up it and spanks the cut through point for four. Broad to Mooney, one run, tossed up on the stumps, politely driven past Yardy for the hundredth run driven. Collingwood chips it back to Eion Morgan, the Irish lad playing for England who fluffs it, very tough chance though. For England, Ajmal Shahzad works this one too deep, square leg for an ambled single. Flighted delivery on the stumps, Swann works it to square leg. Yardy looks to hoick it across the line and misses. Broad opens the face of the bat and steers it down to third man at 106.57 kmph. England have opted for the batting powerplay. Joyce ends a tidy spell. End of a fab innings though.

Ivan didn't love baseball, didn't watch with the rapture he saw on Alastair's face, the intensity of wishing, the attention on every movement from every player, the intimacy of knowing each and his history. Ivan cared that the Diamondbacks got a female pitcher; he'd watch a AAA game in the sunshine at Coney Island; he'd cheer at a bar; pulled for Boston because they still were mostly Dominicans in their club; he'd seen a bright loud game in Cuba, but the concentration he saw in Alastair was one he only felt when in the theater.

Ivan had been back to Cuba since the embargo had been lifted, since the dictator had died, since the elections, since Cubans eradicated poverty and became as gender-equal as Scandinavia. Democratic socialism. He was proud of them, but this fucked-up, flawed, fabulous city was where he belonged, amidst all its inequities and disproportions.

Alastair let out a moan. Ireland won. In their box, the rich Brit owners reacted: "Bloody fucking hell." "Shite. Shite and onions." "Fecking shitebag arseholes." They loosened their silk ties and tossed back the rest of their

Bombay Sapphire martinis. In the stands, men with green, white, and orange painted across their faces, women wrapped in flags representing the orange north, the green south, and white peace in between, sang the national anthem: "Some have come from a land beyond the wave; sworn to be free, no more our ancient sireland shall shelter the despot or the slave." They sang the national anthem again, the English version, not the Gaelic version, because it was easier. Bangladeshis, Indians, Sri Lankans, Pakistanis, all the fans in the stands, all the people who weren't owners or players, tried to sing along to a song they'd never heard, in a language they knew, but an accent they didn't, their arms slung round the winners.

"Sorry," Ivan said.

"I'll try not to be a total arse the rest of the night."

"Sorry for your loss," the bartender came over to say, offering Alastair a hand.

"And congrats to you," Alastair said, shaking it firmly. "From Cork are you?"

"Near to it. Cobh."

They clicked off and looked to the TV over the bar, the news showing the Aviary. The anchor said, "The favorites of the Canon and Cabela's Birds of the World Timed Birding Contest include Clark and Clara Schmidt, Max Shale and Zach Vandenberg, and Basil Bunting and Sean O'Grady."

Ivan said he was rooting for the married power couple, Thad Stewart and Jonathan Walker. A doctor and a lawyer. But very punk rock, even with their middle-aged bellies. Thad had his life list tattooed in Latin on his back, Jonathan had favorites from his life list in portraits all over his body. They each had thousands of birds on their list before this contest, had tattoo appointments already scheduled for after the contest, to update. Murmurs went through any crowd they passed, and Ivan loved all the little flying shapes all over Thad's forearms.

"You're just pulling for them because they're gay," Alastair said.

"How do you know Basil and Sean aren't gay?"

"I don't. But an Englishman and an Irish lad, I don't know."

"Max and Zach? Hey. I like men as much as women, homos as much as heteros. I'm an equal opportunity kind of guy."

Alastair squinted at him. "Good to know," he said. Then, "What's Cabela's?"

"They don't have them in England? They sell outdoor gear, hunting supplies. They build these massive stores with mountains in the middle, taxidermy all over it. Bears and bighorn sheep and elk. Fish in the rivers. It's incredible."

"The great outdoors," Alastair said. "Starting tomorrow I bet we'll be at the bottom of the list. Last place. Leave it to you Americans to turn a leisurely activity into a competitive sport."

"Sure. But I don't need to compete. Last place would be fine."

"I'm not a birder, but I know the lingo," Alastair said. "I went to Kent to see a Golden-Winged Warbler, but I dipped out. Other twitchers saw it, so I felt gripped off. I heard it was a crippler. Some of my megaticks are yanks, some are plastics, some sibes. I've got loads of tart ticks, but I'm definitely not a dude. I can identify birds on jizz alone."

"Are you drunk after two beers?" Ivan asked. But he laughed. He loved the oddity of what he'd just heard.

"There's a Noah's Ark of birds in my own neighborhood," Ivan said. "If the rest of the planet gets destroyed while we're all here, we could repopulate the earth's birds just with what's inside that fence."

"The whole point is they're in here because they can't be out there. But we could repopulate all the people," Alastair said. "All the nations are here."

"But they aren't all procreative pairs," Ivan said. "All the nations will have to mix. More mestizaje!" He raised his glass. His drink was nearly done. He wondered what next. He said, "How'd we wind up a pair?"

"Neither of us had anyone else," Alastair said quickly. Then, "You're here for research for the next film, right?"

"That's what I said. It would be more accurate to say I'm here to find out what the next film is. I..." He finished his drink, signaled two more to the bartender, said, "For the first time in my life, I don't have any ideas. I'm about to launch, and this is what I had. That's it." He wondered if Alastair could see his fear and wondered if he wanted him to.

"At the end of every season, I'm out of ideas. I've used them all. I'm sure I'm shite to live with"—again, he looked down and away—"but the ideas always come back. I said I was here for inspiration, but I'm really here for distraction." After a pause where he seemed to consider what he wanted to reveal, he added, "My husband was supposed to be my partner. But he's decided he doesn't want to be my husband anymore. We're not the type to stay friends."

"I'm sorry to hear that," Ivan said. "Really."

"Me too. It, well, I don't know if it's for the best or not yet. But we haven't been good to each other for some time.

So. You?"

"Never had a partner." Ivan meant for the contest, but it applied otherwise. No person he'd been sleeping with ever fully felt like a partner.

"I often wonder if that's better or worse," Alastair said with a small smile.

"It's better to have been part of a pair. Otherwise none of us would ever do it again, you know? Google paired us for wrong reasons, it seems—I'm scared," he admitted, why not, "and you're sad, even though we both said we were here for research."

Alastair seemed like a man who had it all, but he just lost something. Ivan felt that for the first time in his life, he was about to get everything he ever wanted. Maybe. Maybe not.

Alastair nodded. "There's something about being the first to see this. I'm hoping I'll be inspired despite myself. But the main goal is just to be, elsewhere." Their drinks were delivered and Alastair thanked Ivan for making them appear. "You live here?" Alastair asked. He was looking at the people, Ivan more formally clad than them all.

"Down the block, 183 and Audubon." Ivan felt ownership of his city, his borough, his neighborhood.

"Didn't they make a musical about this place?"

"Yeah. And a short-lived MTV show. The musical aimed for authenticity, but I thought it was pretty corny. *Hamilton* was brilliant, the all-women show was the best Broadway I've seen. Now people don't even remember we're up here."

"They'll remember when the edge of the island starts sinking."

"Maybe. They're making southern Manhattan flood proof, but they think up here can be even more sustainable.

They're going to build eco condos where Inwood Hill Park is now. The last old-growth forest on the island, sacrificed to habitations they think will last. Earthquake-proof, tsunami-resistant, whatever comes, these buildings will be flexible, won't mind getting their feet wet, won't come crashing down. People are camping there this week as a sort of grand finale, a goodbye."

"Will you buy one?"

"I've thought about it. It'll have a micro-grid, solar panels and Tesla Powerwalls to store the energy, and super-efficient appliances with HFC-free refrigeration. When it all collapses after Peak Oil residents will still be able to take the elevator to the sixteenth floor. Good light for window box gardening. A rooftop terrace and garden. Smart glass, solar-heated water tanks. You don't have to give anything up—there's still a washing machine, you can even charge your car for those who still own their own—but this might actually work. Short-term, I'm not sure how long-term. I think they plan to leave a few of the old trees."

"For those who can afford it."

"They'll call it the Uppermost West Side."

Then Alastair said, "I'm staying at what I think is the nicest place in town. The Plaza. Would you like to go back to my place? After this round. It's quite lovely. Maybe you've been."

Ivan looked hard at Alastair's sharp, pristine, desolate face. He'd never been with a Brit before, and while he didn't really want to be someone's recovery sex, he did like this guy. Found him sexy enough, though a bit lean. "As you might have guessed," he said, "I've never been. But, I'd love to see it. Thanks."

He gave Alastair his warmest smile. And Ivan got that

effervescence of knowing what was about to happen, but not exactly.

VI.
Jane Johnson

It's like the best mosh pit I've ever seen. I'm old enough to have come of age with punk, with hardcore, with grunge, when shoving people while singing was a joyous way to spend an evening, emerging with other people's sweat layered on top of yours. Smiling. People got really hurt, but it wasn't real violence. Some people here are certainly thinking of mosh pits, too. The younger ones are just thinking of schoolyard brawls. Fight, fight, fight. People removed earrings, taped over nose rings and nipple rings, slicked back their hair to avoid handholds. People prepared to kick some ass and get their asses kicked. No weapons allowed; that's the rule. Just fists and teeth and kicking and screaming.

"Fuck Monsanto," someone yells while punching someone else in the face.

"Fuck 45's dismantling of the EPA!" another screams.

"Our ancestors did not tend to the earth how they should have!" a woman wails.

"Fuck golf courses in Phoenix!" a middle-aged man hollers, while shoving a young rock chick who probably blames him for the destruction of her environment.

I'm here for research. I have an article due tomorrow night for *The Voice*. I'm watching the swirl, women clawing at each other's faces, a man slapping a woman across the face and her laughing, a man spitting blood with glee in his eyes.

Every Living Species

Anger. The stage of grief these people are trying to process, and then transcend, together. Sponsored by the Dark Mountain Project. They aren't mad at each other, mostly; they're mad at everything that happened before now, to bring us to the brink of destruction. And the idea is that punching a human will be cleansing, even if what you really want to do is strengthen corporate regulations.

I'm not sure if the Dark Mountain Project is cult or catharsis. I'm not sure how I should portray them in my article. It's pretty fucked up, what I'm seeing here. It's pretty marvelous, also. I mean, it might work.

Everyone is in Denial, they say. Anger tonight, Bargaining tomorrow, a Depression session Saturday, and then the last day of the contest, collective Acceptance. And then people will leave this festival with plans, with reality, with knowing what to do in the face of mass extinction. Admitting what is happening and moving past stasis, past paralysis.

I don't know, man. I don't think there's much we can do. Will acceptance that capitalism is unsustainable and therefore humans may or may not survive actually make my life better? I think denial would make my life better. But that's what got us into this mess, anyway.

I don't feel like fighting. But elbowing and ramming people has always felt really good. There's no music. The silent shoving is oddly gorgeous. Like dance. It feels orchestrated. People don't really want to hurt each other. Most people. On the edges of this swirl are brawls and fist fights. I wonder how many opponents will end up fucking later tonight. Sex has a better chance of making us all feel better about the state of our planet than violence, probably. Eros can eradicate Thanatos, maybe. At least temporarily.

But I guess Dark Mountain is looking for a real solution, a way for people to live with what we now know. I doubt this will make me feel better in the morning, but in the face of *What Now?*, *Why Not?* is a pretty valid response. I tuck this notebook in my pocket and walk in.

V.
Arrow Sullivan
and Grant Sullivan

Her father had given Arrow her birthday gift in advance, sent a guidebook to her iPill with two pages flagged, the ones he apparently found the most magnificent: Greater Racket-Tailed Drongo and Rainbow Lorikeet, *I can't wait to see these with you* written in an attached card, *Happy twenty-first birthday* below. And now they were standing in line to register. Across the street protestors held signs that said, "Free the Birds" and "Animal Suffering is Not a Sport" and "This is Not Natural." Three police kept them behind metal barricades that looked like bike racks. One woman had a headful of braids. One man had close-cropped hair and thick glasses. A tall man had his fist in the air. They made Arrow anxious. Obviously, this was unnatural. Little seemed natural to her. Skyscrapers? Energy drinks? Eyeliner? But she knew she was about to see grandeur, a thing most people on the planet never would.

To get to this spot they'd first taken the bus—electric, charged with energy generated from the sun, the main desert transportation as of recently—from Flagstaff to Phoenix. Arrow had looked out the window until the blue mountain at the center of her hometown had become too small to see, then looked out the window to spot the first saguaro on the descent from alpine forest to Sonoran desert, what she'd always done during this trip, since childhood. Phoenix had far fewer people than when she was a kid, but a couple hundred thousand stuck around, those that had converted to solar-powered AC. Then they took a biodiesel plane to LaGuardia.

Queens looked dirty, like any city, blocky and nondescript as Phoenix. But the people astounded her—they moved fast, and they were every color. Something dim and voiceless in Arrow understood who all these people were, why they were in this place. In the airport there were men in suits with loosened ties, women in suits with their heels in their purses, things to be tightened as they rode in green Eco taxis to meetings. There were families returning from their home countries carrying cardboard boxes taped shut, full of spices and jars of condiments they couldn't find in this city, closely inspected by customs. There were hipsters with wide grins because they were so glad to be back from Michigan and Virginia, young professionals and artists going home, they said, to Brooklyn. There were tourists with bright raincoats, fanny packs, and ill-fitting jeans, ready to eat at the Red Lobster in Times Square. On the bus, boys with braids in tight rows, boys with tidy poofs of hair, girls with hair chemically straightened or curled with heat, some watching what they passed through their iPills to learn the names of everything beyond the glass. And a man with waist-length dreadlocks, wearing a fine pinstriped suit, silk tie, offered Arrow and her father his seat, allowed them to take off their backpacks and hold them between their knees.

Then they were up and on their feet again. The subway trains were both grimy and shiny, the subway tunnels bleak and filthy, and when Arrow saw a tall teenager grab the end of a baby carriage and help a mom down the stairs without breaking stride, barely tossing a smile over his shoulder once they were down, showing that this was clearly just a thing everyone there did for each other, she was glad she had a backpack, the one she'd worn when hiking Havasupai, Bright Angel, Zion, not a suitcase to maneuver up and down all those stairs.

The birders were as varied as the people they'd seen on their journey, had skin of every shade, but most wore pants that looked like they could get wet and not stay wet, vests with lots of pockets, tennis shoes, all in shades of brown and cream—the same costume, but what was underneath was so different. They peered through chain-link to see if they could get an early look. Arrow couldn't hear any birdcalls. As they all checked in, they were each handed a jacket, stitched flags from every nation. Arrow recognized the circle of Japan, the leaf of Canada, the stars of China, the crescent of Turkey, the cross of Sweden, but there were many stripes and triangles and crests that she couldn't place. One flag had a ship and one had a bird and one had three legs on it and Arrow wondered if she was going to feel constantly overwhelmed for the next three days.

A man and a woman, both with face tattoos, pinned a flag over the variation of the Union Jack that had been there—black on top and red on the bottom, divided by a white line, all the colors spiraling into each other on the side. *Maori*, Arrow thought but wasn't sure. She pointed to another jacket, said, "That one looks like the Arizona state flag a little." It had a yellow, green, and red horizontal stripe, and a large white star.

"Burma," her father said. Then, "There should be a separate contest for flags."

The person behind Arrow in line looked at the nearest

street sign and said to her partner, "I've lived my entire life on this island, and I had no idea the streets went as high as 190th."

"It goes to 218th up there," the man said, gesturing north.

So many people were selling fruit on the street. Cherries, mangoes, kiwis, bananas, plantains, strawberries, starfruit. Arrow wondered if they were still flying this stuff from tropical islands, or if they'd built greenhouses on Staten Island next to the direct-air capture stations. Do we still need papayas? She could give up papayas. But apparently Dominicans didn't want to just yet. The fruit was expensive but not as bad as other disappearing things, gasoline and the sea ice people were ordering to store in their freezers, to maintain a piece of what-once-used-to-be. La Casa Del Mofongo, 99 Cent Super Discount, Carnicería.

The person in front of Arrow in line stepped up to the desk situated at the entrance to The Aviary. A worker in red said, "We'll have to inoculate you against the Avian Flu. The birds have already been vaccinated." Arrow hadn't known this was part of the process. The worker lifted a hermetically sealed plastic package, a one-use needle inside. "Your right shoulder, please," she said. The woman turned and lifted her sleeve, showing a disc of crinkled skin. The worker said, "This one won't leave a scar." She smiled, slid the needle into the woman's arm, pressed in the medicine. "You'll be immune in fourteen hours, right before the contest begins," she said. "The birds were given their shots before they were released inside." You could tell she was saying this for the hundredth time. On the other side of the chain-link fence, the foliage was so dense Arrow couldn't see what was beyond. The proximity of creatures that would never otherwise meet. Arrow hadn't thought about precautions. The woman pulled down her sleeve, and the worker told her, "Rubbing the spot reduces soreness."

"Thank you," the woman said, massaging her arm. The worker handed her a knapsack and said, "Everything you need to have and know is inside this bag." She hefted the contest materials onto her other shoulder. She had no discernible accent, and Arrow wanted to ask her where she was from, but she knew it was none of her business, she, a woman who hadn't seen much of the world.

"Can I read about the vaccine?" Arrow asked. The information appeared on her iPill, and she skimmed for the pregnancy section. It said it was totally safe, thousands of women and babies had been studied to make sure. She was relieved this would not be the way the first person she told found out. Arrow had discovered she was pregnant three days before they left for this trip. She was about eight weeks, she figured, though she wasn't sure, and she hadn't told anyone yet. Not Ed, her boyfriend of six months, not her mom, none of her girlfriends. She didn't want her dad to be the first to know—or the second, after a stranger. There hadn't been time to take care of it before this trip, but she had an appointment for a few days after they got home. Still, a shot that would certainly cause birth defects, she didn't want to do that, just in case. It seemed unkind to damage even something that wasn't going to ever live. Desertification and relocation and famine and drought and fire and tornados and hurricanes and typhoons and tsunamis and UV radiation and rising sea levels and acidification of oceans and the disappearance of glaciers had people saying it was irresponsible to bring children into this world, a world where so many would die so soon. Eighty percent of the world's population would be wiped out in eighty years, by 2100, scientists said. Arrow didn't want to sign her child up for resource wars or starvation or some other horrific end. And she was fond of Ed, but it was way too soon to face a thing like this with him. She'd made the decision without him and was pretty sure she was going to go through with it.

"Okay," Arrow said and lifted her sleeve, got an injection where she would have had a smallpox scar if she were her father's age. He got his shot right below his circle of corrugated skin.

The backpack was heavy. The woman with a red shirt emblazoned with the Canon and Cabela's logos said sunrise inside the park would happen at the same time as outside the park, 6:25 a.m., so they'd be expected at The Henshaw Street entrance, Gate Five, sponsored by The Met and The Mets, half an hour before dawn.

They walked toward camp and had to walk past the protestors. Arrow wondered if this was the first time she'd actively participated in a thing others vigorously opposed. No U.S. invasion had happened when she was old enough to protest, and she'd marched against increasing restrictions on abortion in Arizona, against cutting the budget for higher education, in favor of in-state tuition for the children of immigrants. She was at the Women's March and the March for Science and she protested against every despicable thing 45 then 46 tried to push through, rallied in support of every good thing 47 tried to accomplish. She'd never felt herself to be on the wrong side of a picket line. Her dad read every sign, listened to what they were saying, then said to Arrow, "They aren't going to stop this thing."

"I think they know that," Arrow answered.

"You look at an animal, you know if it's suffering or not. I bet those birds are twittering away in there and don't even know they aren't home." Arrow didn't answer. The birds were given shots. She could feel him studying her face even as they walked forward. "You're letting them get to you," her dad said. And he was right. He was paying attention. He said, "Don't let them ruin our time together, okay?"

Arrow smiled at him then. She'd been glad her mom wasn't coming along because she could always tell when something was bothering Arrow; she didn't want to be found out, but sometimes her dad was more observant than she gave him credit for.

They walked up Broadway and Arrow wondered if it was the same Broadway with the shows or if there were more than one. They passed a Yeshiva, a deli, a seafood restaurant, Quisqueyana Exchange, Lula's Best Nails. The sun was getting low, turning the tops of the buildings golden. Arrow thought, *When the tops of the trees turn orange, that's the time you need to be in the place you intend to stay for a while.* Some buildings were brick, some painted brick, all a little faded looking. The bottom floors had colored awnings, selling things. People must live above. No. 1 Restaurant. Hardware Store. Doña Carmen Bakery. Beauty Salon. Medical Center. One Dollar Super Discount. The edges were ornate, sculpted stone. At one time, they must have been stunning. Some businesses seemed closed, graffiti on the metal shades pulled down over their doors. The streetlights were on, though they didn't need to be.

They passed the Crystal Mini Mart with a green awning, yellow letters, advertisements for lottery tickets, cancer-free cigarettes, and burner iPill tablets taped to the glass door. Grant said he'd get them some beer, "Since you're legal now." He smiled the broadest version of his grin, the one that made his cheeks stick out, the smile Arrow had inherited, though she had her mother's pale green eyes. Arrow had been drinking with her parents long before she was legal, cocktail hour a family custom, and she'd wondered how she was going to handle booze this trip. She knew he had whiskey in his backpack, figured one beer was better than that, wouldn't destroy this baby. In case she decided she didn't want it destroyed.

Her dad left her outside with the backpack, and she watched him through the windows of the tiny shop. Inside was a wooden stand with limes, tomatoes, cilantro, onions, potatoes, jalapeños, plantains, and bananas, all looking a little less than fresh. Racks of magazines. Wheels of scratch-off tickets. Two aisles with canned food, toilet paper, paper towels, Aspirin, cat food, dog food, bread, shampoo, Jesus and Virgen de Guadalupe candles, beans, rice, rotating racks with small chip bags clipped in. Her dad came out with a six-pack of Presidente and a lime and said it seemed like maybe that's what the locals drank; it was from the Dominican Republic.

They followed Broadway to Dyckman, turned left, and entered the park. Arrow was amazed by the hundreds of tents, huge twelve-person domes and smaller ones just for two. People had set up card tables and camp chairs and badminton nets and fire rings. The trees were huge, leaves the size of her palm. Two boys were throwing a motorized Frisbee, and there were dogs running everywhere. Arrow showed their contest ticket to the man checking people in, and he handed them a bundle of firewood, hot as it was, two gallons of water, and said a Community Rules pamphlet and a map had been sent to her iPill. Their hands were very full. He pointed out bathrooms and showers. Arrow thought this didn't really count as camping. He said most of the spots were taken already, but they should be able find one up the path. They walked for what felt to Arrow's feet like a mile before the tents thinned. Her dad gestured with his chin to show he wanted to keep walking, get a bit more separate from everyone else.

After another minute, Arrow shrugged out of her backpack, her t-shirt pasted to her skin. It was far wetter than Arizona. Buildings towered above the trees with shiny leaves at the edges of her vision, and she could hear the low rush of traffic. Her father handed Arrow a beer and they clinked cheers. Then Arrow said, "I think this is a good place for the tent," pointing. Her father started kicking away small pebbles, clearing things that might poke their backs while they slept. He pulled the tent from his backpack, the same one from Arrow's childhood, a green six-person dome they would sometimes pitch in their yard so they could sleep outside in the summer, the only kind of camping her mom liked. He laid out a tarp while Arrow began to click the tent poles into long rods, fitting together the small metal shafts connected by bungee cords. She'd always loved the way tent poles felt in her hands. She fed the poles through the slick fabric loops on top of the tent. Her father stood at the opposite corner. They inserted the other pole, then put ends in pockets stitched in the base, and it stood up, making a little room in the middle of a forest on the edge of a city. The top was mesh, and her father asked if they should put the rainfly on just in case.

"We won't see any stars in this city, but maybe we'll be

able to see the moon. It's slim but worth seeing," Arrow said. They decided to leave the rainfly off. They could always put it on in the middle of the night if a storm blew in. Arrow thought about when she took the man she had been dating, the man before Ed, to her favorite spot on the Peaks, and when he didn't know how to put together a tent, she found herself getting strangely frustrated as she explained. She just figured that was a thing people knew how to do. They'd put the rainfly on even though the sky was packed with stars, even though Arrow loved to watch them flick on and off between the aspen leaves, because she figured if it did start to rain in the night that man wouldn't be able to help her. The monsoons in Flagstaff used to be like clockwork, a storm would start between 2:00 and 3:00 each afternoon, July through September, her dad had told her, but they were more unpredictable these days.

Her father unpacked their contest materials: passwords to download Canon binoculars to their iPill tablets; passwords to send the contest app to their Lozenge software; passwords to download David Allen Sibley's North American guide, expanded to include birds from the whole globe; two Cabela's jackets with the U.S. flag embroidered on the back; and two bottles with built-in filters for New York City tap water. He read the screen of his iPill then told Arrow, "After we take a picture, the alphabetical list of every bird in the world, every bird in the park, will appear, and we select the name. The identification will be confirmed or denied by the central database, but we won't know which we got right and which we missed until we see our personalized page at the end of the competition: each photograph with our identification underneath, corrections where necessary." He lifted his tablet to his eyes and said the binoculars were amazing. Then, "Hungry?" He opened a jar of salsa and pulled out a container of chips, handed Arrow a green pepper to slice while he poured elk meat and green chiles into a pot, added beans and cheese, set it to heat on his camp stove. He only used half the block of cheese, and Arrow knew it would mold by the third day without refrigeration, but they'd brought their solar-powered cooler, wouldn't have to cut off the spoiled bit. She added the pepper strips, and when it was heated through, they scooped the stew onto big tortillas. One of their classic camping meals. The first bite threw Arrow into the past even more than touching tent nylon.

Arrow's first hunt was the year she turned thirteen. Her father only let her put into the lottery for a deer tag, not elk for her first try, and he'd only taught her to shoot a gun. He'd named her after his archery, but she never learned it. She'd always wondered if it was because she was a girl. She could have learned it on her own but never did. She'd asked her father how many shots it would take to kill the animal, and he said if you do it right, just one. One arrow or bullet to the heart, and if you miss the heart, the lungs will be hit.

"Does it take a long time to find the animal? Does it run far?"

"If you do it right, the animal only makes it a hundred yards, at the most. The animal is dead instantly. It's just adrenaline that makes it move at all."

He left it to her imagination to envision what it would be like if someone—if she—didn't do it right. She pictured gushing animals that were hit with a glancing shot, running into the trees to die slowly alone. She imagined the moan a hurt deer might make. He'd killed his first bull elk when Arrow was five. A father who could take down a nine-hundred-pound animal with one arrow to the heart, an arrow he made himself—she didn't think the word *awe*, didn't think in language at all—but even when he was not near her, Arrow felt she walked in his tremendous shadow. When near him, she sought to never tremble in his presence, only to be an apt student, to only ask a question once, to learn things the first time, to do each thing impeccably well.

They'd set up two tree stands on the edge of Government Prairie, far from the human smells of camp, got up before dawn to be there when the deer moved from their nighttime feeding in the grass to their daytime beds in the trees. Arrow wore jeans, a camouflage shirt that was too big for her, and she tucked her hair into a camo hat. He hung a tab covered with the smell of deer urine from each of their brims to mask their scents. The first day they never got a good shot, and her father didn't commend her for sitting still for hours, not talking, being patient and calm. She only had dried apricots for lunch, chewed softly. After dark, they hiked back to camp and ate this exact meal— good luck to eat hunted meat on a hunt—and he had a beer and she had a bottle of sarsaparilla, and he let her have one sip of his. There was no chance to excel, that day.

The next day she was internally more agitated but externally tried to be as tranquil as she could, not fidget. One animal was too far to shoot, but through her binoculars she breathed with it, in and out. Then her father nudged her, and she saw a buck under the tree. Antlers, a trophy. He held out his palm; it was too close for a good shot. It walked away, she didn't make a sound, but as she lifted the gun to her shoulder the animal turned broadside, offering its entire view to her. It was as if the motion of lifting the gun to her shoulder made the animal turn and present itself. She didn't look at her father, didn't need him to tell her, knew where to aim her shot, knew not to wait too long; she looked through her scope and put crosshairs on the part of the animal where there were organs underneath. She breathed out; she pulled the trigger. The entire meadow was flung upwards and outwards. The deer ran farther than she thought it would; she kept her gun raised for a second, long shot—she didn't know if she needed to do it, and then the animal fell.

Her dad clapped her on the shoulder. "That was perfect," he said. "Just right."

Arrow still had dreams that she missed that deer, that her bullet didn't hit it at all and it escaped. She had other dreams where her bullet obliterated the back quadrant of the deer, but it ran on three legs, bloody meat exposed.

They quartered the animal in the field, each carried part of it on their backs back to the truck. Her father gave her the smallest portion, and when they got to camp, he went back twice himself, saying it was too much for her, which it was, but she was glad he said it and not her.

At their house, they hung skinned quarters from trees, bees covering the meat, and brought in a section at a time to dismantle at the kitchen counter. He explained what fascia is, had Arrow touch the cover of the muscles, feel its stretch; he showed her how to cut between joints, which part of the animal was best for steaks, ground meat, stew, which scraps they would take to the butcher in town to make sausage.

Since she'd already missed three days of school her dad

didn't let her accompany him to get his elk, but one day there were three quarters hanging from the trees, one on the kitchen table, and she helped butcher. After they filled both their freezers, after he apparently decided she and her mother were well provisioned for, her father went away without a word.

Because he worked for the railroad, absence was normal: he'd be home for forty-eight hours then away for forty-eight hours. He could get called to work any time, so his sleep schedule and their holiday calendar were erratic—sometimes Arrow had to play quietly as a child because her father was asleep; sometimes they celebrated birthdays early or Christmas late. When she was young and her family was close and happy, her mother joked that he had a second family in Winslow, another wife and a son. "I'm as good as a son," Arrow would say, and it was funny, something they said to show how sure they were that nothing could tear them apart. But when her dad had been gone four days Arrow asked where he was and her mother said she didn't know. After a week, Arrow asked if he actually had another family. Her mother said she didn't think so. "He told me he had to figure some things out. Your father isn't a very talkative man. I believe he'll be back. In the meantime...we'll be okay. I think we have to let him do this." Arrow didn't understand and got the sense she never would. If her mother could call him back, she should, she thought.

She and her mother kept taking turns cooking dinner, like always—a cut of meat from the freezer dropped in the sink that morning to thaw, then grilled, roasted, or chopped and skillet fried; a vegetable, from their garden some months, during the short growing season between freezes at seven thousand feet, or from Safeway other months; and a starch: quinoa or rice or mashed potatoes or her mom's homemade bread. They didn't eat that every night, but most nights; sometimes Arrow's mom would bring home a pizza, or they'd go out for Mexican; Arrow had taught herself how to make venison marinara from a cookbook, and sometimes a bunch of women came over and helped make dozens of tamales to freeze. Arrow had hoped her dad would come back before they emptied their supply, not because she couldn't get more herself, and not because they couldn't afford to buy more at the store, but because it felt to her thirteen-year-old self like a bad omen, like if they ran out and he was gone, he'd stay gone. That much meat would last a long time. Years.

Arrow watched her father drink his beer; she washed down a bite with bubbles, and she thought about how when he came back a few months later, one morning he was just there, drinking coffee, the meat in the sink; that night he cooked dinner, and both she and her mom were happy to see him and tried to not ask too many questions. She was glad, and angry, that something she'd worried about every day was so casually over. Arrow was under the impression he was there for good, but he only stayed through the next hunting season, when Arrow was fourteen. They found a shot elk in the woods that year, too heavy for the hunter to carry out, apparently, though the head was gone for a trophy. Her father got his chainsaw from the truck and quartered it and carried it on his back in four trips. Arrow could still only lift deer quarters then, so she walked next to her father, carrying his pack and hers, back and forth to the truck four times, lifting water to his mouth when he stopped and rested. As they butchered it, he put each roast or steak in the freezer as soon as it was wrapped, but he couldn't get to the left hind in time, so it turned, and he'd sobbed at the kitchen counter, his hands covered in blood. He hadn't been drawn for elk that year, they had been out hunting for deer, and when he said, "You know not to tell anyone about this," she knew taking the elk would count as poaching, but she never told anyone she'd seen her father cry either. He left most of the meat in their freezer except for what he could carry away in his two hands, and what he had to throw away, and then he left again. That time he stayed gone much longer.

Instead of taking the scraps left in the refrigerator to the butcher, Arrow looked online and learned how to make sausage. She made several kinds with different spices in each, filled the casings with her hands so they were lumpy, but she liked that they looked handmade. She kept one package in the freezer as a talisman, a present upon her father's return to show she was resourceful, that she knew not to waste meat, a taken life.

She wondered what kind of person you had to be to be able to behave badly, disappear whenever you wanted. Her mother would never do that. Arrow felt she was most like her father. She wasn't ready to not run away, she knew, so she wasn't ready to have this child. She didn't want to be a parent who left.

And she wondered why she was still afraid to disappoint her father. When he finally came back, when she was fifteen, over a year gone, he said thank you for the sausage but never told her how it tasted.

The elk in Arrow's mouth was delicious and complicated. They put in for a permit every year, still, but with decreased elk populations so few were released that they never expected to get one and never did. They'd brought the end of their quail from last season on this trip and planned to cook at camp the next night; "This isn't a hunt, I know," her dad had said, "but I think we still want to use our ritual for luck." Grant had been bemoaning smaller and smaller coveys for years, and Arrow wondered if this was the year they'd give that up too. They would eat out their last three nights in town, see the sights of the city.

They finished, and her father poured water into the one dirty pot. Arrow couldn't hear individual cars, the traffic an undifferentiated whoosh. It felt funny to camp without a fire, but it was still hot, even after the sun set. They needed their lantern, but neither got up to get it.

Her father dabbed at his face with a handkerchief and said, "Do you want to take a walk?" Restless, as usual. Her father was worse at being still than she was.

Arrow said sure and grabbed her headlamp.

They walked side-by-side up a path, their two beams moving with their steps. Arrow found it strange to camp where she could see so few stars. She looked up. Past her light flickering on leaves, she counted four. She heard no howling coyotes to tell her where she was. Back home, the days were hot, but up on the mountain it still got cool at night. Here, the air had mass, wet weight she pushed through.

A boulder sat in the middle of two crossing paths. An embedded plaque glinted in their lights. They walked up to it, Arrow's hands touching its smooth surface and raised letters, her father's hands on the rock next to the metal. She read aloud, "According to legend, on this site of the principal Manhattan Indian Village, Peter Minuit, in 1626, purchased Manhattan Island for trinkets and beads then worth about 60 guilders. This rock also marks the spot where a tulip tree (Liriodendron Tulipifera) grew to a height of 165 feet and a girth of 20 feet. It was, until its death in 1938 at the age of 280, the last living link with the Reckgawawanc Indians who lived here."

She didn't stumble on the Latin name; Arrow had taken plenty of botany and biology. But she did not know how to pronounce the name of the tribe. She felt like she'd stepped on a grave, shivered while surrounded by humidity. Arrow felt ownership of her region. Responsibility. Stewardship. Who owned Manhattan? It was purchased. That didn't answer the question.

Arrow had met Ed in an Indigenous Studies class, and when he asked her to go get a burrito one night she was hesitant to ask what he was, what kind of brown his skin meant. He told her that first date, without her asking, that he was Hopi but not raised traditionally, raised in Flagstaff, though his grandparents still lived on the reservation, were still traditional, and his parents were somewhere in between. Arrow figured people must wonder that about him; he must have to explain to a lot of people. He told her things they would later learn in class—at one time there were only 350 Hopi people, but now there were over thirteen thousand, and they're matrilineal, lineage passed through the mother—and it bonded them when later they heard their teacher say things they both knew, though Arrow never forgot she knew it differently than Ed did. She told him about taking a Forestry class and how she already knew much of the material because her father had taught himself, then her. Arrow couldn't settle on a major, might not graduate, couldn't figure out what courses would help her know what she wanted to do with her life. Physics. Dance. Gender Studies. She couldn't decide what would matter on a heating planet. At this point, the world didn't need more climatologists. Ed didn't speak much about his heritage, it was just a part of him, but sometimes he spoke his first language with people on campus, artists in town, and Arrow wondered if he wanted her to know that part of him better. He hadn't taken her to meet his grandparents, though she got along well with his mom and dad, and her parents adored Ed. Especially after he fought the fire on their land—his summer job, when he wasn't at school, and he was on call the day their acres burned. He ran into danger as his job, while everyone else waited for danger to come to them. Arrow hadn't asked Ed how long he planned to fight fires. This child would be half-Hopi, but since she was the mom, it would be considered Bahana, white. She wondered if Ed had ever considered having kids with her. She looked back at the stone, wondered what it would feel like for people like you to have been almost eradicated. Or made extinct.

Arrow and her father looked at each other, and their headlamps shone in each other's eyes and they both squinted then angled their heads away so they were facing each other but not making eye contact.

"These people don't exist anymore?" she asked.

"This says more about the tree than about the tribe. But it seems that way." Then, "We may all not exist soon." People were finally starting to say this, admit the possibility.

"The Hopi believe we're in the fourth world now," Arrow said, reciting what she'd learned twice, first from Ed, then from school. "Each world before, people were told how to live rightly in it. But each time they did the wrong thing—stopped living in harmony with the animals, stopped living in harmony with each other. Each time, the world got destroyed but a few people got saved, and they started over. In each new world, they learned something new, how to cultivate crops, how to build cities, commerce." Arrow thought of the manufactured park behind them, the congregated animals. "Destruction brings evolution," she said. "Most Hopi believe we get seven worlds, but Ed was taught that this is the last one. Just four. That's what they believe on his grandparents' mesa. We better get it right this time." The Hopi also believed their prayer cycle controlled the weather, brought rain in a land with no lakes, no rivers, the land their god told them to inhabit to keep them holy. Arrow hadn't asked Ed how they felt about drought, what that had done to their relationship with their faith.

Her father said, "We're way past the point of getting anything right. But I like the idea that the ones who aren't destroyed can evolve. I can believe that."

He walked forward, and Arrow followed him. The trail led to the river, flowing water wide enough to feel oceanic. Dark water always thrilled Arrow, and spooked her. She grew up landlocked, had always been amazed by such an expanse. She thought of tsunamis, hurricanes, tornados, wildfires. She thought of what might be below the lapping, reflective dark. She knew there were machines harnessing tidal energy, but what creatures? They let their lights shine out over small waves. She knew the south part of this island was different now, had read about barriers and sea walls against the rising tides, reefs and wetlands and marshes built to absorb storm water, porous streets, solar roads, some buildings abandoned, their foundations in the sea, but up here, she didn't feel in danger, and she wondered how long that would last on this part of the island.

Back home, the wind before the calm had been even worse that year than most. Monsoons were wind, not rain—wind that carried hot, humid air which hit their tall, cool mountain and dropped its moisture. Arrow knew that, but the monsoon winds were calm. A soft journeying, movement you didn't notice except for the gathering clouds, a breeze. The winds before monsoon season began were a force every year, ferocious whipping through trees, gales and gusts. Fifty miles per hour for days at a time. Everyone held their breath, knowing how a spark would spread. When they all made it to July 1st without a conflagration, it felt like a blessing, a benediction, every year, and Arrow would start up a mental litany: cloudburst, downpour, sunstorm, deluge, torrent, shower, sprinkle, rain rain rain. Every year, the first clouds that gathered didn't drop water but instead electricity, and they all hoped for the best. This year, a bolt struck near their land and caught. They'd almost made it.

Ed and his team were there within minutes. The fire wasn't there yet, but they knew it was coming. He made Arrow and her mother and father leave in their pre-packed vehicles; he made them drop their hoses and buckets and evacuate. Arrow begged him to let her finish soaking the sides of the house against blown embers but he said she knew he couldn't do that. "Go. I'll do my best. You have to leave." Any firefighter would have said the same thing. She didn't kiss him, just let him run toward their house—their two-story A-frame, the front entirely windows, the glass reflecting the trees that weren't aflame yet—with his hose.

She stepped into her truck, the guns and bows in the bed; her mom had the photo albums and pictures off the walls; her dad had the dogs, and none of them looked over their shoulders as they drove away. What Arrow felt wasn't fear but a terror so sheer it was the equivalent of numbness. She thought, *If I never see this land again, I hope I've looked enough times to hold it.* She knew her father felt rage, and she could feel her mother's protectiveness. They met at a Motel 6 on the other side of town, brought their things inside to guard against thieves, and decided to share one room even with the three quail dogs. No one mentioned food, but they split a bottle of cheap whiskey; Grant offered a good bottle he'd been saving for a special occasion, the last bottle of Pappy VanWinkle Family Reserve he'd been able to find anywhere, but Arrow said Evan Williams was fine with her, and no one mentioned she wasn't twenty-one quite yet.

At three a.m., her phone rang, and Ed asked, "Did you sleep?"

"Hardly. Tell me." She could feel her parents listening in the half-light. Ed said they knew they couldn't stop the fire, so they let it pass. The porch was singed and most of the trunks burnt, there was a lot of ash but it didn't become a crown fire. He didn't think they'd lose any trees, maybe a few where the cinders got hot and burned the roots. But the fire passed quick.

"You and your father did good with the land, Arrow," Ed said. "Tell him I said so. The fire did what it was supposed to do." He was leveling his voice, controlling his modulations, and his effort at calmness hinted to her how shaken he was. "Be prepared for a shock," he said. "There's a lot of black. But everything is okay."

"We'll go there now. Thank you, Ed. So much." He said he didn't do much and that he'd see her that night, and she was glad he wanted to. Then she said, "I love you," a thing they had been saying easily lately, and he echoed her words.

She repeated everything verbatim, and her mom hugged her dad close, more worried about him than the land, Arrow knew. Arrow wondered how they'd spent the night, if her father could let himself be touched or if he needed a pocket of space around him.

Seeing the dark trees was worse than she'd thought, but she could tell they were alive. Her dad kicked the deck with his boot and said they'd have to replace some boards but not the whole thing, and Arrow agreed. The dogs nosed around, and their ashed muzzles agitated Arrow. She kept saying, *We made it. We made it.*

Grant picked up a handful of cinders and said, "Still warm. The roots may be ruined."

Arrow thought, *There will be another.* She covered her face with her hands and sobbed, and her mother came to her and held on. Her mother was thinner than Arrow, with strong, ropey arms. She was always willing to comfort her tempestuous daughter, much more even-keeled than Arrow or her dad. Arrow wished she'd inherited her mother's tendency to rarely cry, her ease in caring for others. She and her father were better at tending to forest. Her father stood apart for a while and then came and wrapped himself around both of them, Arrow in the middle of her parents, and she felt like a child.

That night Ed had a bottle of Booker's out, mid-range whiskey, the best he could afford, and Arrow said, "Sure.

Let's celebrate." Neither said, but they both knew, that bourbon's flavor comes from the charred inside of oak barrels. They each had a few, and she found there wasn't much to say so soon, so she reached for him, touched his ribs outside his shirt, then under, his unsinged eyebrows; she lifted off her shirt and slid off his pants. She ran her fingers along his snakebit leg like she'd done dozens of times before. She never avoided touching it, the gap where flesh had rotted away, the leg that kept him in an office the day his buddies died, the day a fire went over them. Rattlers had evolved—they used to shake and make sound to warn away cattle from stepping on them, but humans killed the noisy ones, so they learned to stay silent. Ed had stepped on one while hiking alone in grassland. Before they were together. He could have died but didn't, and Arrow was the only one to have seen the leg, how bad it looked. He'd told her the story on an early date. "They died in their shelters," he'd said, "even the ones who got inside." Arrow had asked how—if the shelters had failed, she wanted to know what was possible—and he answered, "The fire was too hot. Too long. They were cooked." After she said, "Oh," he added, "I don't feel bad I wasn't there. I wish it hadn't happened, but I couldn't have stopped it." She said he shouldn't feel bad. There was nothing he could do, he was right. "The leg," he said, "it's missing muscle. The skin is scarred. It's ugly. You'll never see me in shorts. No one will." Arrow told him she was sure it wasn't ugly at all. It was an injury. It was just what he looked like now. "No one has seen it," he said. "I mean, only doctors." Arrow took that to mean he hadn't undressed in front of a woman since the accident. She wasn't sure Ed had had sex at all until a few weeks later when they finally slept together and it was obvious he knew what he was doing. That time she touched his leg and every time since. He let her. She felt privileged to know something about him no one else did, and she thought she'd convinced him she didn't mind the wound at all, which was true.

The night after the fire, Arrow thought she might cry again, but then Ed was inside her, his big hands splayed on her wide back. And then she was crying again but it seemed okay with him. She lifted herself up, and he told her she was beautiful, and she laughed because she probably had snot in her nose and soot on her face. She ground her body hard against him and felt fragile and hungry, full of gratitude and fear, and Ed could tell and used his hands, another kindness, another gift of release.

Every day that week, she helped her dad clear the land, and then went to Ed for the same tender and tough sex. She moped and pouted and apologized, and Ed said it was okay, a close call is its own kind of grief. At the end of the week, her parents sat her down for a serious chat. They said the land could burn again, probably would. It might be worse next time. Or the beetles would kill all their trees. They could still sell the land now. It was still worth something. But Arrow said no. She wanted to keep the land in the family, and if it became grassland or a wasteland, she would love that version of it. She knew that's what her father wanted, but she wanted that too. "When you two need help out here, I'll move back. I'm not giving this up." Arrow lived in town, just half an hour away, better for school. She could haul water when her dad couldn't do it anymore, bring wood for the stove. They asked if someday Ed would be coming with her, and she said she hoped so. She thought so. She didn't know what he'd say about that, but she thought he was pretty great. They sat on the deck and burnt earth and bark smelled sweet, sugar charred to caramel. They ate Mexican food, and Siobhan convinced them to use their tickets and go to New York. Enjoy themselves despite catastrophe. Near-catastrophe.

It had been eight weeks since the fire, and Arrow was about that pregnant, she figured. She had access to birth control, but the fire made her forget a few pills.

Arrow stood, listened to the dark in front of her. She could smell the sea. She wondered what rain in a city such as this smelled like. Dirty or clean? Her father stood. Arrow turned back to camp and felt her father's light at her back.

VI.
Gaia

I don't know if they know who I am. My name. I carry cans with me, I don't hide. They maybe don't know how good I am. They said, Do my work in there, make it look like real New York. In the Urban Section, the miniature Manhattan they said was going to be a surprise to all the contestants. I told them, "That? That is not real." I said people will like it better without graffiti, clean and tidy NYC. Tourists want to travel to see their urban decay safely away from their hotels. That bus that takes people from Japan and Montana to see third-world conditions on the fringes of the richest city in the nation, Ozone Park, Bed-Stuy, the Meatpacking District. Abandoned buildings, blocks without sidewalks, overgrown lots, weeds, dealers, flooded streets, bad graffiti, just a name, just a declaration, *I was here*, no art. When they drive by my apartment, I flip them off, give the tourists exactly what they want, an angry brown New Yorker who lives in filth. They said they knew what they were doing. They offered an amount, and it was enough. They said I could do whatever I wanted. I wrote intricate words that only someone like me could read. Apocalypse. End Times. Ruination. Disaster. Destruction. Devastation. Catastrophe. Calamity. Armageddon. I do not think this park is a good sign. Surreal. Hyperreal. I live outside of it, but it reaches outside of itself. They think my graffiti is about gang territory, but it isn't. No gangs left in this city, even on the periphery. Criminals still, of course.

But the two sides are now us versus them, no longer us versus us. People think they know what my art indicates. But I'm talking about where we're headed. I know the doom that awaits us. I have language to say it. I'm here to see it. If any of my friends were in that contest, they'd see my work and nod. These tourists, I don't know what they think.

Friday, September 8th, 2023

Day One of the Canon and Cabela's
Birds of the World
Timed Birding Contest

VII.
Ivan Ríos and Alastair Askgold
Zone I—Rainforest

"Should we have a system in how we identify them?"

"Utter randomness okay?"

"Great. The goal is just to take a lot of pictures, yeah? We're both just doing research."

"Does that suit you?"

"Perfect." And they stepped in line.

Today, Alastair looked even more proper and out of place in his fitted jeans and seersucker jacket, no tie but a pink silk handkerchief in his breast pocket. Ivan thought it was late in the season for seersucker, but it was hot. Ivan was too wide to fit into Alastair's clothes, so they'd asked their cab to swing by his place, and he changed into another blazer, another pair of jeans, but instead of a t-shirt he put on the indigo fitted button-up he kept ironed in his closest. He didn't care much about fashion, but he figured he might as well offer the designer his best. He put a fitted long-sleeve shirt that wouldn't wrinkle into his bag, another pair of socks and boxers for tomorrow, just in case. He changed quickly since he was already clean. That morning, Alastair had asked if he preferred a rinse or a soak: the ornate bathroom had a shower and a tub. So Ivan steamed up the room while Alastair bathed, then Alastair asked if he could get in at the end to wash off the soap, asked as if it was the most natural request, and it was, both intimate and casual. Their night hadn't been nonchalant; it had been intense, yet it was also easy. Ivan had only gotten four hours of sleep, but the bed was luxurious, and Ivan felt great. He thought that they might be the most debonair pair.

They were last in line. Alastair handed Ivan the sweetened, lightened coffee he'd gotten at the cart on the opposite corner from Ivan's building while he waited—Ivan hadn't invited him up. Ivan thanked him. "I had a poster of the flags of the nations of the world when I was a kid," Ivan said, looking at everyone's contest jackets. Everyone was wearing the thin shell, had zipped out the thick lining. He and Alastair had theirs in their shared bag. "A lot have been added since then. Chiapas. Moravia. Brittany. Chechnya. South Ossetia. Hong Kong. Guam."

"Quebec," Alastair added. "Palestine. Well, they always had a flag, but it was never on the posters. More are trying. Hawai'i. Sápmi." Then he jutted his chin toward two women wearing International Brotherhood of Electrical Workers t-shirts, Local Five insignia on their chests, discussing how the park was made. Where are the wires that heat the rooms? Cables under the soil? Filaments in the fence for the electric sky overhead? They talked like they had worked together for decades, had handed each other fish tape and ponies and hogs heads and horse cocks, were in the business when angled side-cutters stopped being called dikes and started being called lesbos. Each had on a ring, and Ivan didn't know if they were married to each other, or others. He listened to the women tell each other they were good at their jobs, very, but people beyond their capacity had made this place. He assumed by his gesture that Alastair found them more interesting than flags.

They threw their cups in a compost bin and stepped to

the entryway. Their tickets were scanned, then their fingertips, then confirmation of inoculation, then their iPills were swiped across a flat plane of plastic. A woman in a fitted red suit said, "They'll still make 911 calls if either of you is hurt. But no other phone calls or data access. All the information you need and are allowed has been downloaded to your iPill. Please enjoy the Cabela's Birds of the World Timed Birder Contest, hosted by The Aviary." She handed them brown-bag lunches to eat at their leisure.

They walked under the wrought-iron arch, metal bent into intertwining shapes of birds. The Margaret Corbin Circle entrance, Gate One, sponsored by Keens Chophouse. Everyone got to see three zones each of the first two days; then the third day, everyone got to roam freely over the whole park, and partners could split up. But today, they had to stay side-by-side all day. They'd decided to start in Tropical. "Why not feel like we're on vacation?" Alastair had said. "Maybe they'll have a tiki bar inside." Ivan realized he was holding his breath while he walked, anticipatory, so he exhaled, inhaled thick humid air. The trail led under a canopy of glossy leaves into a room made by trees, and the sounds became cacophonous.

On every branch, something bright perched. Parrots and parakeets, macaws and mynahs, cockatiels and cockatoos, wings and crowns the colors of candy, fruit, tropical flowers. Each had feathers that cascaded down below the limb, some blue, some green, some yellow, red, orange, some all of those colors. Some had horizontally striped tail feathers. Some had feathers standing tall on their heads.

"Whoa," Ivan said. He thought of balloon animals.

Each person gasped as they walked under the arch and

then moved to get as far away from each other as possible, to start capturing one little corner of this paradise, this utopia. Some had fuchsia bodies. One was ginger with a fan of feathers in a flat arc above its head. One was turquoise with a black head, thin tail feathers twice as long as its body. One had a head as filigreed as a flower. Cobalt. Crimson. Cyan. Saffron. One looked like a wig of feathers, a huge poof. Ivan took pictures as quickly as he could, lifted his iPill, zoomed, clicked, and when the alphabetized list appeared, he picked whatever was near the top, Accentor, Albatross, Anhinga, just to capture it all.

There weren't rules against helping other contestants, and it seemed several teams were treating this like a regular birding expedition amongst friends. Making sure everyone saw everything. "Have you seen the Rhinoceros Hornbill yet? Follow the trunk up to the first branch that veers left, and she's in there." Collaboration, not competition. But they wanted to name what they could. They were slow; they wouldn't win, but they seemed to be having a good time. One was wearing traditional African fabric. One had long locks tied up in a topknot. One had dreadlocks dyed blonde.

A bird with a plain, dun body carried a wild assortment of feathers behind him, thin lacy ones, thin spiky ones, wide striped ones, ones that thickened into a plume, periwinkle, black, brown. Dinosaur feet. As Ivan watched, the bird lifted its feathers up over its head like a mask, like a crown. Contorted, he walked slowly through the forest, a fan held coquettishly in front of his plain face. From the back, he looked like a beast, two spread feathers like buffalo horns. He looked like a sea creature. "Who's he courting?" Alastair asked. They looked but couldn't see the one he was trying to woo.

Ivan understood such elaborate plumage as a tool for attraction, audacious costuming, not so different from humans. Though bird mating reproduced the desirable trait—women like bright red, more scarlet males are born. When Ivan first noticed that his mom was darker than his dad, when he learned that interracial marriages had been illegal generations ago, were still suspicious in some places, he told his mom that eventually everyone would marry someone unlike themselves and all the babies would become the same shade of brown and racism would disappear. His mother laughed with delight at that. He said to Alastair, "Women show off the fancy plumage in our world, but in theirs, the males are the fancy ones."

"I know some pretty fancy men," Alastair answered. "I want more ungendered clothes next season. Fancy, but for whoever wants to be. I'm behind the trend on this, late to the blurring. Though, a man wore a gown in my last runway show." He clicked a photo of something green behind green leaves.

A teenager had a flared mohawk and was smiling in front of a cockatiel, all goofy and thumbs-up, photobombing the identification his partner took. She had hair in long black braids, a feather extending from each, and Ivan figured they were looking for a bird with a tail like that next.

Alastair walked to branches full of nearly identical birds, and Ivan followed. Each body was a simple mix of shades, but each thick beak had a different combination of bright stripes. One's beak was mostly turquoise and green but with splashes of red and orange. One had a red bill, with a black band near its face, a patch of yellow, a patch of blue below the blue ring around its eye. "Those are Toucans," Alastair said. Ivan watched as he lifted his iPill, zoomed and clicked a gorgeous photo, scrolled leisurely through the list that appeared, and said aloud, "Fiery-Billed Aracari." Then, "You can just click on a letter and get lower in the list. It's amazing how long it is."

Ivan smiled. He saw a team, a young girl and older man, trying really hard to figure out what each was. She was dressed like she didn't give a shit, in jean shorts and cowboy boots and a pastel plaid pearl-snap button-up, but was accidentally stylish, even at fourteen. Ivan nodded in her direction, and Alastair grinned. Now that was fashion.

She looked at her iPill and said, "It's either a Choco Toucan or Black-Mandibled Toucan or a Chestnut-Mandibled Toucan."

"Let's say it's a Choco Toucan because I like that name best."

"I can figure it out."

"Do you want to spend this contest paging through a guide you can look at anytime? Or what you will see only once in your life?" He gestured to the air and trees and songs in front of him. Ivan wondered if that was her father. He thought he was giving good advice.

"Alright," she said. Then, "You're right." She touched a name, and Ivan didn't know which one she decided was best. He clicked a photo of her and wondered if the judges would keep it, called her Keel-Billed Toucan.

Alastair captured a bright bird and said, "This must be a Yellow-Rumped Flowerpecker. I'm certain of it." Another. "A Blue-Crowned Motmot."

Neither bird was yellow or blue. Ivan was having fun. "We're in the tropics, but there are no bugs," Ivan said. "I wonder what they eat." He was thankful not to be swatting mosquitoes. He took a picture of a white bird that had a flare of yellow feathers, scrolled down the list of bird names and asserted, "That's a Helmet Bird." He photographed a purple bird with black wing tips and a black mask and declared, "That's an Edible-nest Swiftlet."

"It's not," another contestant said with a smile. She was a big woman who wore it well in a sleeveless dress that didn't try to cover the rolls on her arms. Neon pink nails. "Edible-nest Swiflets echolocate. Like bats."

"Wow."

"We're not trying to get them right," Alastair told her.

"I understand," she said. "I just think that's a fun fact people should know."

"I'm glad to now know it," Alastair said, grinning.

Damn, he's charming, Ivan thought.

Alastair pointed at a gigantic cerulean parrot-type creature and said, "Superb Fruit-Dove." An entirely indigo bird was an Eichhorn's Friarbird. The small black bird with riotous tail feathers was a Tawny Frogmouth. They decided that a bird with a teal head, red body, blue feet, and two tail feathers that curled into circles must be a Lafresnaye's Vanga. And the one with a yellow head, green lower jaw, blue beak and cascading feathers was a Rufous Ovenbird.

"Lichtenstein's Sandgrouse."

"Hyacinth Macaw."

"Cuban Grassquit."

"Pauraque."

"Common Poorwill."

"Limpkin."

"Dark-winged Trumpeter."

"Buffy Fish-owl."

"Sun Parakeet."

"Rough-faced Shag."

"Blue Tit."

"Fluffy-Backed Tit-Babbler."

"European Shag."

"Dickcissel."

"Now you're just being silly."

They laughed so hard Ivan had to wipe away tears, until another pair of contestants asked them to be quiet. The birds didn't seem bothered at all. Alastair was easy to be around, and that made him sexy beyond his shape. Though, Ivan had been pleasantly surprised by how much he'd enjoyed his ropey body last night. Going home with someone shortly after meeting wasn't unheard of for Ivan, was fairly regular, in fact—he'd never had a good reason not to follow his impulses. But he wondered if it was a big deal for Alastair. He wondered if he should ask, or if that would make it an issue when it shouldn't be.

Ivan saw a city bird, a regular pigeon, he thought, but with an orange chest, pink head, green body, and magenta feet. He showed Alastair and he asked, "Is it painted?"

"I think they just come that way." This one Ivan wanted to know, so he looked through the guidebook. Pink-necked Green Pigeon. Of course.

Did he feel inspired yet? Maybe birds were over for him. More pigeons—no, the answer wasn't there. It was foolish, he knew, to wonder if he was stirred, moved, in the moment itself. It wasn't so easy to label motivation, to recognize the trigger for the next thing. As much he wanted to think, *Yes! This!* he knew that wasn't how it worked.

Tonight was the night. It was okay to not know what next for now. To keep from feeling panicky Ivan looked into the leaves and found something a brighter green than the tree. Living jade against living emerald. *Satanic Nightjar*. How wonderful.

Ivan realized what was disconcerting about the light. It had no angle to it. Dawn wasn't shifting, changing, things weren't being lit differently as the sun arced overhead. The fabricated sunshine came from everywhere above, the fabric sky a brilliant blue but no singular globe. It had been a long time since Ivan had been up at dawn, and he missed seeing the revelation, objects changing as a beam reached them. So little light in this city, inside the canyons of the skyscrapers, so long since he'd left it. He felt connected with everybody inside this cage, knew eventually that each—in their own time, but each sometime today—would realize the sky wasn't right. This place a diorama, not nature. But it felt nice to stare upward, feel his face warmed, even if by manufactured heat, not an orb of flame. Alastair stood next to Ivan, lifted his chin, and Ivan wanted to see the planes of his face ignited but didn't want to turn, be too obvious. Alastair said, "Sunlight. But no sun. Blocked by a screen that makes its own new light. How strange and wonderful."

How lovely to be thinking the same thing. Ivan turned to him then, and Alastair's paleness was phosphorescent, his severe face not softened by the false sun, but exposed. Ivan felt ravenous attraction, wanted his fingers in Alastair's hair, wanted to press his thumbs hard into his cheekbones, he wanted to pull Alastair to him, push his pretty mouth down. Last night, Alastair was always in control, even when being commanded. Ivan wanted to find out what next, what else. One fluorescent white cloud floated above but cast no shadow.

They kept walking. "Is that Pope Francis?" Ivan asked.

"I wouldn't know."

The guy was in long white robes, had a face Ivan knew from *Rolling Stone*, six bodyguards. The more radical he got, the more the religious folk wanted him dead, but no one could have guns in here. "It is."

"I guess that makes sense. Since he's named after a lover of birds."

"I wonder if there are other people here with bodyguards."

"I heard James Franco is here."

"I'm so over that guy. No one even wants to kill him anymore, they just want him to go away. Running for governor of New York? Getting a degree in climatology? Christ." Then he stopped, pointed, said, "Whoa. Look at those feathers," because there were just so many gushing out of a small body, reaching out into the air in every direction, and then he felt silly. Alastair smiled and said that must be a King Bird-of-Paradise, and Ivan thought he might be right, based on name alone. Ivan thought of Spanish kings and queens looking at parrots for the first time, the splendor of the so-called new world brought back over the sea, and he could understand their marvel.

VIII.
Jhonny Quiñones-Balaguer

I understand they are meant to return. Bred to, it's inside of who they are. I don't understand the rules of breeding, I think those will make sense someday. When I pointed to two I thought would be pretty together, would make a baby half of each of them, my father laughed, and I didn't know why. Because it was impossible? Because they would make funny babies? I thought it would be nice to pair our whitest bird, the lightest one we have, all solid, with our shiniest bird, the one with the most colors. I thought it would make a bird like a pearl, a bird that looked like no color, but when the sun hit it a certain way, you'd see rainbows. It seemed like that would be such a nice bird to hold in my hands. When my father asked which two we should breed and I pointed to my ideas, he laughed. I don't know why it was funny. He has lots of ideas about how to make the best baby pigeons. He tells the other people who have pigeons who come visit. Pairing birds so they carry both the originals of an older good bird. Like making a bird again through other birds. Fifty-percent copies and runty inbreds and darker feathers have more melanin and so are stronger, and the best birds wriggle when you pull their beak, he believes that. I would never pull a bird's beak. I can feel their hearts when I hold them in my hands. Always faster than mine, but when I hold them they're not scared. I know that hearts speed up when scared. I never quite understand what makes me scared. Someday, I'll understand what kinds of birds can make what. My father calls my cousin a half-breed, and I don't understand what that means except my cousin has darker skin and curlier hair than I do. My father said once he was glad I had his hair, not my mother's. I love my mother's hair, it smells like only my mother does so when I smell that smell I know I am safe. My father has told me not to be a crybaby, to be a man, but sometimes things are scary. My mother has said I am only eight, but I don't know what the edge of having to be a man all the time is. The point of pigeons is they come back, but it seems such a risk. I understand we can't race them if they don't know how to come home, this is the first test to see if our new birds are good enough to compete. But what if they aren't? Then I just lost a friend. I didn't want to release the bird on a school day because I wanted to be home when she came home. I've been waiting since I walked home from school. I was worried I missed the return, but I didn't. We can't tell how fast they are on the roof, but when this one sped away, she seemed fast. We released five, and I love them all, but I have a favorite. My father just calls her Number Three.

My father says pigeons with small pupils are the ones that win distances. Big pupils might win short but never far. He checks the eye of each, bird but I learned in school that when light shines in your eyes, the middle part gets smaller to protect you from it being too bright. I can't see my own eyes, but if I look in the sun it gets easier after a second, so I think it's true. Sometimes when my father holds a bird to measure the parts of its eyes the sun shines in, and I think he might be getting a false result. I think you can a tell a winner other ways, but it's hard to explain. I know I'm not supposed to stare at the sun, so I don't do it often. When we go on fieldtrips at school some of my classmates have to put on sunscreen to protect their skin, but my mom says mine can protect itself. She says we're from a place where the sun is hotter than here and made our ancestors' skin dark to guard them. She and me are from there, not my father. He's from here, he says, but I know his ancestors are not from an island. The part of the eye that's my favorite is the part that doesn't move, the colored part. Mine is almost as dark as my pupil. My mom's has a little green. Dad's dark like me in his eyes, though not his skin. Mom told me that's called the iris, and I said I thought that was a flower, and she said it's both. If I ever get to name a pigeon for real, not just in my head, I'll call her Iris if she's a girl. I'm saving that name.

We have a feral pigeon which means she's wild. She just showed up one day and stayed with us. I wonder why more don't. We have lots of food and water and shade.

Pigeons have been used to smuggle messages and things into prisons. I don't think we know anyone there, but mom says everyone does. Some people eat pigeon meat and call it squab. I know sometimes things have names that make them seem like other things. I know lots of things no one knows I know.

We buy different kinds of birds, fantails and trumpeters and tumblers and highflyers and rollers and beauty homers. My father thinks it's obvious what's what, but I never know. I hold names for the birds in my head so I know who's who, Shell and Butterfly and Silent and Shane and Lucy and Lace.

From here, from our roof that came with our apartment, you can see where those other birds live. My father calls it a circus, but I don't think the birds do tricks.

Our birds do wonderful things in the air, but we didn't have to train them to at all. They just know how they like to fly. They also know how to come home. My father said he only had one ever who didn't, and a house cat must have got him, or a window he thought he could fly through. They never choose to not return. That's what has me worried— it might not be my bird's fault. They have to feel what it's like to be on their own if they're going to race. I can't see those other birds, just the place where they are, a big fence. There's cloth over the top that changes colors throughout the day. Mostly blues, sometimes it shifts a little pink or orange. Smears of color, not in tidy patches like on my best birds, where there's every color, but you can tell where each is. It's pretty over there, to watch it move, but it looks out of place. The trees are just green and the buildings are just gray and that makes sense. The cloth looks like a robot. I would like to see other birds besides pigeons, and mom said we might, and my father said we won't. I wonder if it's something to save my allowance for, I couldn't tell.

If this bird doesn't come back dad says we have almost as good other racers. The other four, he said he might be surprised. He doesn't seem bothered when a chick gets smashed in the nest or a mom and dad don't sit on an egg so it gets cold and never hatches. When we found Joe dead in the cage, dad just put him in a plastic bag in the trash and didn't seem upset, told me the trash wasn't being picked up for four days and without the plastic, maggots would get him and be stinky. I wonder what makes you not mind things like that. I liked Joe because he was black and white and so didn't look like a pigeon at all, like we had our very own penguin. Rich people pay a lot of money for a view like this, my father tells me when we're up here. My mom put a little table and chairs on the edge away from the pigeons' lofts, so we could have snacks and drinks and watch the neighborhood lights click on. Mom and dad haven't lived their whole lives here, but I have. Mom always says she'll take me to see the real city from the top of the Empire State Building, and dad says, "What more do you want? This is Manhattan. As real as it gets." I guess everyone wants to live in Manhattan, and we're lucky we do. Mom says other buildings lower on this island are made of glass and reflect the sky. She said the place with all the birds, that cloth is supposed to be the sky. We watched it get built, and now we look down on the sky. I said it looks nothing like the real sky. Our sky. We have clouds and sometimes they turn colors like my best birds. People say pigeons are green but they aren't really, not only, they're blue, like the edge of a sky, but only sometimes. Pigeons aren't gray exactly, but where they are they're like clouds before a storm. When it rains, I feel like I'm somewhere else. Sometimes I worry birds will get caught in the net of the bridge we can see from here, named after an old President, the first one, but they never do. When you watch for one, you realize how many birds live here. I've been seeing them since I got home. Other birds, not mine. It's bedtime for birds soon.

This pigeon is very blue so I can tell a lot of the other birds aren't her. Dad's at work, so mom let me stay up here and brought me dinner and stayed for a minute with me but didn't say much. She lets me do what I want to do. Soon the light will come right at my eyes, not from overhead, and I think that will tell my bird it's time to come home. I named her Estrella after a signer I like. Pigeons sing little songs but not like people. It doesn't hurt my eyes to look at sunrays, only at the actual sun. There are lots of dark birds around here, and lots of regular pigeons. I am not worried, but I am watching. Sometimes I feel like I could step off this ledge and I'd be able to fly, I've paid so much attention to it, but I know that's not true. I never feel heavy, but I know I am compared to a bird. I see so many windows. Some birds fly in a flock so I know that's not my bird, but it's pretty to watch. Starlings, my mom told me. She knows things you wouldn't know she knows. I told her this one's name and she said it meant star. I don't speak the language she and my father sometimes yell at each other in. She said she doesn't want me to grow up with an accent, I'm not light enough to pass but a good voice goes a long way. I don't understand—who doesn't have an accent? It doesn't seem something to ask. Pass. I'm not sure what she wants me to walk by. She won't let me wander the neighborhood by myself so I just look from up here. Standing on the roof of a building I do feel tall.

There's something that doesn't look like everything else, and I try to watch it move. It looks red so I don't think it's my bird, but it's a bird and I've never seen one red before. A bright splash, nothing else like it around. Maybe it's something I've never seen. I hope for it to come closer. I hope for my bird to come home soon. I wonder if this bird ran away from the circus. Or maybe it's her, mine, red from the sun on her feathers. Stars make their own light, and it's the moon that reflects. I can't tell if it's coming toward me or flying away.

IX.
Arrow and Grant Sullivan—
Zone I: Polar

Everyone was wearing waterproof, breathable, Gore-Tex contest-sanctioned jacket sheaths, and for a moment Arrow felt like they were all lining up to parade into the Olympics. She was surrounded by stripes and crescents and crosses and triangles, stars and suns and birds and trees, script and swords, bright colors, contrast, but she could name so few of the nations. She wondered how many of those stitched birds still survived in their home countries; the grizzly still on the California flag had been extinct for nearly a century.

Their tickets were scanned, then their fingertips, proof of inoculation was provided, then their iPills were swiped across a flat plane of plastic. A woman in a fitted red suit said, "They'll still make 911 calls if either of you is hurt. But no other phone calls or data access. All the information you need and are allowed is on your iPill. Please enjoy the Cabela's Birds of the World Timed Birder Contest, hosted by The Aviary." She handed them brown-bag lunches to eat at their leisure.

Arrow and her father walked side-by-side under a wrought-iron archway behind a team with Union Jacks taking up a quarter of their backs, the rest of the flag white stars on blue, and all Arrow knew about them was that they were from a former colony. As they stepped past the fence line the sounds of garbage trucks and taxis and delivery vans and bagel shops opening their gates were replaced by chirps, twitters, calls and songs, birds far from home announcing dawn.

"Here we are," her father said with a grin. Arrow felt as if they were walking into a funhouse or a big-top tent.

When he'd bought their tickets, Grant had decided that their first day they should see something they never had before, then something familiar: Polar, Needled Forest, Desert. Arrow was charmed; it was exactly what she would have picked herself. Arrow followed the trail that would lead them to snow. After about a mile a person in red stood near a table laden with coats. He handed them long down jackets, booties to put over their shoes, gloves, hats, sunglasses. The boots had rubber traction on the bottom, and as they walked out into the blank expanse Arrow liked the feeling of not slipping along the path.

Arrow spun in a small circle but saw no birds. Small human figures dotted what seemed an impossibly wide landscape, too huge to be inside a park inside a city. Far in the distance she could see the edge of The Cloisters, brick and ancient stone against ice and snow. Arrow searched for the equipment that made it, the engines that kept it frozen, but couldn't see any. The gloves made her hands clumsy.

Something buoyant and bright flew overhead. Arrow turned and lifted her binoculars, gasped. It wasn't colorless, it was so light it made white a color, sunlight glaring off its feathers. It was two feet tall, its wingspan twice that, wingtips spread at the end like fingers, tail flared like a warning. It landed at the edge of their vision, and Arrow and her father turned. A line of beak cut down a feathered face, it had yellow eyes, its face so flat it seemed devoid of attunement, but the bird looked at them as if aware of not only their movements, but their thoughts. It settled into stillness, but its body still held the inkling of flight, readiness to release itself from land. And though it was the purest alabaster, paler than the snow, it looked ready to devour something, made Arrow think of white wolves, polar bears, mythic buffalo.

"That's a Snowy Owl," her father said. "I know that one." Arrow couldn't talk. "It could eat our dogs."

They watched it in silence. It watched them. Arrow said, "I'll let you do first honors."

"Thank you," he answered. He aimed, shot, then scrolled down the S's. It took a long time to get to the Sn's. He showed Arrow his identification, and she said, "I'm not sure what else it could be." He clicked the name, and Arrow said, "That was fun." Then motion overhead made them look skyward. Bodies white and pale gray, orange beaks and feet, black hoods, forked tails, they looked like a flock, not a swarm, civilized in the way they followed each other across the sky, landed together, seemed to know each thought the other was having. The owl calmly turned its head in their direction.

Arrow said, "Arctic Terns."

A couple approached, their flag jackets obscured by down. "I agree," the woman said in an accent vaguely Scandinavian. "One of my favorites."

"You have dozens of favorites," her partner said.

"Hundreds." She announced, "These birds see more daylight than any other creature on the earth. They travel so that it's always summer, always long days. From the Arctic to the Antarctic and back every year, nearly seventy-one thousand kilometers. And they live a long time, many make thirty, so two million kilometers traveled in a lifetime."

"Whoa," Arrow said. Then, "What's that in miles?"

The couple looked at each other and shrugged. Arrow reached for her iPill to look it up, then remembered.

"They should be traveling now," the man said. "They move south August through November. But they're here, trapped."

"They must be so confused," Arrow said. "Disoriented. How awful." Then, "I never realized birds don't have facial expressions." She stared at the flock, their frozen mouths, still cheeks.

The owl and the terns observed each other, their feet indifferent to the snow they stood on. Arrow was pretty sure one was a predator, the others prey, but maybe owls ate smaller things. She and her father were no experts, weren't here to compete. They could use the money, but she knew they were outmatched. She knew it had been expensive for her father to bring her here, so Arrow felt pressure to make it worth it. An investment, like her car or her education. This didn't feel unwieldy like those things, exactly, but she found herself wondering about the damage of capture, like the harm of even electric cars, the cost of college. Nothing felt innocuous to Arrow. Maybe it hadn't, ever, but her worry felt more extreme the past few days. This was supposed to be an experience to savor. She told herself to relax.

Arrow found it strange to see birds and no tree in sight. "May I?" she asked. Her dad nodded. She zoomed in to frame one perfect bird, its eyes alert and calm. She took its photograph and made her first identification. She wanted to see each and every thing and see each thing fully—she felt the itchiness of desiring the next, maybe even better bird, and the converse longing to let this, just this, sink in.

The terns lifted collectively, swirled away. The owl followed. It started to snow. "This isn't possible," Arrow said to her father.

He answered, "Well, I guess it is."

"Nice to meet you," she said to the couple, who were looking up.

"Nice to meet you," they said toward the sky.

Arrow and Grant kept walking and the snow turned to ice then they saw chunks floating in a sea. "Penguin! Penguin, penguin, penguin!" Arrow pointed, jumping up and down in her booties.

"Have you not been to a zoo?" her father asked, laughing.

"This is like finding them in the wild!" There were all different kinds, walking around, leaping in the water, swimming. One jumped on the ice and ate a fish it'd caught. "I love them!" she said.

Her father laughed, and it was substantial and light, both. He laughed like he couldn't help it, and like he didn't at all care how it sounded. Arrow found the sound delightful. She didn't think of her father as a laughing man.

"The biggest ones are Emperor Penguins," he said. "I don't know the rest."

Arrow pointed to individuals in the mass. "The next biggest ones are King Penguins. The ones with white around their eyes are Adelies. The ones with crazy yellow hair are Macaronis. White eye-shadowed ones are the Gentoos. Little black lines over their chins are Chinstraps. And the little ones with spiky black hair are Rockhoppers."

"Impressive."

"I studied. I figured Polar Penguins were the only

species I could learn all of. There are only seven."

"Are you trying to win?"

"No. But we might as well do as well as we can. Didn't you teach me to do my very best at all times?"

Her father shrugged. "Maybe. Maybe I taught you that."

"You did." Arrow wanted him to confirm she was right about him in some ways.

Arrow took the pictures, made the identifications, felt victorious. Then she thought, *I don't want to birth a child into a world where penguins only live in zoos.* She'd only ever seen them in zoos, before today, but she knew they were out there, on their own, right now there were others outside of this box, inside no container, and that seemed to matter. But for how long? She wondered if she would have to depend on Ed for money. Her parents for anything but shelter. She wondered how fat she would get if she did this. *Right now I'm still me.*

She took off her glove, leaned down and touched the ice. "This will never melt," she said, her palm warming a tiny slick of water. "They won't let it."

Her fathered was looking at the guidebook. He said, "There all sorts of other birds that we could see here. Petrels and prions. Shags. What's a skua?"

Another pair of contestants arrived ten yards down the shore. Then two more, then a few more. Nothing identifiable but a small chunk of a face, voices of those who spoke. Soon there were a dozen teams near enough to eavesdrop. Arrow realized this zone must be acres, but most birds would be here, near food. She figured they didn't bring predators, seals, whales, but the penguins must not know that, must still be thinking they could be attacked at any moment, pulled down. One man showed his screen to the woman he was with, and she nodded, apparently agreeing with his identification. They didn't say it aloud. If they had, Arrow wondered if she'd cheat, but realized she'd need a picture first, wasn't certain what bird they were focusing on in the water.

The woman closest to Arrow said in a voice with an unplaceable lilt, "We've heard a rumor that four species aren't here. They looked all over the world and couldn't find four of the known living species." She had beautiful blue eyes, and that was nearly all Arrow could see of her face, her hood cinched around the rest. Arrow figured she was from a place without snow. Arrow was glad so many people spoke English, felt bad that she could reach out in no other language.

"Which ones?" Arrow asked.

"People don't agree which are missing. There's been no formal announcement. We're wondering if they'll even tell us if some aren't here. It seems they wouldn't want us to know things weren't done perfectly. That we can't see them all." The snow stopped falling, and Arrow shook it from her jacket.

"A pair in line with us this morning," her partner added, a man with nearly identical eyes, "said that they weren't going to try to identify birds from the entire contest, but only ones to add to their own life lists. They won't win, but they thought they'd come pretty close to completing their lists this weekend. In their lives, they think they'll be able to see every bird that exists."

"What's the current total?" Arrow asked.

"The official number right now is 9,189," the man said.

"That we know of, right?" she asked.

"Yes. That we've discovered. That we know are still

here."

Arrow nodded. That's about what she thought, about eight hundred less than when she was born. There seemed nothing more to say after that, and the pair wandered off. Arrow looked into the water and saw a mass of movement, nothing discernible beyond penguins.

Her dad showed her a picture in the guidebook, pointed, and asked, "Is that that one?"

"Which one?"

"The one in the water, by the rock."

"Which rock?"

"The one jutting far into the water."

"Which one?"

"That large one. There." He pointed, and Arrow followed his sleeve to his hand to his finger, then traced an arc through the air to a rock with a small white bird on its tip.

"The little white bird?"

"No, the brownish-gray one to its left. I think it might be a skua." Arrow squinted. Her dad took a picture and showed her on the screen. "That one."

"That probably is a skua. But do you think it's a Brown Skua or South Polar Skua?"

"Couldn't it be a Pomarine Skua?" he said, pointing to the Sibley.

"It looks like one, but they aren't in the Polar region, so it wouldn't be here."

"The Brown is darker, and this one looks pretty dark. Should we pick that?"

"Good with me."

He clicked. "No wonder they give us hours in here. Birding is hard. Are you cold? Is that bag too heavy?"

The bag was barely starting to bother Arrow, starting to grow a twinge in her shoulder blades, but she didn't want to admit that, so she said she was fine. She was surprisingly warm and said so. A group of four white birds with thick bodies waddled onto the shore, unfolded their dark wings, lifted into flight one by one. They were gigantic.

"That looks like the biggest seagull in the world," her dad said.

Arrow checked the guidebook. "Wandering Albatross. Largest wingspan of any living creature. Did you get a picture?"

"No."

She grimaced.

"Sorry," he said. "I was watching them and forgot."

X.
Officer Smith

MONTH	September
DAY	8th
YEAR	2023
HOUR	10:57 a.m.
OFFICER NAME	George Smith
BADGE NUMBER	1290
PRECINCT	34th
CRIME SUSPECTED	Carrying a weapon
PERIOD OF STOP (MMM)	8 minutes
STOPPED PERSON'S IDENTIFICATION TYPE Young dark Hispanic man	
DID OFFICER EXPLAIN REASON FOR STOP?	No
WERE OTHER PERSONS STOPPED, QUESTIONED, OR FRISKED? No	
WAS AN ARREST MADE? No	
OFFENSE SUSPECT ARRESTED FOR N/A	
WAS A SUMMONS ISSUED? No	
OFFENSE SUSPECT WAS SUMMONSED FOR N/A	
WAS OFFICER IN UNIFORM? Yes	
ID CARD PROVIDED BY OFFICER (IF NOT IN UNIFORM)? N/A	
WAS SUSPECT FRISKED? Yes	
WAS SUSPECT SEARCHED? No	
WAS CONTRABAND FOUND ON SUSPECT? No	
WAS A PISTOL FOUND ON SUSPECT? No	
WAS A RIFLE FOUND ON SUSPECT? No	
WAS AN ASSAULT WEAPON FOUND ON SUSPECT? No	
WAS A KNIFE OR CUTTING INSTRUMENT FOUND ON SUSPECT? No	

WAS A MACHINE GUN FOUND ON SUSPECT?	No
WAS ANOTHER TYPE OF WEAPON FOUND ON SUSPECT? No	
PHYSICAL FORCE USED BY OFFICER – HANDS No	
PHYSICAL FORCE USED BY OFFICER – SUSPECT ON GROUND No	
PHYSICAL FORCE USED BY OFFICER – SUSPECT AGAINST WALL No	
PHYSICAL FORCE USED BY OFFICER – WEAPON DRAWN No	
PHYSICAL FORCE USED BY OFFICER – WEAPON POINTED No	
PHYSICAL FORCE USED BY OFFICER – BATON No	
PHYSICAL FORCE USED BY OFFICER – HANDCUFFS No	
PHYSICAL FORCE USED BY OFFICER – PEPPER SPRAY No	
PHYSICAL FORCE USED BY OFFICER – OTHER	No
RADIO RUN No	
ADDITIONAL CIRCUMSTANCES – REPORT BY VICTIM/WITNESS/OFFICER No	
ADDITIONAL CIRCUMSTANCES – ONGOING INVESTIGATION No	
REASON FOR FRISK – VIOLENT CRIME SUSPECTED No	
REASON FOR FRISK – OTHER SUSPICION OF WEAPONS Yes	
ADDITIONAL CIRCUMSTANCES – PROXIMITY TO SCENE OF OFFENSE No	
REASON FOR FRISK – INAPPROPRIATE ATTIRE FOR SEASON Yes	
REASON FOR STOP – CARRYING SUSPICIOUS OBJECT No	
REASON FOR STOP – FITS A RELEVANT DESCRIPTION No	
REASON FOR STOP – CASING A VICTIM OR LOCATION No	
REASON FOR STOP – SUSPECT ACTING AS A LOOKOUT No	

REASON FOR FRISK – ACTIONS OF ENGAGING IN A VIOLENT CRIME No	
REASON FOR STOP – WEARING CLOTHES COMMONLY USED IN A CRIME Yes	
REASON FOR STOP – ACTIONS INDICATIVE OF A DRUG TRANSACTION No	
ADDITIONAL CIRCUMSTANCES – EVASIVE RESPONSE TO QUESTIONING No	
ADDITIONAL CIRCUMSTANCES – ASSOCIATING WITH KNOWN CRIMINALS No	
REASON FOR STOP – FURTIVE MOVEMENTS No	
REASON FOR FRISK – REFUSE TO COMPLY W OFFICER'S DIRECTIONS No	
ADDITIONAL CIRCUMSTANCES – CHANGE DIRECTION AT SIGHT OF OFFICER No	
REASON FOR FRISK – VERBAL THREATS BY SUSPECT No	
REASON FOR STOP – ACTIONS OF ENGAGING IN A VIOLENT CRIME No	
REASON FOR STOP – SUSPICIOUS BULGE Yes	
REASON FOR STOP – OTHER No	
ADDITIONAL CIRCUMSTANCES – AREA HAS HIGH CRIME INCIDENCE Yes	
ADDITIONAL CIRCUMSTANCES – TIME OF DAY FITS CRIME INCIDENCE Yes	
REASON FOR FRISK – KNOWLEDGE OF SUSPECT'S PRIOR CRIM BEHAVIOR No	
ADDITIONAL CIRCUMSTANCES – SIGHTS OR SOUNDS OF CRIMINAL ACTIVITY No	
ADDITIONAL CIRCUMSTANCES – OTHER No	
BASIS OF SEARCH – HARD OBJECT N/A	
BASIS OF SEARCH – OUTLINE OF WEAPON N/A	
BASIS OF SEARCH – ADMISSION BY SUSPECT N/A	
BASIS OF SEARCH – OTHER N/A	
REASON FOR FRISK – FURTIVE MOVEMENTS No	
REASON FOR FRISK – SUSPICIOUS BULGE Yes	
VERBAL STATEMENT PROVIDED BY OFFICER (IF NOT IN UNIFORM) N/A	
SHIELD PROVIDED BY OFFICER (IF NOT IN UNIFORM) N/A	

REASON FORCE USED	N/A
SUSPECT'S SEX	Male
SUSPECT'S RACE	Latino, maybe African American
SUSPECT'S DATE OF BIRTH (CCYY-MM-DD)	2004-03-17
SUSPECT'S AGE	19
SUSPECT'S HEIGHT (FEET)	5
SUSPECT'S HEIGHT (INCHES)	11
SUSPECT'S WEIGHT	165
SUSPECT'S HAIRCOLOR	Black
SUSPECT'S EYE COLOR	Brown
SUSPECT'S BUILD	Thin, muscular
SUSPECT'S OTHER FEATURES (SCARS, TATOOS ETC.) N/A	
PERSON STOP HOME ADDRESS TYPE	Apartment
LOCATION OF STOP PREMISE TYPE	Subway station
LOCATION OF STOP PREMISE NAME	181
LOCATION OF STOP ADDRESS NUMBER	N/A
LOCATION OF STOP STREET NAME	N/A
LOCATION OF STOP INTERSECTION Fort Washington and 181st	
LOCATION OF STOP CROSS STREET	N/A
LOCATION OF STOP APT NUMBER	N/A
LOCATION OF STOP CITY	Manhattan
LOCATION OF STOP STATE	NY
LOCATION OF STOP ZIP CODE	10033

MONTH	September
DAY	8th
YEAR	2023
HOUR	1:12 p.m.
OFFICER NAME	George Smith
BADGE NUMBER	1290
PRECINCT	34th
CRIME SUSPECTED	Carrying a weapon
PERIOD OF STOP (MMM)	21 minutes
STOPPED PERSON'S IDENTIFICATION TYPE Young African American man	

DID OFFICER EXPLAIN REASON FOR STOP?	No
WERE OTHER PERSONS STOPPED, QUESTIONED, OR FRISKED? No	
WAS AN ARREST MADE? Yes	
OFFENSE SUSPECT ARRESTED FOR	Carrying drugs
WAS A SUMMONS ISSUED? No	
OFFENSE SUSPECT WAS SUMMONSED FOR	N/A
WAS OFFICER IN UNIFORM? Yes	
ID CARD PROVIDED BY OFFICER (IF NOT IN UNIFORM)? N/A	
WAS SUSPECT FRISKED? Yes	
WAS SUSPECT SEARCHED? Yes	
WAS CONTRABAND FOUND ON SUSPECT? Yes	
WAS A PISTOL FOUND ON SUSPECT? No	
WAS A RIFLE FOUND ON SUSPECT? No	
WAS AN ASSAULT WEAPON FOUND ON SUSPECT? No	
WAS A KNIFE OR CUTTING INSTRUMENT FOUND ON SUSPECT? No	
WAS A MACHINE GUN FOUND ON SUSPECT? No	
WAS ANOTHER TYPE OF WEAPON FOUND ON SUSPECT? No	
PHYSICAL FORCE USED BY OFFICER – HANDS Yes	
PHYSICAL FORCE USED BY OFFICER – SUSPECT ON GROUND Yes	
PHYSICAL FORCE USED BY OFFICER – SUSPECT AGAINST WALL No	
PHYSICAL FORCE USED BY OFFICER – WEAPON DRAWN Yes	
PHYSICAL FORCE USED BY OFFICER – WEAPON POINTED Yes	
PHYSICAL FORCE USED BY OFFICER – BATON No	
PHYSICAL FORCE USED BY OFFICER – HANDCUFFS Yes	
PHYSICAL FORCE USED BY OFFICER – PEPPER SPRAY No	
PHYSICAL FORCE USED BY OFFICER – OTHER No	
RADIO RUN No	
ADDITIONAL CIRCUMSTANCES – REPORT BY	

Every Living Species

VICTIM/WITNESS/OFFICER No	
ADDITIONAL CIRCUMSTANCES – ONGOING INVESTIGATION No	
REASON FOR FRISK – VIOLENT CRIME SUSPECTED No	
REASON FOR FRISK – OTHER SUSPICION OF WEAPONS Yes	
ADDITIONAL CIRCUMSTANCES – PROXIMITY TO SCENE OF OFFENSE No	
REASON FOR FRISK – INAPPROPRIATE ATTIRE FOR SEASON Yes	
REASON FOR STOP – CARRYING SUSPICIOUS OBJECT No	
REASON FOR STOP – FITS A RELEVANT DESCRIPTION No	
REASON FOR STOP – CASING A VICTIM OR LOCATION No	
REASON FOR STOP – SUSPECT ACTING AS A LOOKOUT No	
REASON FOR FRISK – ACTIONS OF ENGAGING IN A VIOLENT CRIME No	
REASON FOR STOP – WEARING CLOTHES COMMONLY USED IN A CRIME Yes	
REASON FOR STOP – ACTIONS INDICATIVE OF A DRUG TRANSACTION No	
ADDITIONAL CIRCUMSTANCES – EVASIVE RESPONSE TO QUESTIONING Yes	
ADDITIONAL CIRCUMSTANCES – ASSOCIATING WITH KNOWN CRIMINALS No	
REASON FOR STOP – FURTIVE MOVEMENTS Yes	
REASON FOR FRISK – REFUSE TO COMPLY W OFFICER'S DIRECTIONS Yes	
ADDITIONAL CIRCUMSTANCES – CHANGE DIRECTION AT SIGHT OF OFFICER Yes	
REASON FOR FRISK – VERBAL THREATS BY SUSPECT No	
REASON FOR STOP – ACTIONS OF ENGAGING IN A VIOLENT CRIME No	
REASON FOR STOP – SUSPICIOUS BULGE Yes	
REASON FOR STOP – OTHER No	
ADDITIONAL CIRCUMSTANCES – AREA HAS HIGH	

CRIME INCIDENCE Yes	
ADDITIONAL CIRCUMSTANCES – TIME OF DAY FITS CRIME INCIDENCE Yes	
REASON FOR FRISK – KNOWLEDGE OF SUSPECT'S PRIOR CRIM BEHAVIOR No	
ADDITIONAL CIRCUMSTANCES – SIGHTS OR SOUNDS OF CRIMINAL ACTIVITY No	
ADDITIONAL CIRCUMSTANCES – OTHER No	
BASIS OF SEARCH – HARD OBJECT N/A	
BASIS OF SEARCH – OUTLINE OF WEAPON Yes	
BASIS OF SEARCH – ADMISSION BY SUSPECT N/A	
BASIS OF SEARCH – OTHER N/A	
REASON FOR FRISK – FURTIVE MOVEMENTS Yes	
REASON FOR FRISK – SUSPICIOUS BULGE Yes	
VERBAL STATEMENT PROVIDED BY OFFICER (IF NOT IN UNIFORM) N/A	
SHIELD PROVIDED BY OFFICER (IF NOT IN UNIFORM) N/A	
REASON FORCE USED Resistance to frisk	
SUSPECT'S SEX Male	
SUSPECT'S RACE African American	
SUSPECT'S DATE OF BIRTH (CCYY-MM-DD) 1993-05-05	
SUSPECT'S AGE 30	
SUSPECT'S HEIGHT (FEET) 6	
SUSPECT'S HEIGHT (INCHES) 1	
SUSPECT'S WEIGHT 205	
SUSPECT'S HAIRCOLOR Black	
SUSPECT'S EYE COLOR Dark Brown	
SUSPECT'S BUILD Thick	
SUSPECT'S OTHER FEATURES (SCARS, TATOOS ETC.) Child's face on forearm, Rose	
PERSON STOP HOME ADDRESS TYPE Apartment	
LOCATION OF STOP PREMISE TYPE Sidewalk	
LOCATION OF STOP PREMISE NAME N/A	
LOCATION OF STOP ADDRESS NUMBER 70	
LOCATION OF STOP STREET NAME Haven Ave.	
LOCATION OF STOP INTERSECTION N/A	
LOCATION OF STOP CROSS STREET between 169th and 170th	

Every Living Species

LOCATION OF STOP APT NUMBER	N/A
LOCATION OF STOP CITY	Manhattan
LOCATION OF STOP STATE	NY
LOCATION OF STOP ZIP CODE	10032

XI.
Ivan Ríos and Alastair Askgold— Zone II: Coastal

Ivan was ravenous. Inside a theme park, while the world burned and flooded outside the gates—this newly intimate stranger's home about to be submerged in a week or in a few years, no one knew, wildfires sweeping California, the edge of his nation—Ivan knew how small his desires were. For food. For sex; he hoped to have again what he had yesterday, last night, in the early hours of this morning. For inspiration—how he hoped for meaning to sweep in, something to hold the panic at bay. Something to make to make his small life seem worth it, while daily others died. He admitted the easy hunger to Alastair, and they stopped to eat.

Today's lunch was Ethiopian. Plastic sealed the tray and had names typed onto it, announcing what the pile below was. Doro wat, tibs, besaega, gomen, miser alech, shro wat, atkilt, kitfo. All on top of injara. Mostly plants, some meat, advertised as pasture-raised. Berbere spice on the side, and tiramisu for dessert, a relic of the failed attempt at colonization by Italy, Ivan knew. He loved Ethiopian food.

They'd only had coffee for breakfast. Ivan liked watching Alastair pinch bits of food in torn pieces of bread. He did it so tidily. Ivan had to keep licking his fingers. Every bite was a pleasure. He liked how much spice Alastair added and that he ate every bite given to him. He liked a man or woman who liked to eat.

They headed to their next zone.

Clusters of long-legged birds edged the lake. Silhouetted against the shimmering water, some had their necks extended, that febrile tendon, long as their bodies, investigating the water or the air; some had their necks tucked down, making them seem small and contained. Some had sleek edges, others had feather wisps that straggled out at the ends. Some were blue, some gray with blue patches, and the white ones could only be said to be ghostly, gorgeous and terrifying, attractive and repulsive. Sublime. Some dark ones had their wings held up like cartoon vampires, shielding the sun so they could see into the water to hunt fish. Most just stood, regal. One flew and landed, one flew away.

One tall bird lifted its feathers like putting on a stole, an immediate, elegant gesture, raised plumage the equivalent of lipstick, stockings, pearls, décolleté created by black fabric, though it was usually the men who were so done up in Aves. In Ardeidae the sexes were alike, and Ivan wondered what that would be like—making love to your identical. These birds knew what they looked like by looking at each other; though, maybe female peafowl thought they were iridescent. Ivan was always after his opposite, never attracted to anyone who looked like him. Ivan wondered if birds paired beyond gender, if there were couples in Aves bonded beyond sex.

Ivan was back to grabbing whatever name was at the top of the list, African Penguin, Antarctic Petrel, Andean Condor. He wondered if the judges would think he was loony, but likely a computer was grading them all at this point. He and Alastair stood near a pair who were probably a Visibility Team. Someone who didn't slot into already-known spaces stood next to someone else who did not, either. Each was androgynous, but they didn't look like each other. One was tall and lithe and long-limbed with thick eyebrows and oval, long-lashed eyes, black hair in a wind-tousled coiffure, square jaw and plump lips; the other had a blonde bouffant quiff, broad shoulders, wide, sharp cheekbones, narrow nose, thin hips. Not a heron facing a heron but an egret of unknown gender facing a neutral crane. Ivan figured some felt squeamish wondering what was under those clothes—breasts? penis? vagina? some combination? nipples on a slightly raised surface, which wouldn't answer the question?—but he found them each gorgeous, and while he knew others must be baffled, he knew they'd also dimly recognize the same sensation felt when in the presence of beauty. The two were not trying to be transcendent. They just were.

The blonde wore a t-shirt that read, "I am the future." Ivan clicked a photo, called him or her or zir an American Kestrel.

The dark-haired one read aloud that there were white variants of many herons and egrets, so it was easy to confuse Little Egrets, Great Blue Herons, Great Egrets, Snowy Egrets, Reddish Egrets, Little Blue Herons, and Cattle Egrets.

"Would they trick us like that?" the other asked.

"That determines the experts, right? We're supposed to use their beaks to tell differences, but all these beaks look the same to me."

"So let's ignore the white ones."

Ivan wondered how many experts were in the park, how many were here to win it, and how many just wanted to see it, gaze on opulence. He hadn't seen any real contenders yet, he didn't think, just spectators.

Alastair was clicking away. "Hey! That's a Flamingo," he said to no one in particular, seeming glad to recognize at least one.

Two birds were taller than the rest, had bright white bodies, black legs, black tail plumes, black heads. Both lifted their heads and trumpeted. "Japanese Cranes," a stranger with droopy eyes said reverently. He pointed to a bird with long feathers on its chest, a yellow crest of feathers spiked from its head to its neck, and a red wattle, and said, "That's a Gray Crowned-Crane. It lives in the southern part of Africa. I cannot believe I'm seeing these."

"There's a swan," Ivan said, and pointed to a white bird gliding along the water.

Some birds stayed on the edge, still as trees. Others dove for fish. One stood on a log and raised its wings, sunning and drying itself, though it looked like it was shrugging, or waiting for a pat down.

Alastair was drawing.

One man said to another, "I keep hearing that Green Heron, but I haven't seen it yet." To Ivan, all the sounds were alike.

Then the man stopped listening, and huddled over his partner's camera, their bodies keeping the sun's glare off their screens. "Okay, in that picture, the bird appears to show pale-based coverts—creating a double flash on the underwing—and blunt-tipped central rectrices, both of which support an identification as Pomarine Jaeger."

"But this shot shows the greater under primary coverts more clearly, and they do not appear to be extensively pale-based. Instead, they seem fairly heavily barred, though this shot has some motion blur on the wing. Juvenile Parasitic

Jaegers *can* show barring on these coverts. But juvenile Pomarines can show extensively pale bases to these coverts, perhaps with faint smudging but contrasting strongly with the median under primary coverts and barred and dark only on the outer portion."

"This shows the underwing again but also the bird's central rectrices, which appear at this angle and in reasonably sharp focus to be pretty pointed. What's also visible is that the bird's feet are black only for about half of their length. I believe the combination of pointed central rectrices, barred greater under primary coverts, a smaller head and finer bill, and half-black feet all point toward an identification of Parasitic Jaeger."

"I just don't think we can be sure."

"I'm certain."

"Okay. I trust you."

Everyone around them stilled, listened intently. Some had the awe-struck face acquired when in the presence of greatness. The men walked away and everyone started chattering—Basil Bunting and Sean O'Grady, the team that might win it all.

Ivan couldn't tell if their competition and cooperation were erotic. He looked at Alastair to gauge his reaction, but he was still working, the same concentration on his face as when he'd watched cricket the night before, the same look he'd had in moments last night, but with his eyes closed.

Ivan tried not to be jealous.

When the worker called time Alastair put his stylus in his pocket. Ivan wondered if he'd get to see Alastair's work. Wondered what they'd share. Wondered what was ahead of them that night—they hadn't talked about whether Alastair would accompany him to his premiere at Radio

City Music Hall. Wondered where each would sleep.

Ivan saw a man drop something from his palm, let a scrap of paper slip from his hand while he walked forward. Surreptitious and purposeful. As if to leave a piece of himself behind, detritus in this built place, a mark, a change. *I was here.* Ivan understood the impulse.

He and Alastair headed toward Deciduous.

XII.
Ray Rasmussen

Some people are from here. Some people aren't from here, but this is now their city.

I serve them food from other places. This job's not so bad. I've been serving people all my life. In my home country, then here. Fast food. Prep-cook for fine dining. Been a maid. I've never been fired, but I change jobs often enough, trying to find easier ways to pay bills and buy food. My jobs mostly have used my body and my mind, and I know others have it worse than me. Never a factory. I have had long hours and repetitive labor but nothing that manual.

This work is temporary, of course, extra on top of the serving gig I have at the new place down on 22nd. After the contest, they'll keep some of us in the museum café. If they offer me that we'll see. Like an audition now. I'd like to see it, after this fiasco, but working inside you don't see much. Whether I stay here or not I'll bring the kids to see it. They said we'd get a one-time discount on admission as part of our wages. We ate what we made for lunch, and it was pretty good for group food. Flavorful. They're trying out a bunch of stuff these three days, to see what the contestants like best, to see what we should serve regularly. Food from countries none of us are from, but we all know how to follow recipes.

They act like this is so brand new and extravagant. Climate Zones. Pods prepared for Mars, in case we want to take the Arctic with us up there. But they've had climate zones at the Brooklyn Botanic Garden for decades. Not for animals, for plants, sure. But you walk into Tropical, and it's so steamy. I've never been to Costa Rica but I imagine they got it right. Smells like growing things. Like even the air is fertile, could do things to me, make me produce. More—I've already produced. And the desert. I've also never been to Arizona, the Sahara, the Mojave, the Gobi. But they have different sections labeled in there, different desert landscapes contained in one room. The air there feels like it's taking something from you. The plants are different in each section. Tiny little things barely alive in one place, in the rocks, succulents, then tall trees, and down the path a saguaro, an organ pipe. The worker who trained me, Cheyenne, told me that there's a leaf in there that smells like rain so I plucked one once from the bush, when no one was watching. We can't have everyone doing that, sure. Creosote it's called, and she was right. A room that pulls moisture out of my face and a plant that smells like what clouds make. What we don't have enough of. Amazing. I felt like I could squeeze the leaf and drink. I get that the Aviary is a feat of engineering. So much goes into making this all look natural. I'm just saying it's not the first time something like this has been built. The most elaborate, and worthy of celebration, sure, if it works. I was a custodian there at the Brooklyn Botanic Garden, eventually got promoted to cater-waiter. Serving people at fancy parties in our atrium. They wander the plants with cocktails, they come into a glass room and we serve them above-mediocre group food. Steaks, potatoes, shrimp. In a tuxedo. Women and men in tuxedos. A great look on some. Not on others. I liked it on me, felt dapper, even if the fabric of the cheap one I bought was close to plastic. Ugly, comfortable shoes, but no one looks at a waiter's feet. Weddings, mostly. Sometimes two a day. Rich people with their terrible taste in music. It was an okay job. An okay crew. Restaurant workers are the foulest, people don't realize. They tell racist, sexist jokes all day to keep the three doubles in a row bearable: a Jewish wedding then an Asian wedding then a gay wedding then a Broadway wedding then a lesbian wedding then a mixed-race wedding, Friday through Sunday in summer. We have something awful to say about all of it, to keep us laughing even as we feel bad for laughing.

One time the garden hosted a corpse flower, very rare. I went in on my day off to see it, stood in line for over an hour to get a whiff. My kids came with me. Amazing what we'll make a spectacle out of. A flower that blooms once every hundred years. It didn't smell nearly as bad as they said it would. It looked eerie and alive though. Then the next day all my coworkers could do was make dick jokes about the center stabbing out of the petals, even those who hadn't seen it. I kind of loved them, that crew. My kids hadn't been impressed with the corpse flower, hadn't thought it as strange as I had. That flower temporarily brought here from somewhere else. Brought back. The cacti will spend their whole lives here, but they weren't born here. My mom and dad were illegal until they died, brought me here right before the border tightened even more. I became legal through my moral character, went to college, worked in the cafeteria the whole time, studied History which I loved, but it didn't turn into a job better than one my other skills offered. People need to eat more than they need to understand the ongoing effects of colonization, apparently. Coming here wasn't my choice, but I did want to stay. My children were born here, so they're legal. Above our heads, birds travel. The birds inside this park will never go home. Immigration and migration. It will be interesting to see how nations change from inside their own borders now that it's so much harder to cross them. Nations built by people crossing borders, legally and illegally. Now, we're all here. I looked up the Latin name, *Amorphophallus titanium*, basically amorphous huge strong cock, as far as I could tell, or loving unbreakable cock, I guess, but I didn't tell them that, my kids or my coworkers. I tried to not give them fuel for any fire, but also joked around enough that they wouldn't turn on me. God help the serious ones. We don't know each other well enough here yet to joke, to talk shit, but those who stay past the contest, I bet the same thing will happen. Inappropriateness as bonding. Acting like none of it really matters as a way to get through the day.

XIII.
Arrow and Grant Sullivan—
Zone II: Coniferous

"This is…" As they walked into the Coniferous Zone, Arrow said, "…where we're from." She spun in a small circle, had the sense of recognition in an unexpected place. "This looks exactly accurate. Just like home."

Her father answered, "They sure got the Coconino right. They must have hired forestry guys. This looks healthy. Like the forest north of town they've done all that work on."

Some parts of the Coconino were burned to cinder. Other parts were scorched but wouldn't fall. This place was the ideal, what would save all those acres. "Like our land before the fire," Arrow said.

The tang of pine needles and the savor of bark filled the air. Dead spines and cones littered the ground; they must have been swept up and bagged in the forest these trees were taken from, since they wouldn't have had time to shed in the few days they'd been planted in this place. *Pinus ponderosa*, Arrow thought. Some were so massive two of her couldn't meet hands around their trunks. Arrow hoped the disruption, the digging up and replanting, wouldn't cause them to turn red-needled and dry, dead like so many in the forest surrounding her home, groves dying from drought, not fire. Not yet.

"Well," her father said and started walking. Arrow didn't have anything to add to that.

Every Living Species

The park was very terraced, tiers and ridges and layers stacked. They'd kept the architecture, the paths, the arches, the stone walls and switchbacks and sheer rock surfaces sliced and squeezed into place to make mini mountains and mesas. As they climbed Arrow felt like she was in a canyon, but verdant, not variations of crimson striations.

"Steller's Jay," she said and pointed. A team with Swedish flags on their jackets overheard. They were blonde and slim, a man and a woman, and Arrow wondered if everyone really did look like that in Sweden. The woman clicked a picture and scrolled down, she and her partner searching for how to spell what they'd heard the American girl say. Arrow didn't care. Anyone could try to cheat off her—she wouldn't help, but she wouldn't hinder them. This jay was all sharp edges, crests and tufts. In childhood Arrow had thought their name was Stellar, as in astral, traveled from a faraway place, from a blue globe like her own but flown across a long gap of black sky. When she was a teenager she thought they were so punk rock, blue bodies and coiffed black spikes. They looked shellacked. "Don't they look smart?" she asked.

"Why smarter than any other bird?" her dad asked back.

"Probably because this is the first bird that ever looked me in the eye, and seemed to recognize me."

"It's the bird you look the most like."

Arrow smiled into the ground because she didn't want him to see how much that pleased her. She knew he meant that she'd had blue and black hair plenty of times, lacquered points, but she wondered what other affinities he saw. She'd loved her heliotrope hair, but the day before they left for this trip she'd had it done bright red, nearly an ultraviolet fuchsia, with cobalt streaks. She wanted an exaggeration of her parents' hair, a more intense version of her mom's Irish red, her dad's black Irish locks so dark they had had a blue sheen to them, before the salt-and-pepper. Having a vivid version of the hair of the two people who made her would help her resolve that the lineage would stop with herself. Help her say goodbye to this person inside of her who wasn't yet a person. Just a possible person. It was juvenile to dye her hair and not just talk to her parents, she knew this, but it proved her own damn point. She wasn't ready. She looked straight up. "They didn't get the sky right. Not bright enough." It wasn't the blue of home, the shade between sapphire and aquamarine, deeper than a robin's egg, that piercing sky purer than water.

"It's not sky, it's fabric."

"Yeah. But it's so nice that's not the real sun." It looked and felt just as hot but no UV. Arrow hadn't walked around Arizona without sunscreen, a hat, shades, and long sleeves in years. Arrow told herself to pay attention to how this felt on her skin. She rolled up the sleeves of her t-shirt, exposing her arms to the shoulders. She wondered if she was the only person out of the two thousand there wearing tie dye. She pointed. "Red-Bellied Woodpecker."

"Where?"

"Near the branch by the big branch."

"Which one?"

"The longest branch to the right, between it and the one above it, the one that's pointed toward us."

Her dad moved his binoculars. "Where?"

"More to the right." Arrow reached over and tried to position his binoculars. "Against the trunk."

Every Living Species

"There!" he finally said. "You're right." He captured it. The Swedes had wandered off, weren't eavesdropping anymore. The woodpecker walked down the trunk and banged its beak against a branch, the pleasant sound of pummeled bark reverberating through the forest. She wondered who noticed. Arrow thought of the woodpeckers that sometimes woke her growing up, pecking their house, finding no bugs in the walls but still thinking their house was a tree. Arrow laid her hand against a trunk. The false sun had warmed it, just like at home.

She leaned in and smelled the tree, and her father smiled at her then smelled the tree closest to him in kind mimicry. In childhood Arrow told people ponderosas smell like vanilla, but when she smelled them herself she would differentiate: some were banana, some blueberry, some cinnamon, toffee, caramel, honey. Variations of saccharine richness—it didn't make sense, this candied bark of a pine, famous for the gritty gin scent of its needles. When she was a child she thought only she knew, thought she discovered it. All of her school friends lived in the city, so when she brought them to her house in the woods it was a revelation for them when she told them to lean in and breathe. The trees back home still smelled lovely, even though their sap had been diminished by drought, some so famished the bark beetles could climb through the barrier. Beetles planted eggs inside, and when larvae hatched, they ate the phloem, the layer between the bark and the timber. Trees carried water through the phloem, so the trees perished from thirst. Her father knocked the bark off a tree on their land, dead from beetles, and said, "It looks like someone has taken an engraving tool to it." His voice full of awe. Beauty and devastation.

Arrow said to her father in that false forest, "If our land back home burns, again, worse, we'll have to come visit it here."

He nodded. Then laid his head against the trunk, next to his palm.

Two other contestants with U.S, flags on their jackets had been watching her and her father; they leaned in and smelled the nearest tree. One woman raised her perfectly manicured eyebrows, the other's smile was enhanced by the fact that she'd painted her lips a deep cherry. Arrow was delighted with their delight, felt she'd brought a touch of her birthplace to two strangers, something they wouldn't have known on their own. She walked and put her hand on her father's shoulder, said, "I know," and he lifted his head and followed her forward.

Then they stepped into a swarm of hummingbirds. Arrow covered her face as if they were bees, stingers forward, then dropped her hands. There were ruby ones, emerald, and she followed one with her eyes, a copper sheen. Several were iridescent rainbows, throats shimmering concentric red, orange, yellow, green, blue, and purple, and when she saw them she grabbed her dad's arm. Arrow wanted to reach out and touch one, feel that tip of a beak. One flew up to her face, looked directly at her, hovered. She was afraid it would stab her cheek. It darted away and the swarm spiraled off elsewhere.

"Those do not live in Arizona. I've seen, I don't know, the little orange ones and green ones. Nothing like that," Arrow said, breathless.

"Looks like some of the rainforest hummingbirds made friends with their North American counterparts."

"Do you think they escaped their zone?" Arrow

imagined birds moving out of their habitats, a parrot on the shore, a gull perched in a spruce. She wondered if workers would gather the birds after the park closed, carry them back to where they were supposed to be. "Those hummingbirds would probably never meet in real life." She remembered on a hunt a hummingbird trying to drink from the pink plastic fletching glued to the metal shaft of her father's arrow.

"Probably not," her dad said. Then, "We didn't get a single picture."

"That I'll remember," Arrow said. Everything was still. Arrow couldn't see any birds, but had the feeling she often got in the forest: that there were eyes behind every branch, bodies shielded by needles. Her father kept walking and Arrow followed, let him lead her through her forest. When he touched a branch, she reached out and touched it after him. Her father had taught her how to hike safely in the alpine desert: always carry water; always carry food; always carry matches, you never know if you're going to sprain an ankle and have to spend the night; a storm can spring up any time, and as hot as any day is, the nights above seven thousand feet are cold enough for hypothermia; always carry a fleece jacket—cotton won't dry, wicks warmth away from skin, but fleece is synthetic and doesn't stay soaked; if you're in the tundra, where the flowers are smaller than your little fingernail, and a storm comes up, you're the tallest thing around—get below treeline immediately, but if you're stuck in a meadow and you feel the hair on the back of your neck or arms stand up, get into lightning position: crouch as low to the ground as possible and balance on one foot, so that if you're struck, the lightning has a quick path through, will do the least possible damage.

Arrow recited this litany in her head, Broadway less than a mile away.

Two people were chatting while walking, a pair of strangers getting acquainted, Arrow assumed. "I like it when the birds come to me. I'm a backyard birder, really. I wouldn't have done this trip but my kids sent me. I have two lists—backyard life list, everything that's come to where I am. I do have another list, the bird experience list. Watching a hawk eat a sparrow, each year's first migratory bird, I mark those kinds of things. This will be its own list, I guess. There's a robin. Hear it? They sound like old Irish ladies saying, 'Cheery-up, cheerio. Cheery-up, cheerio.' Lose the doom and gloom."

The other held her iPill by her face, ready to flip down her binocular app at any time, and Arrow wondered if that was the posture of an expert or someone more anxious than she should be. "There's a catbird," she said. "I can't see it yet, but I hear it." And for the first time, Arrow heard that eponymous growl.

Grant walked into an aspen grove and Arrow followed, the leaves flicking green and silver in the light wind, marks like black eyes on the white bark. Quaking Aspens, *Populus tremuloides*. Arrow felt tremors she recognized, leaves shimmering in the slightest breeze.

"I thought we were in the Needled Forest," a voice inside the grove said. He had wild red hair and a big red beard, stylish nerd glasses, and a pierced lip. He was a big man, but he walked through the trees gracefully; he was sloppily dressed in torn jeans and a cardigan stretched to asymmetry, classic Chuck Taylors.

His eyes were bright behind the sheen of his lenses when he turned toward Arrow as she said, "Aspens only grow around pines and spruces and firs, even though they're deciduous. So, they should be here, even though the labeling system makes it seem like they shouldn't."

"Thank you," he said, and his smile made his cheeks poke out. "I've never seen anything like them. I didn't know trees came in white." He had a nice voice, soft.

His partner had on a vintage cerulean blue dress and cat eye glasses, her bleached hair done in finger curls. *How fun*, Arrow thought, *the Nineties and the Fifties together*. "We live here," the woman said, "well, Brooklyn, so no trees like this."

"People carve the bark where I'm from. Arizona. Initials, mostly, to say they were there. But you really shouldn't. It lets bugs in, which can kill the tree."

"Okay," he said, "I won't." Arrow wondered if he'd wanted to. The woman plucked a leaf off an aspen and put it in her backpack, then the couple walked away and waved. Arrow wondered what else people were taking with them. She hoped to find a fallen feather.

Arrow sat down, speculated about how exactly they got the forest floor of an aspen grove just right. She pressed her fingertips into the leaves above the soil. She guessed the workers who assembled this patch of trees had never seen an actual grove. Aspens were one organism, she knew, connected underground by roots, each tree really a stem. Her father had taken her to the Utah stand, 80,000 years old, the oldest creature on the planet. Aspens survived fire; even if the trees above were burned, the roots would send up new ones after the heat was gone. These aspens must have been disconnected when they were pulled from the ground and shipped here. They wouldn't die, but everything's life was risked to be in this place.

Arrow flattened her palms.

Her father sat down next to her. It didn't seem hard for him to move, he didn't seem creaky yet.

"Do you remember when we camped off Hart Prairie Road that spring after that crazy winter?" she asked. "And some of the pines and aspens, the young ones, were still bent over from all the snow that had been piled on them? You lifted me up and I felt so tall, touching the tops of trees. Mom came on that trip."

"I miss your mom," he said, and that surprised Arrow. "She would love all this. But it's nice to have time with just you," he said. It had been awhile since they'd been alone together, away from their land, a while since they'd done something together besides work side-by-side.

He looked up into the straight white trunks, leaves above. He took a picture and said aloud, "Tree Swallow." He handed Arrow her lunch, *Greek/Turkish/Lebanese Cuisine* printed on the brown paper bag. Hummus, babaganoush, lamb kabobs, falafel, tabouli, and salad with feta, kalamata, tomatoes, cucumber, and pepperoncinis were packaged each in their own little rectangle of a compostable tray made from corn. Baklava. Arrow had a hunger she hadn't yet acknowledged, started with the meat, then the sugar, then the vegetables. They quietly chewed, each said once that everything tasted good. Arrow wondered what cuisine from what mix of nations they'd serve tomorrow, wondered if everyone in the park was eating the same thing today.

Then her father said, "What is wrong with that bird?" He pointed.

Arrow looked, then resisted running toward it, trying to scoop it up. A round, gray bird with a bright white chest, a red smear running down its front. Scarlet in the center, fading to pink on the edges, blood oozing from the breast of the bird.

"Is it shot?"

"There's another just like it."

Arrow lifted her binoculars. "They both have the same mark." They moved slowly through the underbrush, lifting leaves with their beaks. Unharmed. Red feathers fading to pink, not blood. "These birds do not live in our forest," she said. "Will you please tell me what they are?"

Her father flipped through the Sibley. Arrow felt her heart racing, but she wasn't sure why. She felt in danger, even though the birds were fine. "Luzon Bleeding-Hearts," he finally said and showed her the picture in the book.

"Of course."

"They live on the forest floor of the North Philippine Islands."

"How'd they get in our forest?"

"The forest they're from is coniferous, too. They're in the right zone."

"I don't know why they trouble me so much."

"They look hurt. It's alright."

Arrow breathed in and out. She felt loose at the joints, as if she could float away or fall apart. She wanted to lie down in the dead and dying leaves and sleep in the sunshine. All the beauty around her felt fragile, as if it could collapse onto her head or burst into flame. She said, "You shoot birds, I shoot birds, but something about these birds spending their entire lives looking like they're dying is really, I don't know, spooky and sad."

"We all spend our lives dying," her father said. He stood, and pulled Arrow to her feet. She was thankful he didn't make her feel foolish. He took a picture of the Luzon Bleeding-Hearts and identified them. Arrow dusted the detritus of leaves off her jeans.

They walked up a steep incline, and the trees shifted from ponderosa and aspen to a mix of pine, fir, and spruce. "We're in Colorado," she said. She pointed, "There's a Columbine." The flower looked like a tube, or a flute, or a tiny crown. Arrow used to make wreaths of them when they camped. All three would wear them. Her mom would only camp one night, insisted they get a hotel the next night, but she was always there on their trips away from home. But she usually let them go without her in Arizona. "You need just-the-two-of-you time," she always said.

One contestant, young, a teenager, tall, lanky, held his body like he'd been doing this his whole life. One foot on front of the other for a stable base, rigid shoulders to hold his binoculars steady, he scanned the forest and made identifications, and his partner right behind him, clearly his father, same body but thickened, clicked pictures and selected the accurate name while his son studied the next bird. Arrow listened. Crested Flycatcher. Cuckoo. Goshawk. Northern Flicker. Swallow-tailed Kite. Scarlet Tanager. Whippoorwill. In the meadow, Bobolink. Godwit. Phoebe. Vesper.

Every living species versus every known species. Some used one term, some the other.

What we've seen versus what's still here. What we've found, what we haven't yet destroyed.

They walked down the other side of the embankment,

saw a group of little sparrows or nuthatches or finches or wrens, Arrow was unable to say which. Two people were snapping away, looked up. "I love the little brown jobs," one said. Arrow looked into the round face, square glasses, cropped hair, and didn't know if she was looking at a man or a woman. It didn't matter. "It's hard to know the differences, but I do." The birder pointed. "House Wren, House Sparrow, House Finch, but that one is a Song Sparrow." Arrow laughed, thought it was wonderful that some people knew things she didn't care to know. They wandered down through patches of cypress, cedar, yew, other trees Arrow didn't recognize with variations of needles in clusters on branches, and then they stood in a patch of redwoods. "Oh," Arrow said.

"Yes," her dad said.

"How did they get the mist threading through the tops of the trees right?" Arrow looked again for machines, but again couldn't see any. "We're in Northern California now, only a few paces away." Arrow leaned her back against a trunk. "When we went to the redwood forest that year for spring break, I kept imagining fairy tale characters walking around in these trees, Little Red Riding Hood and Snow White and the dwarves and Sleeping Beauty peeking around trunks. Hansel and Gretel. I saw them everywhere." Vapor crawled past them, wrapped itself around a tree trunk. "This doesn't seem like the same existence that has skyscrapers and taxi cabs," Arrow said.

A peacock, an albino peacock, and a gray peacock walked into the clearing, lifted their feathers into full display. They strutted around each other.

"Seriously?" Arrow asked.

Her dad took their pictures, looked at the screen, told

Arrow, "Apparently, they're called peafowl. I suppose 'peacock' just covers the men."

"These three are clearly men. Trying to seduce a dull brown lady we can't even see. I'm starting to feel like I'm stuck in an art installation more than a zoo. Or a museum. Or a joke."

Another team exclaimed into their screens that peacocks are actually called peafowl. Another pair, each with short gray hair tucked into a baseball cap, said, "Common Peafowl" before they even clicked a picture, and the man said to the woman, "We haven't seen a Gray Peacock-Pheasant since our trip to Thailand." Arrow wondered if they were in the top ten. The white bird squawked and it sounded like a baby being ripped to bits. Several people jumped.

The air around them darkened and everyone looked up. The sun must have gone behind a thick cloud, but then the fiber-optic screen brightened to compensate, to pretend it was still broad daylight. It turned the air an eerie blue closer to violet, and all the contestants in all the forests, all the deserts, near all the shores, they all felt this peculiar periwinkle on their skin, the real world crowding in but being combated. The mood dampened, and people turned their thoughts toward home, toward fights and mortgages and lingerie and natural disasters, and for a moment, all the people stopped seeing the feathers in front of them.

Then Arrow said, "What is a rooster doing here?"

"That is a very elaborate rooster," her dad answered.

"I didn't expect farm fowl."

"I don't think he's livestock. He's much more lavish."

A woman said, "Red Junglefowl," and Arrow had to ask her to repeat herself because she'd barely understood her accent, then realized she was giving her an identification.

"Thanks," she said. "I appreciate that." And the woman nodded.

XIV.
Zac Begay

They wanted about twenty of each in case some died in the crates. I wonder if the people in the park feel the same hunting to see as we did hunting to capture. I'm guessing not. For us, it was a job but also part safari. A trip around the world in two months. I'd never seen most of those places. Free food and booze at night in whatever port we were parked. Some of the young ones out the next day with stun guns and no sleep and no shower still reeking of all the sex they'd had. I'm lucky I never got a dart in my ass. Wouldn't fell a guy as big as me but still. Dumb kids but they caught their fair share. We were given small bonuses per bird to keep us productive. I caught about twenty thousand, a tenth of what we brought back. Plenty to live on for a while and even vacation but I'm not sure where I'd return.

We saw places where trees had been planted to capture carbon. We're not putting much more in the air, but we've still got to get some out of it. But they'd been planted on hillsides where people used to farm, this was in Uganda, and the growers were hacking up the trees with machetes to get their fields back. In the patches of trees still there we found lots of birds, displaced by the commotion nearby. We'd sailed through the Panama Canal to get to Africa, but on the way from Asia to Europe we took the Northwest Passage. The front of the ship broke ice and the captain told me it was soft because it melted every year—only ice that freezes again and again and again got as hard as concrete. It saved us four thousand miles to not have to use the canal again, and he said the Passage would be clear for longer and longer each year now. Easier to go by sea than across land, I guess.

We saw displaced Dutch refugees in Germany and we didn't take any of them with us, but we took their birds. People from the Maldives in the plains of Australia knew nothing about where the birds might be, and seeing Bangladeshi villages underwater shook me most of all. Throughout Europe we drank wine and growers told us some of their crops were better for the increased heat; others had to harvest early and had batches tasting of raisins. We plucked birds from their vines. I don't know the names of anything I caught. We had to wear bug spray against the mosquitoes that hadn't been killed that winter, who were carrying tropical maladies an Italian man brought back from vacation. No one got dengue fever or Zika.

I wonder about the places we skipped. No monsoons in Darfur for years, so the birds have all moved on. There are places worse than what we saw. I wasn't paid to identify anything, just to track and find creatures and catch what the scientists said we needed. I'd point to a bunch and they'd say yes or no. Sometimes they'd say they needed the brown ones and not the orange ones, but I'd just shoot them all and let the ones we didn't need wake up free, the ones we did need wake up in a cage. I slept with one of the scientists once, figured what the hell, more complicated than a local because I had to see her the next week, but I'm never sure about locals who'll sleep with anyone just passing through. The scientist wanted to talk after, asked if

I felt bad for what we were doing. Displacing thousands of creatures. I said most people were displaced from their origins, weren't they? I hadn't lived on the Navajo Nation in years, but I was still Diné. I wasn't trying to be deep, just stating reality, but she thought on that for a while. She said some of us would have to return every year and capture more of whatever died in the park. She thought they would make babies and be self-sustaining, but not right away. I said sure, sign me up, I'd do a yearly tour. Non-lethal bird hunter is better than some of the other things I've been: mercenary soldier, photo safari leader, caribou hunting guide years ago—all you do in place your clients in a stream of migrating caribou and they pluck the one they want. Of course, that hunt doesn't run anymore, though calling that a hunt is a stretch. I've guided nature walks at National Parks and led backcountry backpacking trips. There's plenty of work for a guy like me who knows a little about a lot of things and has a strong back. The scientist had been to school and knew a lot about one thing—birds—and she was worried. I don't think I did much to comfort her. I have enough money now to do pretty much whatever I want but I wonder what now. What next.

XV.
Ivan Ríos and Alastair Askgold—Zone III: Deciduous

There was a swamp in Deciduous, which Ivan thought better suited to Coastal, but sure, it was surrounded by leafy trees. He understood he was in a park inside a city, but he still instantly thought of alligators. The Living Fossils exhibit was previewed before the contest, and he'd seen them live in glass cages inside a building, crocs and gators unchanged for generations, basically still dinosaurs. And other creatures that looked prehistoric, and were: nautilus and horseshoe crabs and wasps and beetles and shrimp and vampire squid and trapdoor spiders. Things he'd never known about, hoatzin and aardvarks and gar and okapi. All these animals were hanging out in trees that had their own ancient DNA, or whatever trees have, gingko and sequoia and a monkey puzzle tree. The conclusion was supposed to be Everything Will Be Alright, or, more likely, At Least Some of Us Will Survive. They weren't anachronistic, but the room felt uncanny to Ivan, and he didn't feel comforted. Velvet worms.

Ivan wasn't much of a hiker. This was as much nature as he cared for. They wouldn't have hauled reptiles and spiders in here, he knew, but the swamp still made his skin crawl. Green grew on tree trunks and in the water and the fecundity of life, the thought that moss would grow over him if he stayed still long enough, algae, didn't reassure.

He was supposed to be looking for birds. So he did. He

looked up, and the jolt he got stopped him. "No way," he said. He reached out and wrapped his palm around Alastair's bicep and stilled him.

Alastair looked up, his jawline taut. "It's not possible," he said. Then, "Even I know what that is."

"Lord God," Ivan said, and crossed himself for the first time in years. A black bird with a white streak down its side, like a race car or storming night sky. White wingtips and yellow eyes and that crest of red. And yes, the bill like a tusk. They were casually stripping the bark from a tree with mouths made from what made piano keys, dice, jewelry—or used to. So there must be bugs in there somewhere. The females the same without the crimson pinnacle, but both with a punk point of feathers that made them so look like a star, a singer, the lead in a glam band. Ivan had read all about them. Some ornithologists had been certain some remained, but there was never conclusive evidence. Murky recordings, blurred film. Ivan had always thought of them as gone, the hope and conviction of the few delusional. This was resurrected. The Lord God Bird, because of exclamations made upon seeing one. It was longer than his forearm, thicker than his thigh.

Ivan took fourteen photographs, picking the first identification to get the camera screen back. He wanted proof. Did everyone else know this was here? Anyone else?

A team from Jamaica came from the other direction, he knew that flag, and when Ivan pointed up they stopped in their path.

"Ivory-billed Woodpecker," the woman said.

"I know," said Ivan.

"They're extinct," her partner replied.

"We know," said Alastair.

She took a picture and scrolled down. "It's listed," she said. "This is supposed to be here."

Soon two dozen people were gathered under the tree, and they could see three Ivory-billeds total. One was female. There were supposed to be twelve of each species in The Aviary, six procreative pairs. Noah's Ark times three. "And we're positive, absolutely positive, it's not a Pileated?" a man asked, the stripes on his jacket an unplaceable flag to Ivan. "We don't want to all look like fools."

Five people said at once, "Positive."

"Some people must have seen this in the first two rounds," someone said.

"Maybe that's why they cut off our communication, to not start a stampede, hysteria."

One woman was silently crying.

This would be one way to announce that species could be brought back. That the science Ivan had studied had worked.

Without looking at him Alastair reached out and took Ivan's hand. His fingers were long and slim, knobby knuckles, his palm was soft, and Ivan teared up, knowing whatever was next—he'd never forget this. He didn't look down, kept his eyes steady on the unperturbed birds as they foraged.

A worker came to tell them their time was up and people said they didn't want to go and asked dozens of questions at once, and he said, "Look, I'm basically a security guard. I work for Academi. I don't know anything about birds. I'm supposed to tell you that your group can exit today through the Urban Zone and get all your city bird identifications." No one had known there was going to be an Urban Zone. "They built it in as a bonus, a surprise," he said. "Birds that used to live elsewhere but now thrive here." A script, but they hadn't told him what to say about the de-extinction.

"I guess we couldn't finish our lists without a city zone," one woman said reasonably.

"I'd wondered where they were keeping them, the birds from home," a guy with a classic Jersey accent said.

Ivan looked at the closest Ivory-billed one more time, the other two in the adjacent tree. One cocked its head and made eye contact. As they walked away he told Alastair everything he knew about de-extinction.

"It's all in the film, you saw it all, but it's hard to really hear. On purpose, you know, we sped it up, to not bore people who don't care about the science. We just sketched it in. It's basically cloning, called somatic cell nuclear transfer. You reconstruct the species' genome. You get cellular material from preserved species. There are over 1,500 stuffed Passenger Pigeon specimens left on Earth. I don't know how many Ivory-billeds were taxidermied. You get what you can, but you can't get much from them, so you use the closest relative as a blueprint—in the case of Passengers, the Band-tailed Pigeon. The genome is inscribed into a living cell. This is even more complicated than it sounds. You replace chunks of Band-tailed DNA with synthesized chunks of Passenger DNA, then introduce these living cells into a Band-tailed embryo. When the chick hatches, it looks and acts like a Band-tailed Pigeon. But if it is a male, it carries Passenger-Pigeon sperm; if it is a female, its eggs are Passenger-Pigeon eggs. I don't really understand why that is. These creatures—Band-tailed Pigeons on the outside and Passenger Pigeons on the inside—are called chimeras. Chimeras are bred with one another to produce Passenger Pigeons."

"This already happened?"

"None have lived yet. They die quickly. So it's still in process. But it's happening."

"Sounds like a lot of rot to me."

"I think it's terrifying. And fascinating."

"So it's possible to bring back Ivory-billed Woodpeckers, too?"

"In theory. I'm not sure if Pileateds are genetically similar enough. I only studied pigeons for the film."

"It premieres tonight."

"It does."

"Are you nervous?"

"Very."

"Would you like me there?"

"Would you like to go?"

They hadn't released hands. Hadn't looked at each other while walking.

"If I go, would you want to wear a tie from last year's collection? Might do me good to get a bit of exposure in the American market, advance promotion for next year's."

So practical. "I'm not famous," Ivan said.

"But you're gorgeous, and that's a start," Alastair countered. "And this might make you famous."

Ivan hadn't known that Alastair thought him gorgeous. He wasn't, he knew, but he liked being thought so. "Will photos be okay back home? I'm not famous, but there will be paparazzi tonight. Because of the venue and the bands more than me."

"I can't imagine moving on will hurt James more than not moving on did, or make him nastier. It's wonderful our phones don't work in here. I haven't heard from him all day."

They stepped into a simulacrum of Ivan's city.

Pigeons, the standard ones, roosted on the metallic gargoyles of the Chrysler Building, starlings swarmed over a tiny Times Square, ducks and swans swam in a mini Central Park pond. Ivan figured it would be heated all winter, so they could stay. The spikes that prevented pigeons from perching on the Empire State Building were duplicated, so the birds all landed elsewhere. Grackles squawked from the branches of one tree, and starlings mimicked car alarms from electrical wires. Nighthawks nested on roofs, sparrows built nests in the Os of the Broadway Bodega, crows hopped through a small vacant parking lot, and swifts spiraled up and out of a chimney. Purple martins filled the small houses built just for them, houses found throughout the United States, houses they would vanish without. Skyscrapers, apartment buildings, commercial zones and single-family homes shared the equivalent of a block of space, a New York City in the heart of New York City, Manhattan repeated in the margin of Manhattan, the outer boroughs unacknowledged.

A woman said to the woman next to her, "It was nice to be able to bird in the jungle and not have to worry about stepping on a snake. It's nice to be able to walk through a version of this city and know you won't see a rat. No homeless people begging for change."

"But there's graffiti," the other said.

"I can't read it."

"Well, at least no drive-bys," she said.

Ivan pointed tags out to Alastair. "Tragedy. Cataclysm. Obliteration. Damage. Extinction."

The edges were sharp, the interiors shaded, the letters

both jagged and blurred; points and swoops and swerves and precise lines made shapes hard to see as language.

"You can read it?" Alastair was grinning beautifully, looking slantwise at the old ladies.

"That's Gaia's work. I went to high school with her. She used to show me sketches in math class. I always wanted to be her wingman, carry her paints, but I was never cool enough for her." The fake accuracy made Ivan emotional, but he didn't know how to tell Alastair. That this was his city and not. Synecdoche, simulacrum, simulation, imitation, recreation.

They all looked up, and a Peregrine Falcon gripped a pigeon with its talons and carried it off.

"Do you want to show me New York? Actual New York?" Alastair asked Ivan.

"Please," Ivan said, "yes," and what he meant was, *There's nothing I'd rather do more.*

XVI.
Börje Valkeapää

Those of us who have covered our flag with another, we look for each other. A group inside a group. We want to know—where do you say you're from? And what's your official designation? So many of us speak English. At least a little. A convenience, and colonization on display. Neoliberalism. Cultural imperialism. They don't want our resources, exactly, though companies would take our petrol, our iron ore. They want us to increase their capital, less directly. Beowulf Mining. A Brit thinking he knows about Scandinavia. Then and now. A poet and drillers. I am from Sápmi. They say I am from Sweden. My partner, he is from Sápmi. They say he is from Norway. Villages in what they call Finland, what they call Russia, are our neighbors. We speak Northern Sami, I speak Swedish, compulsory education, he speaks Norwegian, but here we've been practicing our English. My friend's father speaks Ume Sami. One of twenty people left in the world who do. It will not last. Thirty thousand people speak our language. I hope it will last. Today, we met Diné people from the Navajo Nation. Their parents and grandparents were sent to boarding school, too, like us. The Long Walk. We met Kānaka Maoli from Hawai'i who said the U.S. occupation there is illegal. A Buddhist monk in robes and a teenager in a Rage Against the Machine t-shirt with a picture of a monk self-immolating had Tibetan flags on their jackets. Finally, Tibet is free. But we have to pin flags over the ones stitched onto our jackets. It makes me wonder how many people don't have a flag to show where they consider themselves to be from. How many places have no symbol? We've tried to talk to many people with a flag over a flag, a symbol of resistance, but who doesn't have that to show, can't label themselves like we do? Colonizers sought assimilation of indigenous peoples worldwide. In some places it worked, in some places it didn't. Some of us disappeared. Most of us didn't. The Maasai were in traditional dress, so we would have known them, but they have a flag, too. The birds have been amazing, but we haven't tried to name them. We've just looked. We're trying to name the people, hear how they name themselves. The Crow call themselves Apsáalooke. I hope I can remember all I have seen here.

XVII.
Arrow and Grant Sullivan—
Zone III: Desert

They paused at the edge of the Desert amidst junipers and piñons. Many-armed cacti and gnarled cholla stood in the distance. Quail crossed their paths. Some had the black curled topknot, some were speckled black and white, some had lovely blue and brown patches. Arrow named them as she clicked a picture of each from overhead: "Gambel's Quail, Bobwhite, Chukars." A man with the Japanese flag on his back tried to overhear, but made a face like he hadn't quite deciphered Arrow's words. *Fuck it, let's work together*, she thought. She went over and showed him on his screen and he thanked her. Her father smiled and nodded at the animals they'd hunted and brought for dinner that night.

Then they walked up a hill and down another, for many minutes, maybe a mile, until all they could see was sand and what could survive on it. A roadrunner skittered by, a cactus wren peeked at them from the hollow of a saguaro, hawks spiraled, hot currents lifting them higher. A machine so cleverly hidden baked the moisture out of the air, cooked the ground and any skin above it. The prickly pear were in bloom: yellow, white, and red petals atop untouchable tubes and pads. The sand was insipid sable, palo verdes were the green of tin trucks left in the sun for decades, spines pricked the air, ocotillo beaks blazed orange and scarlet, the bougainvillea was ink pink, the sky flamed above—in this peroxide landscape some colors combusted.

Arrow pointed straight overhead. "Red-Tailed Hawk." She knew their flight from watching a slow-motion video at the tiny museum in Flagstaff, the same museum where Ed took her to see Native art, jewelry, and paintings from all the tribes. She took a picture of a silhouette when one crossed the sun, hoped that would be enough for the judges to see she was right about this one. In the distance, a patch of sand was covered with knotted, contorted bushes that looked part tree, part cactus, bent and tangled like they were in pain. Plants blown into the shapes of the wind. "Joshua Trees," she said to her father and pointed. Trees from a different type of desert.

"We're standing in Sonoran, that's certain," he said. "There must be a patch of Saharan somewhere. Let's go find the place where there's only sand. I've never seen that." There were no tall trees, just shrubs, so Arrow could see all the other contestants, some mopping their faces, some shielding their eyes to look into the distance, several drinking water. Arrow felt her skin getting baked but not burnt, that burrowing.

Arrow felt like she was on a fieldtrip to the desert. She thought of being taken to Wupatki when she was in the seventh grade, Native ruins an hour from Flagstaff. All the twelve- and thirteen-year-olds glad for a day away from classrooms boarded the bus at seven a.m. with more enthusiasm than they usually entered first-period history. Arrow had taken to wearing thick black eyeliner then and was friends with Jada, a blonde who was bad at school and good at sports. They sat in the back row of the bus. Arrow saw purple cliffs out the window, yellow grass, green bushes, red dirt, all bleached by the sun to a pastel version of their intrinsic shade, and all up against a blue sky so vivid it looked like it would zap you if you licked it. Arrow took pictures and was disappointed when they only showed paleness on her screen, didn't capture the layers and complexity her eyes saw. Indian Paintbrushes grew taller than she'd ever seen them, two-foot-long stems, and she wanted to reach out and cut a bunch with the pocketknife her father had given her for her twelfth birthday. She didn't think she was supposed to have it at school, but she carried it daily in her jeans next to the arrowhead her grandfather had found. As they drove the trees shrunk and curved, piñon instead of pine, and since they were in a national park, the dead ones weren't removed, everything left natural, graphite trunks worn silver and twisted, jagged lines silhouetted against sky.

At the site, they walked through the gift shop, kids already touching tarantulas encased in glass, tossing plastic snakes at each other, everyone ignoring the books filled with drawings of katsinas, descriptions of pottery styles, jewelry, rug designs. Ms. Madden raised her voice once, told the class they'd have the chance to shop after the tour, but right now she needed them to give their silent, undivided attention to the park ranger.

The ranger told them that archeologists believed four different types of people converged on this spot starting one thousand years ago: Anasazi, Sinagua, Cohonina, and Hohokam. He was an old man with gray hair who'd clearly been doing this most of his life. The ruin had one hundred rooms, had been the largest structure for at least fifty miles. The Hopi believe this was one spot where their ancestors stopped on their migration to the place they now live.

Every Living Species

There was a spring at the base of a nearby mesa, and the volcano that erupted in 1064 had lain cinders over the soil, which acted as mulch and kept in precious rainfall. People could grow crops—corn, pumpkins, gourds, and lima, kidney, and tepary beans. They had hundreds of plots because, every year, many would fail.

He said, "Let's go see it," and all the bored pre-teens roused from their slumped postures, started walking. They turned a corner and could see it from above, the walls the color of the ground, rust red, rooms without roofs, a tangle of abutting squares that seemed a labyrinth, a hive, cells of a living creature. Arrow walked right next to the ranger, and when they got near it and he stopped, she kept walking, placed both her palms against the surface, touched sandstone, a mosaic of flat rocks cleaved from the land around them. She put her whole hands against it and felt the absorbed sunlight, the heat that made the stone seem a deeper red, she soaked it into her body, and then she felt the ranger's hand on her shoulder, and he said to her very gently, "We don't touch the building. It is very ancient, and the oils in our hands can hurt it." Arrow stepped back and held her hands at her sides, grit on her palms. She felt as if her skin lit up then, and the skin of the Native people in her grade, all of them glowing, connected, and she wondered what they thought about her fascination, the people who had a reason to be drawn to this place.

They circled the building, looked at metates for grinding corn, heard about the cloth woven and dyed here, how it was traded for shells from the sea and macaws from the south. They saw the oval ballcourt, went into the circular amphitheater, and Arrow saw dancing, felt the thud of feet and drums. "There aren't just ruins," she wanted to say, but of course didn't. "Why aren't you taking us to places where people live?" That's what she wanted to see. The homes of her classmates she'd never been invited into. Arrow wanted to go wherever she could, but she wasn't sure where she was allowed. Lunch tables were segregated at her school.

And then they saw the blowhole, an opening in the earth where cool air shot out. Each kid had a chance to put his or her body over the hole, feel the surge of wind rushing up. The girls with long hair giggled as it swirled around them, colder than the air conditioning none of them had in their homes. As Arrow leaned her body over, she imagined jumping in, falling into a cool lifting darkness, floating down. The ranger said that the hole connected to caverns underground, and when it was the opposite of now, cool above ground and hot in the earth, air was sucked into the hole. She read the sign: "The Hopi believe this is the breath of Yaponcha, the wind spirit. Some believe this feature is the reason people settled here." That seemed obvious, a clear sign of a magic there and nowhere else.

They ate lunch on picnic tables. The peanut butter and jelly on white bread, potato chips, apples, and cookies that the school packed for them made Arrow feel like a little kid. She drank water out of a plastic bottle—they hadn't been outlawed yet—and refilled it, thought of the people who carried water in clay pots, prayed for rain.

The sand here was that same red. Scarlet Macaws were now extinct. The ancestors of the child Arrow carried once lived in that place. She wondered if it was wrong, to want to destroy something that had barely survived. Half-white, half-Native. Would that count as continued survival? Yes.

Her dad shielded his eyes with rigid fingers. "Do you see that black bird with the yellow head?" he asked. "What's that?"

Arrow flipped. "A Yellow-headed Blackbird."

"Well that's the most logical thing I've heard in days. Is that a Cardinal?"

"Where?"

"That red bird in the palo verde."

Arrow aimed her binoculars. "No, it has black on it. It's like a red Steller's Jay. It's beautiful."

"They're all beautiful."

"Yes."

"It's a Vermillion Flycatcher," her dad said, looking up from the guide.

"And I thought Cardinal was a pretty name," Arrow said as she clicked its photo. She knew the experts had most of the birds memorized, rarely used the guide, but she was enjoying these discoveries.

Every time they paused in their walking, her father made her drink water, just like he would on hikes at home. "Even if you aren't thirsty," he always said. "Stay hydrated." They saw a group of glossy black birds, all perched in the same scrub brush. Arrow pointed to the largest one while her dad took its picture. "Raven." The next biggest bird she named as Crow, the one with spots she called Starling, and she paused at the other two. One was between the size of a Starling and a Crow and was such a shiny black it was really an iridescent indigo. The other was the smallest of all and had a spiky crest of feathers. Arrow spent some time with her guidebook, said the littlest was a Phainopepla and the other was a Grackle.

"There are lots of kinds of Grackles," her dad said.

Arrow examined the bird. "Pick the most normal sounding one."

"The other one has red eyes," he said. "Creepy."

A couple approached, both wearing stitched leather boots, the flag of Texas pinned over the U.S. flag on their jackets. They named the five birds in the same way, and Arrow was glad they agreed. The woman said, "Crows are from another world. But Grackles, Grackles are from Texas."

"You don't have an accent," Arrow said before she thought about it.

"Not all Texans are hicks, dear," she answered.

"I'm sorry."

"I know that's not what you meant. I'm from the country, honey. And I did my best to get that out of my voice as quick as I could," she said, turning on her drawl.

A bird with a flare on its wing landed on the branch, and all four contestants said, "Red-winged Blackbird" at the same time.

"Easy, but still a beauty," the man from Texas said, and they went their separate ways.

A bird streaked by, tail held parallel to the ground, and Arrow clapped her hands. "I love roadrunners!" she said. Then, "I didn't get a picture." Arrow wanted to hold it all.

She looked to the top of a tree she didn't recognize and saw her second owl of the contest. Its body was full of feathers striped brown and white, overlapping and cascading, and its little feet gripped the branch, showing strength used to crush the bones of mammals. It looked right at them, a white flat face with rings of brown encircling each wide black eye. It stayed for a few minutes, and both Arrow and her father slowed and calmed their breathing as they looked back.

A stick cracked on the path, and the owl glided away, seeming to hardly flap its wings.

"They're everything people say they are," her father said.

"It looked like it wanted to eat my face," Arrow said. "Isn't it supposed to be sleeping?"

"All the noise probably disrupted it."

Arrow said, "Holy shit. That's an ostrich." It looked more like a horse than a bird, an animal trained to carry human burden, but with a bit of viciousness in the eyes. Its long neck could reach around and bite anything held aloft on its back. Its face was almost pretty, large eyes and lashes, prim mouth, but set on a naked neck above thick, naked legs, above such shaggy, lush feathers, it looked like a Victorian woman caught half-dressed, a working woman lifting her skirt and deepening her neckline to show men which burdens she could carry.

Her father clicked a photo, scrolled, and said, "There seems to only be one kind of ostrich."

"Great," Arrow answered. Six other birders crowded around, snapped shots. Arrow tried to imagine what meat lay under its feathers—red or white? More like a quail or elk? Arrow had heard that an ostrich egg was the equivalent of six or seven chicken eggs. She would love to break that strong shell, see what poured out.

Arrow felt like her life was a fragile orb she held aloft. She thought she was probably a general disappointment to her mother, a kid on academic scholarship but with no real plan for what to do with her life. Her mom kept wanting her to find a purpose, a passion. But it all seemed so pointless. Sometimes Arrow wanted to fuck up so badly that they'd all just leave her alone. Have no more expectations of her. Not need or want anything from her anymore. If she finally just let the sphere crash, dropped it, the exhaustion of holding it up would be over.

Her father had almost done it, but he hadn't. He came back, and while he never asked for forgiveness, he become a good dad again.

Arrow wondered if killing her child would be enough where she could just walk away and no one would follow. If she told them what she'd done.

Arrow walked to a creosote bush and pinched off a few leaves, lifted them to her father's nose to smell.

"Rain," he said.

"After all these years, it still amazes me." She lifted the pinch to her own nose, and the compact petrichor smack made her eyes water. Arrow felt herself stretched between two places—her feet on arid sand shipped into this city, desiccated air pulling moisture from her skin; and standing in the forest of her hometown, smelling the first rainfall of the year, the one that always smelled the strongest, as she watched dancers at the Hopi festival Ed brought her to.

Vendors with names like Kuwanhyoima and Masayestewa sold smooth brown pots painted with thin lines; silver jewelry inlaid with precious stones; silver jewelry with etched black designs representing clouds and rain; pendants of men standing at the entrance of labyrinths; pendants of gods with faces like suns; katsinas carved from cottonwood roots with painted bodies and faces, yellow, blue, red, black, white, katsinas dancing that were part animal, part human, part divine. Ed spoke to some of the vendors in Hopi. Ed and Arrow ate Indian Tacos: beans, meat, lettuce, tomatoes, and cheese on puffed flour fry bread. They'd already learned in class that the Hopi did not invent this food, the Navajo did, when they were made to leave their land, leave their crops of corn and march for hundreds of miles to a place where they were given wheat flour and lard by the government. They made something new with it. After thousands of years of not eating processed flour, the diet of the past hundred and fifty years caused diabetes, obesity, heart troubles, yet fry bread felt traditional, like ancestral food to many people in Arizona. Some people ate theirs with honey and sugar.

They watched the dancers, the Nuvatukay'ovi Sinom Group, named for Snow-Capped Mountain, what had been renamed by the Spanish missionaries for their patron saint, The San Francisco Peaks—right before they forced the Hopi to stop practicing their religion. The dancers' bodies were painted: one yellow leg, one blue leg, red and yellow and blue torsos and arms. Their faces were made white with corn meal, red streaks representing rain. The women wore carved wooden headdresses, painted with symbols for mountains, clouds, corn. Feathers extended from each edge. The men carried gourd rattles, the women had bells tied to their waists. They wore bracelets of turquoise shaped into blossoms, woven bands on their ankles, and they carried feathers in their hands to accentuate each gesture. The woman who introduced them said, "We do not clap at the end of our dances. But we are in a different setting here. So if you want to clap to show appreciation for the dancers, here, that will be fine. And if you don't, that will be okay too." The woman explained that these dances were ceremonial, done only for their own people, usually, to ask the gods for things, or to thank the gods for receiving things. She said that for the Hopi, dancing is a sacred way of maintaining a yearly prayer cycle that brings rain to sustain them in a land without rivers or lakes. She said the Hopi migrated to their land, followed a star placed in the sky for them. After traveling to the four edges of the continent, their god told them to stop in the middle, in a place without water. Living rightly would make it rain, make crops grow. Others did not stop there, went on to the easier lands of the rainforests below, became the Inca, Aztec, Maya. "They are our brothers and sisters, but they are not god's chosen people," she said, "because they did not stay in the hard land, the land we must cultivate with our prayers, the land that keeps us obedient, grateful, and holy." She did not say whether or not that dance was a dance for rain.

The movements were plodding, monotonous, shuffle strides and stamps and swooping arms. The dancers repeated each step dozens, hundreds of times. Their feet traced circles and circles into the ground. People took pictures, their flashes like lightning bolts. Arrow stayed still, felt as if she were in the same trance as the dancers, the repeated movements a meditation. The music was guttural chanting, low singing, rattles, drums, the footsteps of the dancers. She lost the sense of wondering when it would end.

When they finished, everyone clapped, and Arrow smelled it before she felt it, as if the soil and clouds could communicate without touch, as if the earth contained grains of sugar and lead shavings, lifted by the promise of moisture—there was a crack of thunder, and rain fell. The first of the year. Ozone capsules broke open, and something broke in her. As she smelled the caramel-slicked nickel smell of rain in the alpine desert, as the dancers exited the tent into streaks of water falling from the sky, as all the watchers applauded and filled a passing basket with bills and coins, Arrow bent forward and began to shake with crying. Ed, her new love, put his arm around her and didn't ask her to explain. All she could manage was, "Rain is the only thing that makes me feel hopeful." This was four days after the fire. They'd almost made it.

Arrow took Ed to the Celtic festival at the end of July, said it was the closest thing to a culture she had. Both her mom's and dad's families had been in the United States for generations, but since her mom grew up in Boston she felt somewhat Irish. Her dad not at all. Her mother's grandparents had still spoken Gaelic, came over from the Aran Islands, but they didn't teach her, didn't want her marked by accent. Then she moved to Arizona and everyone heard Southie in her voice. It rained a little that afternoon and the man playing bagpipes said it felt like home. They ate chips with curry sauce. They traced her last name, her dad's people, back to county Kerry, Ó Suileabháin the original spelling, but Arrow should change the Ó—grandson of, to Ní—daughter of. Her mom was Keenans and Finnegans, both traced back to County Galway.

In August, deep into monsoon season, they went to the Navajo festival. They ate Navajo tacos and watched the energetic swoops of traditional dancers. While it rained, a punk band played, Blackfire, the Benallys' band: Jeneda, Klee, and Clayson, and their dad Jones who chanted traditional songs. Jeneda wore gold-sequined Doc Martens and said yes, atrocities have happened, yes genocide, yes both were still happening all over the globe, but we must keep hope. We can't let them take away our hope. She said that her people aren't just ancient, they are modern too, and can use modern tools. Like an electric bass and drumset. And the English language, though they sang in Diné bizaad too.

This October, after she got home, after the rains stopped and the air turned crisp in the way that only happens in the high desert, she figured she and Ed would go to the final cultural festival in their small town, El Día de los Muertos. It was what they did. Arrow imagined women in bright dresses with grinning skeletal faces drawn over their own, bright jewels and sequins and cobwebs and hearts and flowers and red lips. Arrow would wear her t-shirt with ribs on it, a cage of bones meant to protect, not to help us move, like our cranium only, a scarlet heart painted inside. She didn't know what she'd bring for the communal altars, and she didn't know what Ed would bring, and she wondered what they would tell each other about what they mourned.

In this contrived desert, Arrow felt the sun and sky of the place she was from all around her, and in her fingers she held the smell of rain. Everything reminded her of everything. She let the creosote drop to the sand she stood on and thought of creosote paste, bushes boiled to black and smeared on railroad ties to preserve them from moisture. She thought of the miles her father traveled, forty-eight hours away from home, only eight of those spent not on a train, required rest in a company-paid hotel in Needles, California. He said very little about his job, only told Arrow that the rhythm of a freight train was soporific—a word she had to look up—but it was his job to stay awake. He said the desert at night was still, though he knew it was alive out beyond the border of his motion. Arrow filled in the multitude of stars, the silhouettes of mountains, mesas, saguaros, coyotes, roadrunners. Every time he had to work he drove to Winslow, an hour away, then rode the train back through Flagstaff. He sounded a special signal when he passed through, long, short-short, long, so she'd know he was thinking of her. She couldn't hear it when she was at home on the family land, but heard it when she was in town. He used the same signal even that year he wasn't living with her and her mom. It would have been easier for them to live in Winslow, but he wanted his daughter to grow up on the land he did. Because she'd tended to the land while her father was away, it was unclear who felt like it belonged to them more.

For her fifteenth birthday, he brought her to the old train station in Winslow, the nicest hotel and restaurant for forty miles. It had been where people spent the night on their train trip out West, their rest before seeing the Grand Canyon and Indian Lands. Albert Einstein, Mary Pickford, and Presidents Roosevelt and Truman had stayed there. John Wayne. It wasn't used as a train station anymore now that just freight came down those tracks, hardly any passengers since people could now drive I-40 the same route. Arrow wore a red, floor-length, spaghetti-strapped dress she found at a thrift store and brown beaded sandals. Her father wore jeans and his dress boots made from sharkskin and a black button-up shirt with a turquoise bolo tie. Arrow loved the broad roof beams and stained-glass scenes of roadrunners and cacti. The restaurant was grand but not fancy, it looked Western but not rustic, and she felt like this big, sprawling hotel with clay-tiled floors was a proper place for a special occasion.

They sat in the bar first, and the bartender brought her father an Old Fashioned without him having to ask. "Your daughter, she looks just like you," she said, and Arrow couldn't quite figure out the tone—maybe awe, maybe wistfulness. She asked for a sarsaparilla, and the bartender brought her the opened bottle with a glass of ice, topped with a skewer of brandied cherries. When she walked away, she squeezed her father's shoulder.

"Is she the reason you don't live with us anymore?"

"No," her dad said, sounding more shocked than she'd expected. "No, Arrow, that's not it at all." She waited for him to explain. "It would be worse if I were there right now. This isn't something I can help you understand. I've needed to be on my own for a while. I'll be coming home soon."

"We don't need you."

"I know you don't." Then, "I'll never leave again."

"I never thought you would." Arrow was proud of how icy—not hurt—her voice sounded. Accusatory. Her life had been destabilized by his absence, but she didn't want him coming home because he thought he had to. She understood enough to know a sense of obligation wasn't going to fix this.

Her father asked her if she had an appetite, and she said yes. The menu was like a storybook. They split an order of stuffed squash blossoms, grown in the garden outside the restaurant and filled with local cheese, and Arrow ordered Hopi Hummus made from Tepary beans grown by Marla Polequaptewa and Piki bread made by Joyce Saufkie, both of Second Mesa, then the Lamb Sampler Platter, raised on the Navajo Nation by Irene Yazzie, prepared three ways. Her dad ordered the wild game platter: boar, elk, and duck. The food made Arrow feel rooted to the land, the ceremony of eating out with her father made her feel tied to him—enamored with and frustrated by him.

Now, she was increasingly afraid she was just like him.

Now, she was in a city with her father, and she knew they would eat quail for dinner that they'd killed in Arizona, after a day of seeing birds, some of which she would never see again in her life. Wherever she went, she carried home with her.

"Damn," her father said. "That's a bald eagle." He looked up and pointed. She followed the line he drew.

She and her father watched it fly. "I've never seen one before," she said.

"Me either."

XVIII.
Asma Zawati

When they teamed us up, they made sure we both spoke English so that we could speak to each other. We have not said anything to each other. There is nothing to say. All I would say is colonization, settlements, 1967 borders, walls, right of return. All he would say is bombs. I would say, Do you not understand why an oppressed people acts violently? When other processes do not work? I understand your people were oppressed, I understand, why must you continue this oppression in my land? Why does genocide not make people better? But it does not. Everyone pretends we can become better than we are. Some say climate change will force us to finally work together. I do not believe. Peace between peoples is only ever temporary. The pressure of environmental catastrophe, less inhabitable land, will make us all worse. Some want my part of the world to become more of a desert, some want us to sink underwater, disappear, pretend it never happened, these two nations that cannot get along. We have had a state for three years. There has been no violence. So many have hope that it is finally over. But we both have lost people to violence. This is not over. I have nothing to say to this man. You deserve a homeland? No one has ever denied that. No one sane has ever denied that. We were here first? We both think so. We will never settle this. God gave it to us, to my people. We both think so. Why do I not deserve a homeland? I have a homeland. I cannot help but think it is smaller than it should be. It is larger than it was. Smaller than it was. It all will flare again. We walk in silence through this fabricated place, he and I, we know about invention, about borders made by others; we walk through this manufactured arena filled with real creatures, people from every corner of this earth. We walk past a pair, one with the flag of Sudan, one with the flag of South Sudan. We walk past a pair, one with the flag of Russia, one with the flag of Georgia. Someone pinned an ISIS flag over whatever was there before. He was asked to leave. This beauty is not for us. None of it will last.

XIX.
Ivan Ríos and Alastair Askgold

They emerged into a New York beginning to turn on all its lights.

Their Eco dropped them off in front of The Plaza, the red velvet stairs, the revolving door, and Ivan was more attentive to details, sober, not as certain he was about to get laid as he had been last night, but hopeful. Not as distracted by his certainty as he had been last night. The lobby was a cavernous pale space, lit with the sparkles of chandeliers.

In Alastair's room Ivan washed his hands to give them something to do. The faucets were gold plated. Real gold, Ivan assumed, though he wasn't sure why. Maybe because the flowers had been changed since yesterday, because he knew marble when he saw it, maybe because the linens were so nice on his skin last night.

These are the things we will have to release. This can't stay this way, Ivan thought.

"Can I offer you a drink?" Alastair asked from the sitting room. "I asked him to bring Brugal for you, scotch for me."

"Who?"

"The butler. He'll shine your shoes. I've ordered up a shirt and pants and jacket from my store for you. I guessed you to be a 36 x 30, a 44 regular. I'll let you choose your tie, if you like. I had him bring several options. He should be here soon."

"That's right, my size." Ivan had no idea what it would be like to have a butler. To know dimensions on sight.

He sipped the Brugal Cuba Libre Alastair made and was touched he remembered. He said, "You look around this place and see either effortless luxury or an old-fashioned, stuffy, overdone décor."

"Which do you see?"

"I see a place not for New Yorkers. This was built for Europeans, to show them what they think lavish extravagance is. Stone. Gold. Jeweled chandeliers and stained glass ceilings."

"What is actual lavish extravagance?"

Ivan wondered if he was being condescended to. He gave a true answer. "For me? Mofongo at La Casa Del. Drinks at a dive. Décor that's not trying so hard looks more beautiful to me."

"Beautiful?"

"Interesting. Worth looking at. Isn't that a definition of beauty? No New Yorkers live like this. Even the richest, the bankers on the Upper East Side, they go to a brasserie and order a Stella. Oysters, sure, but that comes with bread and butter and every table has snack mix on it. Salty. You can get mussels and steak tartare and steak frite and pâté and salad Niçoise, white linen, impeccable service, and that's the greatest pleasure of New York, you can always find a place like that, every few blocks, or an Irish pub with very decent food and right pints, or a street slice. This is the anomaly. Who wants to live at the Plaza? Eloise had no parents. Those books are tragic." Ivan guessed he was sort of insulting Alastair, but yeah, okay, he meant what he was saying.

"I do. Want to live at the Plaza. Forever. A butler

unpacked my clothes. He stocked the bar with Boddington's and a nice scotch, added specific rum when I said I had a visitor coming. He will fold and pack my clothes when I leave. He would draw me a bath with my preferred salts and fragrant soaps."

"Oh hell no. I can draw my own damn bath. I bet those palm trees downstairs aren't even real. Aren't alive."

"This place never changes."

"Everything will."

"This will be the last thing to end."

"Do you actually think you deserve this? You work hard for your money. But this feels reasonable to you?" Ivan told himself to relax his grip on his glass to not shatter it in his fist.

"No. I do not deserve this because of what I do for work. Or everyone does. Everyone deserves this. But staying at a Motel 6 changes nothing. I give plenty of money to charity, if you're wondering." Alastair was very relaxed. This conversation wasn't hard for him.

"That's not what I was wondering. I just. I could never be comfortable here. This is not what I'm from."

"You're angry," Alastair said. Ivan was. He couldn't read Alastair's tone, which made him angrier.

"My parents were immigrants," was all he could say, shorthand for the fact that he got out of poverty, and he knows not everyone can, so he feels awkward and ashamed everywhere, here in Midtown and on his old block in the Heights.

Alastair nodded, said, "This will stay standing whether I sleep inside of it or not." He stepped closer to Ivan, within reach. "Will you stay here with me tonight? With this transplanted European? We'll celebrate after your premiere. Amidst all this false luxury. Us, the only three-dimensional things amongst all these flat surfaces. Tomorrow, you can show me your apartment."

Ivan felt violent. He stepped toward Alastair and hooked his middle finger in his belt loop.

Alastair said, "You're from somewhere else. I got that. Let me pamper you." He wasn't being condescending. He sounded sincere. "We don't know how long we have. Let's enjoy this obscenity tonight. Step outside of reality with me. You'll show me your city tonight, and I'll see more of where you're from tomorrow."

Ivan didn't know if Alastair meant big picture, *We don't know how long we have to live,* or small, *You and I don't know how long we're going to keep this up.* "Yes," he said. "I'll stay here tonight." Because, really, why not?

Alastair held his gaze, held the tension in Ivan's arm which was still linked at Alastair's waist, said, "Later."

The most arousing word Ivan had heard in a while.

He wasn't sure who was calling the shots here. But he wanted this man more than he'd wanted anyone for quite some time.

He wondered if the right thing to do was to show he didn't want to wait for later. Instead, he deferred to the request. Command.

There was a knock at the door. "Take off your shoes," Alastair said. A practical statement that sounded sexy.

The butler brought in clothes and hung them in Alastair's closet then placed two plates on the coffee table. Alastair handed him Ivan's shoes and asked if they could be shined in half an hour. "I'm sorry to rush you, Manuel. But I'd appreciate it."

"Certainly, Mr. Askgold," was the reply.

Ivan wanted to ask Manuel where he was from, maybe they went to school together, was his dad raised in an orphanage, too? Did he ride a raft one hundred miles? Ivan wanted Manuel to know he was a guest, only a guest, but of course he already knew that. He'd stepped into someone else's life. Thank you for the Brugal. Where are you from, güey? Ivan was used to flying his barrio feather on purpose, out of fear he'd fly it on accident. Now, he didn't make eye contact. Which probably made him seem like he thought he was better than Manuel, instead of embarrassed. This could be him, and there was no real reason why it wasn't.

He left. Ivan assumed you tipped at the end of the stay. He wondered how you learned these conventions.

"I ordered the cheese plate and the meat plate. You should have a bite. I almost got the tea sandwiches, they're so excellent, but I'm glad I didn't."

"Because I think only rich assholes eat tea sandwiches?"

"Exactly."

"I'm not hungry."

"But you passing out at your own party is not the press we want. Eat, and then I'll dress you."

The brie was runny, the manchego salty, the stilton briny and rank, the salami rich. Ivan felt a catch of gratitude in his throat and realized it had been a while since anyone had tended to him. He washed his hands again, then walked to Alastair.

"The belt is actual sharkskin," he said. "The suit is the synthetic blend called that. I'm interested in fur, skin, their fabricated derivations." Ivan liked to think of this serious man being playful in his creations. The suit was deep gray with a slight sheen, not shiny enough to be gaudy, but a brightening of the depth of the color. The shirt was crisp, starched, white with just a tinge of blue, a few sapphire threads through white. Alastair watched while Ivan changed.

Alastair helped with the cufflinks. Then he opened a box, satin strips inside. Each a vivid gemstone hue, each a different pattern, crosshatched, striped, chevron, stippled. Ivan chose a purple tie with small dotted stripes, made from tiny stitched flowers. So bold it wasn't girly, but almost. "Good choice," Alastair said, and Ivan assumed he would have said that whichever he chose. Alastair stepped up to tie it and Ivan said, "I know how," and Alastair said, "I know." Alastair lifted his collar and wrapped the fabric around Ivan's neck and wove it into itself and Ivan loved this intimacy, remembered the last person who'd tied a tie for him, though he could do it perfectly well himself, Yessenia, whose nails were painted deep purple, she was wearing a cobalt dress and had her hair up, he remembered the closeness of faces, hands that could strangle being gentle.

Then Ivan watched Alastair dress, a pale blue linen suit and pink shirt and ascot patterned in huge flowers. So feminine, but on his reedy frame it was assertively confident, so strangely masculine. Ivan loved the whimsy. "How long before we have to go?" he asked and Alastair smiled as if to say, *I know what you want.*

"Twenty minutes."

"I love this," he said, gesturing to himself. "But the new work. Isn't it kind of morbid? Now? Birds?"

"I want the collection to be really lush and gorgeous, spectacular, but also really spirited. Almost feisty or absurd." Alastair showed Ivan a sketch of a necklace, a lacquered black bird, eyes ex'ed, upside down, claws in the air, held aloft by a dainty chain.

Ivan laughed. "That's beautiful. I know a ton of chicks who would wear that. Tough femme girls."

"Great. Brilliant. And I've not been just sketching birds. People in the park are dressed in ways I've only ever seen on the History Channel. Tribal, traditional, but then also hipsters in vintage '80s gear. And I loved your neighborhood." He showed more sketches. Women with whorls on the sides of their heads, hair wrapped like butterfly wings or flat squashes, woolen robe covering one shoulder, white buckskin boots. A man's face covered with tattooed swirls, a woman with tattoos on her chin, lips darkish black-blue. A man with a bright beaded disk on his forehead, feathers in his hair, a string of beads looped so it hung to his cheeks, framed his eyes, a robe of feathers and intricate stitching. A young woman with beaded discs around her neck, a headdress of sticks and metal and beads lashed to her head, throat painted red. A woman with slicked back hair, a frizzed ponytail beyond the rubber band, big earring with her name in script across, *Yahaira*, a trend Ivan figured would never die; a woman in a fake fur coat, spray-painted pastel, lace dress under; a tight black t-shirt, cut and tied to fit even tighter, with "Give More Love More" printed on it; tall, tall shoes. Girls with layers of socks, one overall strap up, one down. Scrunchies. Then a page of birds and feathers, close-ups of patterns and color swaths, details of tails and how the feathers overlapped and extended.

Alastair said, "Here's what I've come up with so far, of my own." A few pages of designs, not duplications. A white tank top with *Uptown Against the World* scrawled on it, graffiti style, but readable to anyone, a short, elaborate fabric-feathered skirt below. A woman in a fitted gown, metal feathers as straps, with lines cut into the sides of her hair, a metal nest tangled in. Baggy pants on a female model, slung low but fitted at the hips, with shoes, tee, and hat all the same shade: one woman in the blue of a jay, another in the yellow of a warbler, another in the vivid green of a parrot, all with feathered earrings, curly hair. A man in a wide square dress, long sleeves, patterned with a tangle of feathers. Ivan wondered who had the money for this stuff but knew it still must be plenty of people. He told Alastair it was stunning and he meant it. It didn't feel like appropriation of what already existed, but tribute.

Alastair put a piece of meat in his mouth, put a piece of Irish cheddar in Ivan's. Ivan wanted to lick this pretty Brit, and so he did, and when he took that man's finger in his mouth, oh, the smile he got in return. This man might be ruining the world, but there was something riveting about him. Ivan was wrecking the world, too, surely.

"Ready to go?" Alastair asked, and Ivan said he was.

Ivan hadn't been to the dress rehearsals. Last night showed him that the film was as good as he could make it. But others made tonight's extravaganza. He'd met with the Rockettes' director, they'd gone over each other's ideas for how to enhance the film with movement, Ivan had watched a few early practices, but he hadn't yet experienced the full effect. He wanted to see his own premiere. He and Alastair exited the cab to see the iconic neon sign: Radio City Music Hall, and a line of people waiting for tickets. Long. Alastair jutted his chin at the line, smiled, and took Ivan's hand. The flashbulbs started then, pulse lightning, and they hadn't discussed this part but both smiled, both paused and posed. Alastair said lightly, "Turn toward me. Your left side is your good side, so aim it toward the camera. Smile widely in some. Half-smile in others. We have opposite good sides, so we can face each other. Good." Ivan hoped to see his good side in the papers tomorrow, would always wonder what his other side looked like. Looking into a mirror wasn't the same as a photograph on a screen.

They entered a gilt and ginger lobby, the huge vertical column of space filled with paintings in umber and cerise, chandeliers in white and bronze, a shiny jet bartop with every spirit lit on glass shelves behind the tender in a suit, and everyone smiling. Red velvet stairs led to terraces lined with dark iron railings, led up the levels to the cheap seats, but there was no bad seat in the house: 5,931 maximum capacity, and Ivan wondered if anyone would tell him the numbers. The gold foil walls shone softly, but each surface was gilded so the space felt aflame. Or at least smoldering. Sans serif script lit red and pale green directed them toward exits and elevators, and their footsteps made no sound on Picasso mosaic carpet in primary colors, shapes indicating instruments and mirth. Orange marble veined with marigold, saffron, and ash. It was so old-fashioned, so out-of-touch, not at all up-to-date, this rococo art deco, but there was something comforting and preparatory about the entrance—*you are about to see something.* Ivan felt excited and sick. Alastair was holding his hand still. He guided them to the bar, ordered, and paid—a scotch and a rum neat. They took shots and no one inside knew who they were, but people were watching them.

Statues of metal women, naked, some with the thighs of linebackers, small firm tits, and paintings of old theater scenes—pink ballerinas, fleshy showgirls, white clowns, striped mimes, painted minstrels—adorned their walk to their seats in the front row. A reporter knew who he was and asked him how he felt, and Ivan remembered to express enthusiasm, and to thank everyone involved in the production. These are the kinds of things Alastair could help him with, remembering everyone on the production team. He seemed good at what Ivan hoped to become good at. The auditorium was excessive. The stage was surrounded by ovals inside of ovals, beams extending, meant to mimic sunset on water. Pink velvet cushioned chairs, more space per person than any other theater in New York. It was ridiculous, Ivan knew, but it made him feel expansive. But everyone still shared an armrest. He and Alastair sat, sank, some of the first to enter into the horizontal column of space. "Remember this," Alastair said, and Ivan thought he would.

Instead of putting Radiohead and Tool in the pit, the choreographers put them on the stage, on display: Danny Carey's shining drum kit stage left, what was rumored to be made out of melted-down Buddhist shrines but was actually brass, synthesizers with LED light blinking stage right. Ivan couldn't believe two of the most significant bands of his childhood were about to play music for his film, Maynard and Thom singing together for the first time ever. Lady Gaga and Estrella singing backup, and he hoped the spectacle wouldn't overshadow the story. Live recordings would be sold immediately after the show, and Ivan wondered if he should have one sent to Alastair's iPill. He had no guess to his musical tastes.

The room filled. The lights went down. Ivan filled his chest with anticipation, a breath shared with anyone who'd ever been behind a curtain on a stage. It lifted in cascades, pulled by dozens of ropes. The film began, the shadows of the musicians silhouetted, blacking out small bits of the screen. And as scientists reanimated something gone for generations, the Rockettes came on stage, stiff in their matching medical shifts, and did a stomping, spinning dance imitating automatons. They made stars and asterisks and columns. Their precision was terrifying and robotic. They weren't smiling. Ivan loved it.

The Rockettes left the stage and the film unfolded. The colors were such a stark contrast to the theater in which it was set, though the pigeons' rosy breasts nearly matched the seats' fabric. Ivan was astounded how much better the soundtrack sounded live—the voices murmuring as the babies were born, the voices wailing and keening as the birds attacked. Four high voices harmonizing, in wonder and horror.

Thom Yorke crooned and clapped and spastically danced. Maynard James Keenan moaned into machines and soaringly screamed above his bandmates bashing on their instruments. The time signature changed without warning, just as the swarm changed directions. Ivan heard slivers of lyrics. He knew all the words to all the songs but they were doing a medley. Old songs, blended to sound new, and some new songs. "Just to see what if. Just to see what is." "I've seen too much. I haven't seen enough." "Here I'm allowed everything all of the time."

"Ice age coming, ice age coming."

"This is really happening."

"I must keep reminding myself of this."

"Recognize this as a holy gift and celebrate this chance to be alive and breathing."

"No fault, none to blame, it doesn't mean I don't desire to point the finger, blame the other, watch the temple topple over."

"Overthinking, overanalyzing, separates the body from the mind." "Reaching out to embrace the random. Reaching out to embrace whatever may come. Whatever will bewilder me."

"We may just go where no one's been."

"Watch the weather change."

"I may find comfort here. I may find peace within the emptiness."

Then, in the calm after the attack, after the women found a way to settle it, Alastair very, very quietly sang along, so just Ivan could hear, so as not to disturb their neighbors, and his voice was high and crystalline and sure.

"You can't take it with you
You are not to blame
Reckoner,
take me with you."

There were tears streaming down Ivan's face. He didn't try to show them to Alastair but he didn't try to hide them.

The sorting it out, that would all come later.

This was happening.

Ivan felt himself falling in love at the end of the world. The beginning of the end of the world.

People lifted their iPills with their screens flamed out.

Both bands sang their most gentle and most voracious songs. But everyone was sitting in plush seats. There was no mosh pit. No one banged their heads or thrashed along or danced. So Ivan couldn't tell if they were thinking what he was thinking.

And then the Rockettes returned for the finale; once

everyone knew they were going to be okay, their glitzy costumes and leg kicks to eye-level and huge grins such joyous juxtaposition to the victory on the screen—yes, we won. But.

Their red sequins mimicked the eyes always watching from trees.

The credits normally ran to a somber silence—Ivan had wanted a still space at the end for the audience to uncomfortably settle into—but tonight four new men stepped on stage and started to play a song Ivan knew by the first three notes.

Ivan hadn't known this was going to be part of the show tonight.

There must have been just enough people Ivan's age in the crowd, because as soon as they heard that guitar riff all these heads went up like, "No way." Rage Against the Machine on stage. Ivan grabbed Alastair's hand and dragged him to the front, and he remembered doing this with Maxine in '93 and Jose in '97, and he brought his sister to a show shortly after and they rushed the floor even though they only had seated tickets; even though the security guards tried to catch them, they couldn't. This thing he thought he'd lost, here again. Right at his first line everyone was there for Zach de la Rocha, ready and waiting. Everyone started jumping, and Ivan didn't have time to worry if Alastair had ever done this before.

People were in their finery but they weren't holding back and Ivan only thought for a minute about the precious garments on his body. He turned to make sure Alastair was into this, or to at least give him a nod as he disappeared into the crowd, and Alastair's shoulder landed on his chest and pushed him back and in. Ivan shoved a young girl and she pushed him back harder. Alastair held him up for just a moment then thrust him into another flailing body. Ivan got cracked in the jaw, but he wasn't bleeding, and someone fell and was helped up then both his hands were on Alastair's skinny chest, but he was hard to move. They both spun into the spiral then Alastair swirled back against it long enough to clack Ivan and a guy near him and they both smiled. Everyone's fist went in the air. Everyone yelled, "Still in a room without a view." Everyone turned on each other.

Zach looked down to see if he needed to call girls to the front, but everyone was fine.

Then Ivan was fighting Alastair and himself and no one, and it felt really good. He threw an arm and hit Alastair but didn't hurt him, and everyone was fighting everyone else and themselves and no one. A guy was whirling his tie over his head, and a woman's strap on her dress had torn, but Ivan was still all buttoned up.

Maynard stepped forward to that deep bass line, and everyone stilled. Ivan loved how everyone knew what to do. They sang along. Two women's voices through the men's: Estrella's voice piercing, earning her name; Lady Gaga staring down the crowd, the edges of her mouth smiling. "Yes I know my enemies. They're the teachers who taught me to fight me. Compromise, conformity, assimilation, submission, ignorance, hypocrisy, brutality, the elite. All of which are American dreams." People were yelling. Ivan wondered if they were about to start a riot.

Ivan placed a hand to his heart in gratitude. Alastair found him again and his sweaty arm was around his shoulders and he pulled him in for a kiss and no one seemed to know who Ivan was or care, but here he was in the middle of it all.

When the lights came on Alastair still had his arm around Ivan's neck and the armpit of his suit was ripped out. Ivan nodded to it, said, "Sorry."

"Not a problem. I know a good tailor."

Then Ivan said, "I wouldn't have guessed. About you. Alastair."

"London has punk music, still," he answered. "I came of age gay in the nineties, too, Ivan." He had small fabric burn on his cheek and god it was gorgeous.

Ivan felt elated. Everyone was laughing and sweaty. Ivan overheard, "The movie was kind of silly, but man, I haven't moshed in years." Another, "Amazing to see those bands for the price of a movie ticket." Someone else, "That was fun." All this joy and anger and catharsis wasn't really for him, because of him. It was because of the other artists.

Alastair seemed to be hearing the same things. "It was good," he said. "Really good. The reviewers will talk about the film itself. Tomorrow people will see the film without all the show. It'll hold up. It's really good."

"Thank you," Ivan said, but he felt punctured.

In the Eco, Alastair tried to cheer him up. "You're the vanguard. Soon we'll see advertisements for dinosaur safaris."

"That's sick."

"We saw Ivory-billeds yesterday. It's all happening. You don't think someone would pay ten million pounds to shoot a brontosaurus?"

"Too easy. They're slow."

"One million for a brontosaurus. Ten for a t-rex. Fifteen for a velociraptor. Twenty to shoot a pterodactyl from the sky."

"That's fucked up."

Ivan was smiling, even as his brain spun, thinking of best- and worst-case scenarios for the reviews, ticket sales. He didn't want to go home yet. "The ballet is over. But 'What Still Remains' is showing late," Ivan said.

"I'd love to see that."

Their Eco took them to The Armory, a huge space for big exhibits. Industrial, none of the glamor and gold they'd just been in.

On the way Alastair was scowling at his screen so Ivan asked, "What?"

"James is trying to sell our place so that neither of us has to buy the other out and stay there, but real estate is a nightmare now. We're likely going to lose a lot of money and I care but not really and he cares very much. I think we should just set the thing on fire and be done with it."

The thing Ivan always had to offer but never had—a decent place in Manhattan—would not matter to this man. Ivan had never cohabitated; no one had ever had a key; he'd had sex with plenty of people he'd brought home in every room in his small apartment which was big for this island, never a lot of drama when things were over. His sister thought he was afraid of commitment, was always wanting to set him up with her friends but was hesitant to get them involved. She wanted her brother in love. "I have companionship," he'd tell her. "I'm not lonely." Which wasn't the truth—he was lonely, terribly lonely, but none of the people he met for drinks or museum exhibits or film openings made him feel any less lonely. They were company, and he liked conversation, and he loved sex, but there hadn't been someone yet whose absence really mattered. He watched Alastair's face while he wrote his ex-lover, ex-husband, ex-partner, back, and clearly Alastair had had had something Ivan hadn't, but he wasn't sure that was a thing he wanted. A thing that when taken could matter so much. Ivan had always felt a little distant from other people, even his sister, and Alastair seemed not distant at all from this person thousands of miles away, and Ivan did not want that, he did not, and he wondered if Alastair had or if it had just happened.

They walked into the exhibit space not touching. They saw pictures of a pink lake in Australia. A red beach in China. Bluebonnets still came up in fields in Texas. The Blue Ridge of Appalachia was still blue. Havasupai was still cerulean.

Glowworms were thriving in New Zealand. They loved the heat. The Northern Lights carried on.

Cinque Terre was high enough on hills, cliffs, that it was still there, the sea closer but not touching.

They saw photos of reflections of the sky in salt flats. Caves full of crystals. Sand dunes where the footsteps of visitors got erased every night by the wind. All the images hung on cables, larger than life.

They saw castles that hadn't crumbled. Ruins of ancient civilizations that weren't gone. The Taj Mahal hadn't fallen.

Niagara Falls still powered the Northeast.

Wind Cathedral in Namibia and Antelope Canyon in Arizona were still majestic. And empty. Meant to be desert. The Grand Canyon wasn't going anywhere. The light still changed above it and shaped it daily, shifted its shades. Deserts were growing, but it wasn't all desert yet.

In so many places you could still see the stars.

Buddha statues. Huge Jesuses. Some temples were still

okay. Some cathedrals. Some mosques. Some synagogues.

So much magnificence still.

"But isn't the whole point who cares, if no humans are here to see it? I don't think this all means as much to tigers."

"No more tigers soon."

"Well."

"That didn't cheer me as much as I'd hoped. Your film is more honest, even though it's made up."

"Thank you," Ivan said. Touched. And hopeful. That's what he always wanted.

They went home, thirsty but not for booze, hungry but not for food.

"That went well," Alastair said.

"Maybe. We'll see what they say tomorrow. This feels like my big chance."

"We all get more than one chance."

"Okay. My best chance."

"Fair. And, truly, I loved it. Just so you know." Then Alastair asked, "Any ideas yet, for what's next?"

And Ivan was glad Alastair didn't avoid the thing you're really not supposed to ask another artist. "No ideas," he said. "My mind is blank." Ivan looked at Alastair, jacket discarded, ascot off, fitted pants tight at the thigh. "I'd be terrified if I weren't distracted."

Ivan went to undo Alastair's belt, said, "I've been wanting to do this all day," and got a beautiful grin of permission. Why not fuck a man at the window overlooking Fifth Avenue? No one was looking in, but they were both looking out, at lights and a fountain and horse-drawn carriages, still, green taxis and people walking and beyond, Central Park, with unknown things happening inside.

XX.
Sterna paradisaea: Arctic Tern

Tired is not a word we use. I learned the word from another bird, bigger than us. He chased me for a long time, to eat, and said out loud "tired," and I got away. But we don't use the word. I don't know how many others of us know it. For us, the flapping is what we do, from the time the sun rises to the time the sun sets, twice every cycle of the seasons. We continue motion knowing that this too will end, and it doesn't do much to think about it. Eventually, we stop, but we never say it's because we can't keep going. We stop because it is natural to stop in that place.

We learned to make the journey the same way we learn everything. We don't explain to each other, we just watch, and learn what the feelings deep within mean, what to do about them. I have a feeling, I don't know what to do to change it, I watch another in the flock consume water, and when I do, it releases the feeling, and I learn, though I still don't have a name for that need for water. I don't know the name for the feeling until someone says to me, "thirst," and then drinks. We rarely name our feelings. I know thirst. I know hunger. I know tired. We meet our needs mostly without stating what they are. We have words for almost everything, but to use them too much embarrasses us. I talk to myself in my head. When I have that feeling in the sky, and water is days away, I learn to pay no attention to it. I do not say to anyone, *thirst*, because what could they do? I learn to not focus on the feeling, though it never leaves. I don't have a name for doing that, that ignoring, I've never heard what it is called. I don't know if it's better or worse to forget but not fully. Better. It must be awful to not be able to sink the thought down a level, to have it shouting every minute: *You need water, you need water, you need water! Thirst, thirst, thirst*—awful to have that ringing around in your head. That happened one time, and I think I had reached the desperation place. Without water, I would have not been anymore, soon. That shouting, it was hard to endure. I could not stop the flock. I could not get the thing my body was telling me I must have. It was nowhere near. I had to wait, and wondered if I would drop from the sky. When we landed, and I drank, I didn't know how to tell someone that that might have been the end of me. What would it be to hear that shouting more often? To not be able to quiet desire?

The feeling the others get, the thing that tells them it's time to begin, it's time for us to leave, journey, the feeling that tells them this travel is necessary, is worth it, is less risky than staying home, I have never had that feeling. I have never heard it named. I leave when the others say it's time, without my body ever telling me I must.

We lose some each year. No one says we would lose less if we stayed. Everyone seems to know we would lose more. After our months in the place we are going, no one suggests that we stay. We go back and forth, trusting that we will keep most of us if we do, add more of us. No one complains about the distance, or the effort. No one says we could have our babies in the place where we mostly live. I don't know if others feel it, the tiredness before starting, the awareness of what's ahead. Maybe it is only me.

Maybe if we were to stay, we would suffer. More. We

suffer during the long flight, at least I think others who aren't me do also, but if we stayed, they all must know we would suffer more. I think the days are not so cold this year as they were last year, and the year before, at this time. I think we could stay. But maybe the suffering we endure during the weeks of flight is tolerable because we know. We know it will end. We lose track of days, we lose track of hours in flight, we forget when we last ate, drank, slept, we grow delirious with the beating of wings, but we know we are on the way somewhere we can rest. Maybe if we stayed in the place we left, each day we would just be glad for survival, each day glad we made it through, each day not sure what the next would bring. Never sure how long it would last, how long we would have to last for it to be over, not knowing how much worse it would get before it would stop.

We do not have names for each other. I called her my daughter, and I knew which one I meant. I do not remember each of them distinctly, all of my children, each daughter, but I knew when I spoke of her, she was not the daughter of last year, and she was not the first daughter I bore. She was this year's daughter. And I only had her, only one lasted, but if I'd had two, I'd call each my daughter, and I would know the difference between them. But were I to speak of them to others, they would not know which I meant when I said *daughter*. To them, it would not matter—a daughter is a daughter. They are the same. To me, they are not the same, but for us they fill the same role. If I had a son last season, last time I was in the place we were going before we got brought to this place, I could differentiate there. My children would be different, because they are different to the group. Each would be born, pushed from my body, each would have cracked itself out of a shell, each would have fledged, flown, not fallen, each would have followed me on this journey, learning the route to teach to their young next season. What would make them different would be what they say. How they would say it. He would sing, *The sun grows strong each day, as we fly towards the winter place.* The last thing she said to me was, *Where are your other children, like me?*

I told her that once I teach them, across one cycle of seasons, they leave me, and start their own families, and the group no longer distinguishes who came from whom. They no longer stick by my side. They know everything they need to know, and I must create more babies to teach. She realized she would leave me when we got where we were going, she would choose a mate, have babies. She asked me if I still knew who was from me, which ones. I said if I thought about it, I could know, but that is not something we think about. It is not something that matters. We raise our young and teach them our ways. Everyone helps, but babies learn best when they have one chief teacher, one to focus all attention on. We know this. But then, after that, we are just us. A group. All the same. All responsible for all. No need to trace lines.

I needed food, but it was not yet time for food. *Hunger.* I could wait. I wondered if some creatures had things when they wanted things and didn't have to wait. I wondered if it was only me that would like to stop and rest. I wondered, if I said I wanted to stop, would it be considered against us all? We all know there is no place to stop when we travel the long journey. Just water below, but not the kind that stops thirst.

I was afraid to tell anyone that I was doubting why we

did that thing, that I was finding it hard. All those years, no one had ever said that it was hard. They said, Get ready. They said, It will be soon. They said, I feel the air telling me it is nearly time to go, and all agreed. No one said what I was thinking, I worry that this year it will be too far. No one said, I would rather stay here. We do not know what our home is like when we are away. We could find out. No one said, I would like to disregard the wisdom of the ancients, which they have placed in my body. To leave, I will suffer, and I worry about whether I can endure. This year, I cannot make it.

I wonder if I made this happen. If I asked for it. Somehow. Because now we are not in the place we were going. We are somewhere else, someplace none of us know. Some of us were pulled from our flight and brought to this place where we can fly, but we cannot continue our journey. Not all of us. My daughter, this year's daughter, is not with me anymore. My mate, who helps me keep the eggs warm each year, who helps me raise each year's daughter, each year's son, he is not here. Some of us are here. Some of us were taken. Some of us were not. We do not understand what has happened. I fear it is my fault, the result of my desire, the result of my body being tired. We have said nothing about what has happened. We either have no name for it, or are afraid to use the name we have.

I cannot see my own body. I can turn my neck and stretch out a wing and see that, I can see my feet. When we fly, I look to the bodies next to me, and assume I look like that. Our bodies are all like each other's, but on each body, it is not all the same. I do not have names for all the shades that we are. We know how each one around us will move and we move together, we swerve we swoop we slot into formation, we land, and we all lift together, and we don't run into each other. We know how to do that. No one else notices how magnificent it is. It is just a part of their day.

Now, we are near others who are like us, but not us. They sing similar songs, but not our songs. We don't have names for the shades we are, but we can say, We are darker than they are here, lighter there, and, They have something we do not. When we were put here we were ravenous, or I was, my attention was drawn to the all-dark bird, the speckled bird, the bird with nothing like our color on him anywhere, the bird who is a color that seems to be the opposite of ours.

If we had arrived in the place we were going, we would say to the others there that we are glad to see them after such a long absence, we are glad to see they have multiplied, we are delighted to see them looking so well. We would wish them prosperity and many progeny this season. They would say the same to us. The others are like us but aren't us. They look similar, but not the same. They have the same shape, but not quite—longer legs, different beaks, bigger wings. But we don't know what to say to the others here, the strangers near this lake. We don't know how to ask if they are as confused as we are, if they were traveling too, but if their journeys were stopped. Maybe some of them are from this place?

I will try not to mourn my daughter. This trip, our last as a family, I thought maybe I could say things to her, ask her things, see if she wondered what I wonder, if she got that from me. She looked at things not only like she wanted to eat or mate or drink or run from them, but like she wanted to see them. I thought maybe that tilt of her head meant she had thoughts like mine. I will try not to mourn my mate, the way he provided for me and my children. I fly to a branch in a small tree where I will stay this night, and I land, and it sways with the weight of my body. I do not still.

XXI.
Arrow and Grant Sullivan

A typical species becomes extinct within ten million years of its first appearance.

99.9% of all species that have ever existed are now extinct.

The natural background rate of extinction has historically been one to five species per year. Just seven years ago, in 2016, the earth was losing dozens of species daily, one thousand to ten thousand times that rate. Now, hundreds of species disappear daily.

This is the midst of the sixth wave of extinction in the past half-billion years.

Sea urchins disappeared in the Ordovician extinction 440 million years ago.

Early fish disappeared in the Devonian extinction 365 million years ago.

Nearly all sea creatures and three-quarters of land vertebrates disappeared in the Permian extinction 245 million years ago.

Ancient squid and clams disappeared in the Triassic extinction 208 million years ago.

Dinosaurs disappeared in the Cretaceous-Tertiary extinction 65 million years ago.

This extinction doesn't yet have a name.

Of the approximately six thousand modern species of mammal, 115 have gone extinct since 1600. One in five mammals faces high risk. Scientists give large carnivores—

tigers, lions, grizzlies—three-quarters of a century to live; two at the most.

Of the over ten thousand identified bird species, 811 have already gone extinct.

Some scientists predict eighty percent of the human population will be gone by 2100.

Arrow read these facts, printed in navy on a baby blue wall, in the lobby of the Museum of Natural History, at the entrance to the Extinction exhibit. The vaulted lobby was big enough to house a dinosaur, marble columns, paintings, and everyone oohed and aahed over the bones assembled into a massive shape, and no one said aloud, *This thing no longer exists.* Cascading down the wall, alongside the other side of the entryway, a poem:

"Essay"

So many poems about the deaths of animals.
Wilbur's toad, Kinnell's porcupine, Eberhart's squirrel,
and that poem by someone—Hecht? Merrill?—
about cremating a woodchuck. But mostly
I remember the outrageous number of them,
as if every poet, I too, had written at least
one animal elegy; with the result that today
when I came to a good enough poem by Edwin Brock
about finding a dead fox at the edge of the sea
I could not respond; as if permanent shock
had deadened me. And then after a moment
I began to give way to sorrow (watching myself
sorrowlessly the while), not merely because
part of my being had been violated and annulled,
but because all these many poems over the years

have been necessary—suitable and correct. This
has been the time of the finishing off of the animals.
They are going away—their fur and their wild eyes,
their voices. Deer leap and leap in front
of the screaming snowmobiles until they leap
out of existence. Hawks circle once or twice
above their shattered nests and then they climb
to the stars. I have lived with them fifty years,
we have lived with them fifty million years,
and now they are going, almost gone. I don't know
if the animals are capable of reproach.
But clearly they do not bother to say good-bye.

— Hayden Carruth

Arrow felt afraid, and compelled to enter. As if it were a haunted house.

After Day One of the contest, she and her dad were thrilled and restless. "Okay," Arrow said, looking at her iPill. "The ballet and opera have already started. It's First Friday, so the galleries are staying open late." She listed the options and was surprised when her father said he was interested in the Extinction exhibit. "You want to see how bad it is? How bad it's going to get?"

"Well, yeah. I guess a lot of people do, to have an exhibit."

Then, "Can we go wearing this?" Arrow asked. She had on jeans, worn cowboy boots, and a tie-dye t-shirt from a local brewery in Flagstaff. Her only jewelry was the long ,etched-silver earrings and bracelet Ed had bought her at the Hopi show, things she'd casually admired, and when he bought them for her, it felt like a signal of their alliance, symbols that represented clouds and rain, what became her daily decoration. Her dad wore jeans and a button-up over a t-shirt, not the kind of button-up a businessman would wear but the kind built to last, and work boots. They must have not been the same pair, but they were the same kind as what he would wear when she was a child, boots that laced through holes in the bottom and hooks in the top, boots that when he came home from driving trains, Arrow would help him pull off his feet, the joke being that he was too tired to do it himself, and she had to use the leverage of her entire little body to pry them off but she would because she had abundant energy and was glad to see her father, and now she realized the joke was probably closer to the truth than she then knew.

"I don't see why not," her dad said. "We'll take showers in the morning."

Their green taxi dropped them off in front of steps leading up to a building with columns. Arrow felt intimidated, but her father walked right up them, showed his pass at the door. The exhibit brochure was downloaded to their iPills, and when Arrow read that the museum had left the dinosaur wing exactly as it always had been, the best in the world, she said they should go there first. Move chronologically through destruction.

Hanging from the entrance to the Dinosaur Wing were birds, stuffed gulls. What was still here. Arrow laughed.

The complete skeletons may as well have been dragons, were so much larger than Arrow ever thought they could be. She could stand under the bellies of some. Horns on their noses, frilled skulls, spiked tails, they were as delightful as the cartoons of her childhood, stunning and spooky. A fossil of a flying dinosaur that flapped its feathered arms and legs, four wings, plumed edges pressed into stone, documentation that some of these reptilian creatures would become avian.

Her dad walked toward the next room and Arrow followed. The museum used its famous diorama style. The painted background was soft blurs, intricate and detailed but prettier than the real world, less sublime. Real animal pelts stretched on a frame, feathers, so that the animals appeared alive, in their natural environment, behind glass—the brushed scenery reduced the realism, but the animals seemed nearly sentient. Apparently, it didn't work nearly as well in the human exhibits, Arrow had read—shiny faces, no way to recreate human skin.

Arrow looked at colossal creatures and tiny ones. They all felt consequential, their furred and finned bodies, their glass eyes that once could see—if not like she saw, at least something like what her eyes showed her. They walked or swam or flew on this earth she now inhabited, and the enormity of it, the thousands of stuffed bodies surrounding her, made her feel a swift hysteria, but she knew if she ran she'd regret not facing what was in front of her, what was behind her species. Toolache Wallaby. Verhoeven's Giant Tree Rat. Lesser Stick Nest Rat. Blue-Gray Mouse. Christmas Island Shrew (officially critically endangered but has not been reliably seen since 1985). Cebu Warty Pig. Nendo Tube-nosed Fruit Bat. Balearic Islands Cave Goat. Queen of Sheba's Gazelle. Addax. Hokkaidō Wolf. Formosan Clouded Leopard. Bali Tiger. Cape Lion. Mexican Grizzly Bear. Bactrian Camel. Quagga. Western Black Rhinoceros. Malagasy Hippopotamus. North African

Every Living Species

Elephant. Wooly Mammoth. Mountain Gorilla. Baiji Dolphin. Gray Whales. Yellowfin Cutthroat Trout. Gölçük Toothcarp. Ash Meadows Killifish. Axolotl. Xerces Blue Butterfly. A wall full of flower fossils.

Arrow couldn't believe there were children here. But she guessed they didn't know what they were looking at. To them, this was just a bunch of animals.

Then Arrow's hand reached out, her fingers touched glass. "Wait. Dad? The elk in Arizona are extinct? What does that mean?" Merriam's Elk, the sign said. It looked like the elk she knew, the elk she had hunted and eaten, but they were huge. One's muzzle was lifted, throat extended in a bugle, and Arrow wondered how many people in New York City knew that elk sounded like whales.

"The elk we hunt aren't native," he answered. "They were brought in from Yellowstone when our indigenous elk were overhunted. Management is a lot better now. That's why it's so hard to get an elk tag."

Arrow wondered why she never knew this, why she assumed that one thing she knew intimately had always been where she was from. Arrow loved elk the way some girls loved horses.

The Extinction Wing wasn't exhaustive, was just a suggestion of what was gone, mammals and amphibians and reptiles. There wasn't room for all of it. But the Extinct Bird wing was comprehensive, so some contestants could complete the weirdest life list—seeing the entirety of what was no longer alive, all of it. Arrow walked in then turned around and walked out, sat on a bench next to a stuffed Dodo, its dumb little face, its ridiculous stubs of wings, its beautiful plumpness.

Her dad came out a few minutes later. "That one's

awful." Then, "Can you handle more?"

"I don't know. Sure." They walked into the Extinct Peoples wing and the first sign Arrow saw read:

Aboriginal Tasmanians (Tasmanian: *Parlevar* or *Palawa*) are the indigenous people of the Australian state of Tasmania. Trugernanner (1812–1876) and Fanny Cochrane Smith (1834–1905) were the last people solely of Tasmanian descent. Today, some thousands of people living in Tasmania and elsewhere can trace part of their ancestry to the Parlevar, but they have mostly European ancestry, and did not keep the traditional Parlevar culture.

There was a picture of two dark-skinned people in European clothing—bonnets and suits and poofed skirts. There was a painting of one dark-skinned person in traditional dress, animal skins and beads. Arrow looked around her. Bo. Capayán. Giraavaru people. Harla people. Jangil. Khodynt. Koningo. Minuane people. Sadlermiut. Ware people. Guatemala: Acala Ch'ol, Chajoma, Chinamita, Kejache, Ko'woj, Lakandon Ch'ol, Manche Ch'ol, Pipil people, Toquegua, Yalain. Russia: Anaoul Yukaghir. Asan people. Chud. Kamasins. Mators. Merya. Meshchera. Volga Bulgarians. Volga Finns. Yurats Samoyed. Azerbaijdzhanlylar, 1 member. Ankalyn, 1 member. Izhorians, 227 members. Khamshetsy, 1 member. Kerek, 6 members. Russko-ustintsy, 4 members. Votians 63 members. Yakhudoi makhali, 22 members. Yakhudi, 2 members. Yaskolbinskie Tatar, 2 members. Yugh people, 16 members (Yugens 1,Yugis 15). Alyutors, 23 members. Kamasins, 2 members. Kerek, 3 members. Extinct peoples and peoples doomed to become extinct, soon.

Visitors were meant to wander in and out of spaces,

into curved corridors and rooms in the middle of a bigger room. The exhibits were interactive—here you touch a cloth no longer made, here you smell a dish no longer cooked, there were speakers broadcasting languages no longer known and music no longer played. It was all very frank and straightforward and Arrow felt like sobbing.

As she was leaving, she read above the exit: "The general consensus is that there are between six thousand and seven thousand languages currently spoken, and that between fifty and ninety percent of those will have become extinct by the year 2100."

Arrow waited for her father again on a bench. She was glad there weren't dioramas of people in there at least, just flat photographs and paintings. She read about the history of the museum on her iPill. They'd done shows on mythic creatures, the fossils that made us believe in dragons and phoenixes, the narwhal leading to merpeople, why we want so badly to believe a Pegasus is possible. Extreme mammals. A whole exhibit on gold, one on pearls. Bioluminescence. Einstein and Shackleton and Darwin. The butterfly exhibit featured live animals. In this museum, Lonesome George died—people watched the Pinta Island giant tortoise go extinct, and that seemed to shift something. Life at the Limits showed the few species that would survive. The Natural Disasters exhibit was so casual—each will happen again. All of them. Volcanoes and hurricanes and tornadoes and tsunamis. Children could watch a map of the five boroughs showing the damage of Sandy, then Kamilah, death counts. Arrow didn't know why she came to this exhibit, naturally next in the progression. She should have known this was something she didn't want to know.

When her father walked out, he said, "I need to get out of here."

"Yeah. Okay." Her iPill suggested they go one of two places next: an exhibit of photographs of viruses that could destroy the human population at The Whitney, or *What Still Remains* at The Armory.

"I don't think either will help," he said, and she agreed.

Arrow summoned a green taxi to take them back to camp.

She climbed into the Eco's driver's seat, her dad the passenger seat. The map on the dash showed where they were and where they were going, gave an approximation of how long it would take. Arrow knew even in a human-driven taxi she could look out the window, didn't have to be responsible, but sitting in the driver's seat but not watching the road was even more fun. Out the window were taxis as far as they could see, beads on a string, all green except two yellow relics, emitting carbon dioxide, drinking the last of the fuel laid down when the dinosaurs disappeared, for those who still trusted humans more than the machines they made.

Arrow didn't find the city beautiful. It was filthy, as much as they'd seemed to try to clean it. There was bulbous, undecipherable graffiti everywhere. She tried to make the shapes into the alphabet but couldn't. Peeling advertisements. But it was entrancing. Impressive. Everywhere, there was something worth looking at—the corner of a building's cornice and mullioned windows and chaotic storefronts and that woman walking like she was the only person here. The city seemed solid and stolid and unchanging and mercurial.

Her dad said the quail from their most recent hunt should be thawed by now, and he'd cook them over a fire and make wild rice and ranch-style beans and they still had beer at camp. Arrow said that sounded great.

"You have arrived at your destination," a pleasant voice told them as they slowed to a stop. Arrow wondered about the choice to go with such a bland intonation, wondered if New Yorkers missed the chance to chat with a driver with an accent. The voice was female, and Arrow wondered why all the devices and machines that served us were women. She'd taken few taxis in her life, but none had been driven by a human woman.

"You may take the water produced by this hydrogen fuel cell vehicle with you, if you wish. You will find the tap near where the exhaust pipe would be in a conventional car. If you do not pour this potable water into your own container, it will be added to the city's water supply at the end of my shift. Thank you for using Eco. A receipt has been sent to your iPill." Arrow hadn't brought her water bottle but had her father tip some of the water into her hands. It didn't taste like anything. The rest she left to the city.

As they walked into the park, her father's eyebrows knit together. "What's that?" he asked, pointing. At the opening of the path was a small pale mass with feet. He walked ahead and picked it up, and it was droopy in his hand, newly dead, white and gray with a shiny green head.

"Can you tell what killed it?" Arrow asked and he said no. "A pigeon. One of the few birds we didn't see in there today."

"We could cook it with the quail," her dad said.

"What? What if it was sick?"

"I bet it hit the window of the building," he said. "One of the few places in the city where windows reflect trees, not other buildings."

"But we aren't sure."

"We ate the birds that hit the windows of our house."

"But we saw that happen, so we knew." Dozens of birds had broken their necks on the glass of their home over the years, flown into the front wall of windows which overlooked and reflected the forest, thinking they were still flying through trees.

"I don't want to waste it. When I pluck it I'll be able to tell if the meat is okay. People used to eat pigeons all the time." He looked around to see if anyone was watching, shielded the bird with his back, lifted it into the top of the backpack and gently zipped it shut around it. None of the dozens of people on the street noticed.

As they walked toward their tent, they passed dozens of people, over one hundred, sitting in a circle with hundreds of flickering candles. Some were wearing all black, but others were in bright clothes, stripes and patterns, saris and kilts and costumes. Some were lying prone. Some were groaning, wailing, sobbing. Many were writing, many were conversing. Arrow couldn't hear what they were saying. A man stood on the edge of the crowd in an elegant suit and invited them to join. He handed them each a sheet of paper—Arrow hadn't seen a flyer in so long—and offered to download more information to their iPills. "We're the Dark Mountain Project, people who grieve for the loss of life on the planet, who stopped believing the stories civilization tells itself. We're moving through the last four stages of grief during this contest to help people push past the first stage: their Denial." He gestured to the crowd. A showman. "Tonight is Bargaining. People are negotiating with the universe, describing what they would give up in order to save humanity, to save the animals. The bonfire in an hour, where we will throw in the contracts we've drawn up with whatever gods we believe in, will remove all of those delusions."

Arrow read the first quote on the paper she held. "They think we're saying: 'Nothing matters.' But in fact all we're saying is: 'Let's not pretend we're not feeling despair. Let's sit with it for a while. Let's be honest with ourselves and with each other. And then as our eyes adjust to the darkness, what do we start to notice?' —Paul Kingsnorth"

Her father looked at her, waiting for her to speak. She appreciated that he thought she might want this, this might help her. "No, thank you," she said. "But thank you for inviting us."

When they got back to camp her father poured himself a whiskey from a flask, and Arrow read the reverse of the leaflet. He offered her some whiskey, and she shook her head. "I have already accepted that today is as good as life on earth will ever be, it's all downhill from here." And, "What do you do when you accept that all of these changes are coming, things that you value are going to be lost, things that make you unhappy are going to happen, things that you wanted to achieve you can't achieve, but you still have to live with it, and there's still beauty, and there's still meaning, and there are still things you can do to make the world less bad? And that's not a series of questions that have any answers other than people's personal answers to them." Arrow wondered if she would like this Paul Kingsnorth person, or not.

Then, "We do not believe that everything will be fine.

We are not even sure, based on current definitions of progress and improvement, that we want it to be. Read our manifesto at http://dark-mountain.net/about/manifesto/"

"Rearmament

These grand and fatal movements toward death: the
    grandeur of the mass
Makes pity a fool, the tearing pity
For the atoms of the mass, the persons, the victims,
    makes it seem monstrous
To admire the tragic beauty they build.
It is beautiful as a river flowing or a slowly gathering
Glacier on a high mountain rock-face,
Bound to plow down a forest, or as frost in November,
The gold and flaming death-dance for leaves,
Or a girl in the night of her spent maidenhood,
    bleeding and kissing.
I would burn my right hand in a slow fire
To change the future...I should do foolishly. The
    beauty of modern
Man is not in the persons but in the
Disastrous rhythm, the heavy and mobile masses, the
    dance of the
Dream-led masses down the dark mountain.

— Robinson Jeffers, 1935"

Arrow hadn't made it to Glacier National Park before all the glaciers were gone.

Arrow watched her father start to pluck the pigeon. Some of the feathers were dun, some a dull gray, others a green overlaid with pink shimmer. She'd never seen a pigeon up close, such a beautiful, disrespected bird. She thought of Audubon, who killed animals in order to study them, in order to make his beautiful paintings, who threaded wire through wings and stitched skin and posed the creatures he captured. There was a street named after him somewhere in this neighborhood.

Her father started cooking and Ed called. Her dad told her to go ahead, he could handle quail and rice. She wandered up to where the light stopped.

Ed and Arrow exchanged pleasantries. He asked if she was having fun, said this seemed like her kind of adventure. She told him a few details about the contest, skipped the exhibit they'd just seen. He said he'd checked in on her mom and she was fine. "She makes salsa just like you do, chopping vegetables without really watching. I thought she'd slice a finger off but I should know better, having watched you." It was nice to hear his voice, but he seemed off, distracted. She wondered if she was projecting. Finally, Arrow just asked, "What? What is it?"

"I have to tell you something."

"Okay." Quickly Arrow went through worst-case scenarios: he was cheating on her, he was sick, he was leaving her. Whatever he told her, she hoped it didn't mean she had to tell him her secret. "Tell me," she said. "It's okay."

"When I fought the fire on your land, it went over me. The fire."

Arrow had figured that to be true but hadn't wanted to make Ed admit it to her if he didn't want her to know. So she said, "Do you want to tell me what it was like?"

He did. "We train for this yearly. Unzip the carrying

case, pull out the shelter, and shake it open. Step into it, pull it over your head, and lie down with your face close to the ground, where the air is cleanest and coolest. Use your elbows, knees, and feet to pin the shelter down against wind created by the fire. It's very hot and very noisy. It lasted about five minutes, though I'm not sure how long it felt like. They tell us in training it will last about five minutes. Things fall on top of us. It can last up to fifteen minutes, they tell us. Because sometimes if it seems like it's taking too long people run, not really to escape but to get it over with. This was fairly fast. None of my crew ran."

"That sounds terrifying," Arrow said. She meant it. How awful. "I'm so sorry that happened to you, Ed." Then, "Why didn't you tell me before?"

"I didn't want to see your face. I was afraid you'd be more upset than I am. Was. I thought you'd feel guilty that it was your land, that you'd somehow feel weirdly obligated to me because of it. But I didn't want to keep this from you."

Arrow understood her face to be grimacing, scowling, looking horrified, something like that. She was upset. "But I don't feel weirdly obligated to you," Arrow said. She felt a catch in her throat. "I mean, I do feel obligated to you, but it's a choice. I don't feel like I have to be with you. And the fire—I knew it was a possibility. I know it is every day you work. I'm just so sorry it happened for the first time on what's mine." *On what might sometime be ours*, she thought but did not say. "I wish it hadn't happened." All there is ever to say about grief, sorrow.

"It finally happened," Ed said. "I don't have to wait for it anymore." He sounded relieved.

That's what this was about. "Okay." Then, "Are you going to keep this job forever, Ed?"

"I don't know."

Arrow didn't tell him whether she wanted him to or not. Danger was unavoidable. She sat in the quiet of his breathing.

Then he said, "We've never been apart this long, Arrow. Since we've known each other. It's nice to miss you."

She hadn't realized that. She told him she missed him too. She opened her mouth but found she had nothing else to say. They wished each other goodnight, good dreams, good days the next day. She had no desire to tell Ed she was pregnant, no wish to go through this with him.

Arrow and her father ate the birds with their fingers, and again she was thrown into her childhood, this meal in her mouth tasting exactly as it had then. She spit out a bit of buckshot stuck in a quail breast and complimented her father's spice mixture, a peppery, paprika-rich combo he'd rubbed into each bird's oiled skin. He handed her the edge of a wishbone. Arrow thought, *Please let the world be worth living in*, and with slippery fingers they twisted it between them. He won. She wondered what he'd wished. "Again," he said, and handed her another from the pile of bones at his feet, airy enough to allow flight. Arrow won this time, and she would think he let her except there was no real way to tip a wishbone pulling. She'd thought the same wish in her head.

They split the pigeon, and it tasted just like quail. Gamey and delicious. This may be the last time they ate quail. They always expected to get more, but this may be the year they finally found no coveys. Ed could have died, but he didn't. He could have been cooked in his shelter.

Her dad offered her a beer, and Arrow took one. The firelight was lovely but Arrow felt damp in her shirt. She held the chilled glass against her forearm, one and then the other. They sat and didn't have much to say to each other. A fire was a distraction, crackling timber and flames something to watch in a space without television, no computer screen. Arrow wondered if they were both also seeing a fire that wasn't really there, how much her dad was thinking of home. She decided not to tell her father what Ed had told her; she didn't want Ed burdened with her family's pity, or more of their gratitude. She could almost imagine what it felt like for fire to pass over her, nothing but reflective fabric between her and burning. But her mind stopped short of how bad it would be. How blistering, suffocating. Air came in and out of her lungs easily, here in this forest, trees taking in carbon dioxide, trees producing oxygen, and she couldn't quite envision what Ed had endured on her behalf. But, of course, it wasn't for her. It was his job.

He offered her a second beer and when she shook her head he noticed she'd barely taken a sip of her first. He looked puzzled and she just shook it again.

"Are you feeling okay?" he asked. "You had an appetite."

"Yeah, dad, I feel fine. Thanks."

"Are you feeling restless?"

"I guess so. Yes. Today was a little overwhelming, I guess." So much death. So much almost death. And when they got home, Arrow would stop potential life. They sat in silence until Arrow said, "Dad?"

"Yeah?"

"I have to tell you something."

"Okay." And he gave her his full attention.

"I'm pregnant. Nobody knows."

"Not even Ed?"

"No. I don't want to keep it."

"What? Why? Is it Ed's?"

"Is that relevant?"

"But you like Ed. We like Ed."

"I like a lot of things. Not enough to birth a child at the end of humanity."

"Humanity won't end."

"It might." The fire was fading, so her father's face was dim. Neither got up to add a log.

"At this point, we aren't sure."

"But we're sure things will get bad."

"Why are you telling me?"

"I was hoping you'd be the one to agree I'm not cut out for this."

Her father was picking the label off the bottle of his beer. She'd never seen him do that before. "Why do you think I would think you weren't up for this?"

"Because I'm just like you. And you know that. And you walked away from your family and I think I'm the kind of person who would do that, too. I've never committed to anything. You either."

"I am committed to you. And our land. You know that." Her father finished his beer and got up for another, put more wood on the fire so the flames flared. His bright, gilded face said, "I've always done the best I could, Arrow. With everything. Don't let your perception of my, what? Failure? Be your excuse."

"It's not an excuse. This is a thing I just can't do. Maybe killing my child is the best I can do." Arrow held her palms to the fire even though she wasn't cold. "And it's not a child. It's just the potential of a child."

"You're more like your mother than you know. Good at tending to people. You could do it."

"Why would you want me to do it? I've never known what I wanted to do with my life and that was fine. It bothered mom, I know, my lack of ambition or passion or whatever, but not me, and not you. You've always let me be aimless. I don't want this to be the reason I pick something. Decide to do something with my life." She thought of Ed not wanting her to feel obligated. "I don't want to live my life because of duty to someone else."

"I understand that," her father said. Arrow wondered how much he sacrificed to return to her and her mother. "But I can't believe you're not even considering this."

"I have considered it." The night felt the same temperature as Arrow's body. She felt held by thick air. "I don't know what I want. I don't want to sacrifice my life to someone else. I don't want to sacrifice my child to catastrophe. I don't want to sign a human up to see the end of humankind. A kid who can't choose."

"I think Ed has a right to know. I think your mother has a right to know."

"No one has a right to my body but me."

"Fine. Fair."

Arrow wanted approval from her father. Arrow wanted comfort from her father. Arrow wanted to know the world would continue to be worth living in. No one could promise her anything.

Her father wiped his brow.

"I'm glad you were born, Arrow. Are you glad you were born?"

"Yeah. Yes. I am. But there's still food in the grocery store."

"That's what you're most worried about?"

"Sort of. Yeah, when I think of the future, that's the first scary thing that comes to mind."

"We can grow food."

"Not enough to live on."

"All that's a long way off."

"It doesn't feel that way, dad. It really doesn't. It all feels right on the horizon. Like, I'll have to deal with some of it, but a child born now—they'd have to deal with all of it. They might not be glad to be alive."

"I would want to see it," her dad said. "The end of the world. Not the planet, some life will survive, but if humanity is going to end, I'd want to see it. See how we say goodbye. I'd rather see it than not have lived."

Arrow hadn't exactly considered that. She felt a fear that ran like silver in her bones.

"I'm glad you told me, Arrow."

"I'm not."

"Well."

Then Arrow felt bad. She wondered what the cult they'd seen in the park would tell her to do. Family planning was promoted in the third world but no one had yet told Americans to stop having kids.

She wondered if what she actually wanted from her father was permission to make a hopeful choice.

They sat still together until embers shimmered, cinders that cast no light to see by but filaments in a dense pattern illuminating and darkening, like a city seen from above, blackouts and power surges in turns. Arrow saw a dying civilization, or, at least, a city slowly returned to primitive methods of sustenance. With the animals gone, what would people eat? With water gone, what would people grow?

The heat kept flaring up, the wood lit and alive, fibers suddenly bright, like crystals. A fire takes longer to die than expected, always. Arrow kept watching. She wondered what her father was seeing. Probably just wood turned to ash, kindling charred to carbon. Natural.

Saturday, September 9th, 2023

Day Two of Canon and Cabela's
Birds of the World
Timed Birding Contest

XXII.
Not Your Average Aviary
by Jane Johnson
for *The Village Voice*

It sounds like an idea cooked up by Jean Baudrillard, George Saunders, Jorge Luis Borges, Josephine Waldorf, and Walt Disney: let's make a smaller version of every ecosystem on the planet, smoosh them together on the island with the eighth-highest population density, wall it in wire, and fill the container with birds. Colonial Williamsburg meets Snow White's forest, a labyrinthine hyperreal synecdoche. What is happening in Washington Heights and what does it mean?

As if this whole endeavor wasn't perplexing and po-pomo enough, the organizers decided to launch The Aviary as an alt-Olympics: every country on the earth, according to most accounts, is here, alongside Peace Teams and underrepresented groups. If we get out of this one without a drive-by or knife-fight I won't be the only one impressed. Starr Saphir always said that birds take away sadness just by looking at them, but can birds really make Dermot Ó hÉidin from The Republic of Ireland and Eóin McGowan from Northern Ireland forget the Old or the New Troubles? Sure, enough Catholics were born and are about to be old enough to vote for unification (Brexit was almost enough, almost—I thought it would happen back in '19, but now I'm really calling it), but if you think that shit's about to be over you're more optimistic than even The Aviary's inventors.

(If you don't know who Starr Saphir was, you must not be a birder *and* not a New Yorker.) Protestors stand next to the new Whole Foods, which is filled with fruits from across the globe—out of season, shipped in green to ripen under fluorescent lights—and yell that the Canon and Cabela's Birds of the World Timed Birding Contest, sponsored by The Aviary, is "unnatural."

I talked to Lisa Hyde, who was responsible for organizing all the teams from the United States. She said:

"We wanted to get every kind of American there was. You know, African American. Hispanic American, Asian American, Scandinavian American, Arab American, everything, German American, French American. But people in the office started saying how experiences really differ within those labels. Like, a Mexican American and Guatemalan American can't be said to be that similar just because they're both from Spanish-speaking countries. Spanish American, Paraguayan American, I mean there are differences. And Turkish American isn't really covered under Arab American. People say the Scandinavian countries are all alike, but Danish American and Norwegian Americans probably don't agree. Finnish is a totally different language, you know. Other countries don't have this problem like we do. And the term Native American doesn't nearly cover the diversity of the experience of this nation's first peoples. We talked to all the federally recognized tribes, 606 of them, but some said they had better things to do. We settled on sponsoring an indigenous team from each of the fifty states. All I can say is we did our best. Some people will not feel represented at this great event. And we think representation is empowering. When you see someone like yourself doing something, you feel more like you can do it, too. No other country is like ours, no other place has so many kinds of people who can call themselves one thing—American. It's fraught and we don't want to claim an easy diversity has been accomplished here, or that diversity will ever be easy. But we wanted to celebrate it."

Some indigenous people from this country and abroad have shown up to the contest in jeans and fleece, while others sport traditional gear: Maoris with face tattoos, Tafadzwanashe and Tapiwanashe Fichani in prehistoric Zimbabwean loincloths (except in the Arctic zone, where they agreed to don down covers), a pair in beaded regalia made by their grandmothers: one Spokane, one Coeur d'Alene. This Olympics of identification has made at least this author consider all the things I haven't seen.

Pageant or festival or spectacle, NYC itself has never seen anything like this. Banksy is going to retire, and for his farewell tour, he's been painting a bird each day somewhere on the walls of this city. I've found his American Robin in Bed-Stuy and his Vulture in Alphabet City. Tequila Mockingbird is performing a drag show of songs she wrote herself, lyrics made up of vintage tweets. Rumor has it she'll be giving everyone vintage Angry Birds apps at the event then holding a contest. I want to see it all, all of it, but I picked four things to go to—on the *Voice*'s dime, of course. First, Brandon Ballengée's exhibit *Frameworks of Absence*. He's found original prints of Audubon's drawings, some colored by John James himself, of birds that have since become extinct. Ballengée cuts out the birds then frames the print so that it makes shadows on a blank canvas behind it. The most interesting ones for me were the Carolina Parakeet—I hadn't known the United States had a native parakeet, hadn't known it was extinct, and I couldn't learn its colors from Ballengée's art; and the Ivory-billed Woodpecker—which contestants learned today isn't extinct after all. Never was, just hiding from us. Or, brought back. No one is yet sure.

I went to The Cloister's exhibit of illuminated manuscripts, early Christian conceptions of birds. The Cloisters is so weird anyway: you walk through the Heights, which feels like another nation; then Fort Tryon Park, nature; then you walk into something ancient. In the display cases and on the walls are rings, reliquaries containing pieces of a saint encased in a metal hand, gold, silver, jewels, tapestries, frescoes, unicorns, dragons, sarcophagi, stained glass, bits of cathedrals, abbeys, monasteries, nunneries, convents, chapels, altars. Ivory. Things made nearly a thousand years ago, taken apart, shipped here, and reassembled. Now surrounded by an arctic landscape. Polar is edged along the Cloisters, and the scientists have promised that the ice abutting the stones from Medieval monasteries won't hurt a thing.

My day, The Cloisters was even weirder. Japanese teenagers swarmed, whether from Japan or from the Bronx I don't know. They were dressed in costumes, wide-legged pants with straps and chains, tight shirts with collars and zippers, trench coats of finely woven fabric, elaborate vests with high necklines and laces that pulled the waist in tight. Some girls were dressed like baby dolls in frilly, short skirts and platform pumps and puffed sleeves and chokers. One had wings. Their hair and lips were pink and blue and silver and red, pigtails and braids with bows and mohawks flared out in straight lines. They slunk around as if things from the twelfth through fifteenth centuries were their natural habitat, as if only they understood that this was how things should be. They wore contact lenses to make their pupils big as dolls', to make their eyes look like animation. One wore white lace gloves.

I went inside to look at statuary and at places where monks and nuns once resided, to see what they once believed.

Pages from medieval bestiaries were displayed throughout the rooms, juxtaposed against the stone and stained-glass from places where people prayed and lived and did not make love. There were drawings of peacocks, black and white with feathers spread, colorful with feathers lowered. Below them, a sign read, *Peacocks weren't common in medieval Europe, but most Europeans knew what they looked like from drawings in books like this one. It was rumored that the cooked meat of a peacock never spoiled, which evolved into the rumor that eating peacock meat would lead to immortality. The hard flesh of the peacock represented the minds of teachers, who remained unaffected by the flames of lust. Its voice was terrible, causing fear in the listener, like the voice of the preacher who warned sinners of their end in hell. The eyes on the peacock's tail signify the ability of the teachers to foresee the danger we all face in the end.*

Hawks were called Accipiters. Eagles were called Aigles, Ailles, Aisgles, Aquilas, Aygles. Alerions were birds the color of fire, with razor-sharp wings. There was only one pair in the world. When she turned sixty years old, the female laid two eggs, which took sixty days to hatch. When the young were born the parents, accompanied by other birds, flew to the sea, plunged in, and drowned. Annes de la mer are now known as Barnacle Geese. They grew from trees. Ardeas were Herons. They are wiser than all others because they do not have many resting places. They are afraid of rainstorms and fly high above the clouds to avoid them, so when a heron takes flight, it means that a storm is coming. Arondes were Swallows. They knew when buildings were about to collapse and left before that happened. If the eyes of young sparrows were injured, the mother had the medical skill to make them see again. A Caladrius was an all-white bird that lived in the king's house. If it looked into the face of a sick man, it meant that he would live, but if the Caladrius looked away, the sick man would die. To cure the sick man, the Caladrius drew the sickness into itself, flew up toward the sun, and the disease was burned up and destroyed. The Caladrius must not be eaten. Cocks can tell time. Crows (known as Cornix, Cauue, Corneille) were monogamous. Their voice predicted rain and could foretell the future. When the crow found a corpse, it first pecked out the eyes. Nightingales—known as Luscinia, Lousegnol, Lucina, and Rosignol—sing so enthusiastically that they almost die. I overheard a woman say that Medieval conceptions were really screwed up, and I thought but didn't respond that it would be amazing to look around and feel like you understood everything, its relationship to other things, what it had to teach you.

And, finally, I picked the two fanciest possibilities because I never get to do stuff like this. I'm a working writer. Today, I went to the matinee of The American Ballet Theatre's performance that honors the birds and their spectrum: *Swan Lake* and *Firebird*, along with a black-and-white Balanchine and the colorful *Duets* by Merce Cunningham. Both the men and the women in attendance were done up in plumage. A tall man wore a crisp linen shirt with blue stripes, a camel sweater vest with red piped edges, chalk-colored khakis, madras bowtie with matching handkerchief folded in the pocket of a herringbone blazer, cufflinks, boater hat, boater shoes. A slim man wore a white tuxedo with tails. Women wore sequins and lace and organza and silk and denim.

Agon was first. They staged it the same way as its premiere in 1957: twelve dancers, only one of whom was black, the magnificent Justin Baker, and his presence on the stage felt only slightly less fraught than it might have back then. His solo with prima ballerina Wendy Kistler was anxious and intimate, erotic and strenuous. They were partners and combative—she knighted him with a leg like a sword on his shoulder, they twined and twisted limbs, he spun her, and she bent and straightened her knees at peculiar angles and she was utterly dependent on him for balance and for movement. After their slow, sustained battle ended in a seeming stalemate the other dancers entered the stage. They were lithe, willowy, languid, supple, lissome, svelte, sinuous, agile. They made it look easy, like their bodies were made for this. Then the dance was over and everyone stood and clapped and shouted bravo and brava. It was just as good as the original, which I've only seen on film.

Years ago I loved seeing Misty Copeland do Odile/Odette, so blasé as white swan, her Beyoncé bitch face on as black swan. ABT was right to promote her to principal right after that debut—the house was yelling like they were at a football game (appropriately so, respectfully so, just with more enthusiasm than one usually hears at an opera house). There were far more black people in the audience than I've ever seen at the ballet. *So how will ABT top that?* I wondered. Oh my, they did the right thing.

An all-male *Swan Lake*. En pointe.

We haven't truly seen men dance en pointe without parody. The choreography was classic, modified for the male form, but not much. They penchéd and jetéd and bourréed. Men partnered each other romantically and seriously. The corps had every shade of skin—finally not just a black star, but a casually black swan as part of the flock. Yellow, golden, tan, bronze, auburn, olive, and onyx skin under bright white costumes. And bare-chested, no less, a note taken from the fabulous Matthew Bourne. I won't say this was better than Bourne, but there was something audacious and delightful about seeing pure classic ballet so casually and drastically altered. And goddammn, Shaun Stevenson as Odette did all sixty-four fouettés pirouettes. I've never seen anyone do that—not just sixty-four spins, but sixty-four fouettés. You bet the audience was hooting and hollering.

Nobody knew they were going to do that. The audience lost its mind. What a time to be alive. Everyone was perfect. Their shoes didn't even look stiff.

The second half was about color. John Cage's music started, again music that was more sound than melody, a modern incarnation of Stravinsky's violin. Again people walked in a way that was half dance, half what everyone did daily. Instead of wearing matching rehearsal gear they wore ugly bright colors in peculiar combinations: a man in a black unitard paired with a woman in a yellow top, red skirt, black choker; a man and woman each wore green tops with yellow legs and she wore a light green skirt; a purple unitard and an orange unitard; a red unitard and blue unitard; one couple wore purple and green tops and bottoms, in opposite combinations; one woman wore a goldenrod leotard and skirt, and her partner wore periwinkle. The colors were so vivid that the varied skin tones of the dancers were less glaring. They weren't trying to be beautiful. They were exploring shapes. One woman moved with a very alert body, alive in her chest. Their partnerships were about being caught and being released. Bodies would do the same things at the same time then move independently. Their movement and the music seemed to be happening separately, simultaneously but not in unison. The slow turning of a body by someone else. Grabbing her knee to her chest. Grabbing her under her arm. Like a child in the arms of a larger father, kicking her feet. Like lovers. An arm escaping. Dragging and lifting.

Then *Firebird*. The original Chagall sets. The lead, first danced by Osage Maria Tallchief, later wife of Balanchine, now danced by Anna Not Afraid, Apsáalooke Crow. The ballet is a fever dream, monsters with bulbous green bodies and monsters with round yellow faces and tall monsters with blank faces, and one red body, whose feather is protective. Her solo was astounding—go see it, tomorrow's your last chance if it isn't sold out, but I'll tell you: she steps into the spotlight, steps into an arabesque that she holds for longer than she should be able to, and then she bursts into flame, real, actual fire, she leaps a circle around the stage, complicated spins and flips, rotating her body around its own axis, then she leaps from the stage, long jetés with legs parallel to the ground below her. The best dancing I have ever seen was last night.

And then I got a seat at Yekaterina Steele's restaurant, Metal. Oh, how I have craved to eat this woman's food. And to bask in her presence. That she basically named her restaurant after herself—I've known she was a badass I wanted to meet.

The block in Brooklyn where she built Metal is a little forlorn, but when you open the door on the corner of Hoyt and Schermerhorn all you see is gleam. Copper pots hung from wrought iron, burnished aluminum tables, actual silver silverware. Plain white china and black silk linens and lead crystal glasses. Orchids the only adornment.

And the music she plays—metal. Current and vintage. Cattle Decapitation and Skull and even Tool. It's not club-loud, so you don't have to yell over it, but luxury does not equal classical music in this space.

She does tasting menus, and tonight's was fowl-free. But first, cocktails. A tattooed woman with skinny arms and bangs straight across her face asked me what spirits I preferred, and to please give her some adjectives for how I was feeling tonight.

"Whiskey, buoyant and lucky," I said.

I watched her chip ice, squeeze juice, peel, grate, and shake the ingredients in a metallic cylinder, then pour opaque liquid in a glass and add a bronze straw that also served as a spoon. "A Goldfinch," she told me. "Peated Scotch, honeyed scotch, grapefruit, peel of bitter orange, grated ginger, and a chili-oil float."

It tasted like spiced candy saved from a fire. I loved it.

Then twenty rounds of food, a never-empty glass of Prosecco.

Sweet cool pea soup topped with Parmesan foam, flashing with salt.

Bluefin *toro* tartare with a dollop of mustard and soy.

A single sultry Kumamoto oyster reclined on crème

fraîche and *yuzu* gele.

Frog-leg and veal-brain beignets.

Lump crab wrapped in crispy *kataifi*.

A shot glass: avocado mousse, cured salmon in mignonette cubes, maple foam, salmon roe.

A fried calf brain popper.

A bite of octopus with a coin of palm heart cooked in extra-strength dashi.

Langoustine tempura with Iranian saffron.

Fried monkfish liver with sansho that numbed the mouth.

A mini sardine caught in a potato-chip cage.

Folds of soy-milk skin with soy and wasabi.

A single seared scallop with morels, green almonds, white asparagus, and shellfish foam.

Madai with a Japanese risotto made with sea urchin, coconut, and garlic.

Japanese snapper with garlic chives and orange miso.

Veal raviolo topped with truffles shaved into confetti.

A sliver of rib eye atop a funky layer of ripe Langres cheese.

A single portion of lamb slow-cooked to velveteen, bright red inside, over a sauce of miso and espresso.

There was no yellowfin, but we all understood.

Sea bass with sweet peas, as if to second the point, to close where we began.

An airy parfait, layered mango mousse, coconut froth, candied cashews, and rum-soaked brioche.

I touched my flushed face. I felt like I had a fever. Dizzy like I'd been walking on a high wire. Jungle travel. Something important had happened.

We aren't facing scarcity. Not yet.

Yekaterina came over in a white shirt and black pants, Prada, unstained, no chef's coat. Her bright blonde hair was in an abundant, tidy bun. She asked how things were and I simply said astonishing, thank you, and she nodded.

I thought to myself that the Peace Teams and Visibility Teams should all have to eat incredible food and get drunk together, that that might solve the world's problems quicker than talking. But surely some don't drink.

New York City is fabulous in both senses of the word—really great and not to be believed—and watching its citizens extrapolate the weirdness of northern Manhattan to every corner of the boroughs has been my biggest pleasure this week. But to remember why all this began, I asked some birders why they do this.

Jonathan Franzen, novelist and avid birder, said when he first walked in the woods of Central Park and started seeing all the creatures he'd never noticed before, it felt like the trees were hung with ornaments, "One of those rare moments as an adult where the world seems more magical instead of less." This contest, for him, is that on a large scale—there's the idea that you can see them all: there aren't too few to make it easy, not so many to make it impossible. "If there were as many types of birds as there were beetles, there would be no birdwatching. Because it would be hopeless," he told me. Most birders never expect to see them all—but some will, a treasure.

I asked the youngest contestant, thirteen-year-old Anya Ångström, why she watched birds. "Because they're so alive. And I guess I feel somewhat protective of them." It seemed she thought her presence calmed them, let them know at least one person in the world was not just watching them, but watching out for them. Her mother,

Erikha, her partner, touched her daughter's shoulder and said quietly, "I think we know this is all fading. I think we're hungry to touch something before it slips away. Or rather, as it slips away." She said it as if this was not something her daughter yet knew, and as if a quiet voice would continue to keep it from her. A local contestant, Cherie Smith, echoed those sentiments: "There's so much to see that it can trick you into thinking mother nature is doing just fine. But I do the Christmas Bird Count, and I know that a quarter of the bird populations we see in Central Park have declined in recent years by fifty percent. The planet is not doing fine. We're in peril. And then I come to this contest and it's all here. All of it. This doesn't persuade me that we're all okay. It persuades me someone is planning to take an ark or a pod to the moon, preserve just a few of each thing."

Not all contestants mused about the brink of destruction or sci-fi solutions. One handsome man rattled off the seven joys of birding to me: "The joy of beauty; the joy of nature; the joy of scientific discovery; the joy of hunting without bloodshed; the joy of puzzle solving; the joy of collecting; the joy of the Unicorn Effect—you've read about something, seen its picture in books, then you see it in real life. It's like seeing a movie star."

Starr Saphir, who should probably have the last word on all things, told my predecessor here at *The Voice*, Michael Wilson, when she found out her cancer was terminal: "I could keep this up for hundreds of years, I think, and not get tired of it. Birding. Though no one gets to find that out. But my diagnosis, it has heightened my joys. Seeing all this, I love it even more than before, which I didn't know could happen. I have a fury to see as much as possible now." A tiny bird landed on the bench next to them. "House Sparrow," she said. "On the streets of New York. Look how inquisitive the little guy is. If you get tired of looking at the common birds you might as well pack it in, you know."

A few years later we're all feeling this, on a community scale, a grander scale. It's a party, sure, because why not enjoy it while it's still here? But there's sorrow, certainly. Fear. The Dark Mountain Project is holding a Four Next Stages of Grief in the evenings during the contest. They claim most people are still in Denial, but they want to help people move forward, the ones who are ready. Thursday night they had an Anger Fest in the park. People screamed, some emerged battered and bloody. One man, Jonas Bergman, said he understood that he was actually angry at all the humans who lived before him and made bad choices, all the corporations who used resources unwisely, polluted, but he couldn't hit them, "And getting in a fight with a stranger, man, that was cathartic. Don't worry, he was willing. It was good for him too." I moshed with strangers, shoved and spun and charged and collided.

"Fuck Monsanto," someone yelled while punching someone else in the face.

"Fuck 45's dismantling of the EPA!" another screamed.

"Fuck golf courses in Phoenix!" a middle-aged man hollered, while shoving a young rock chick who probably blamed him for the destruction of her environment. Women clawed at each other's faces, a man slapped a woman across the face and she laughed, a man spit blood with glee in his eyes. I didn't participate in the real violence, just the orchestrated swirl of what we used to do to a soundtrack of punk, grunge, hardcore, but that night we swirled in silence. It felt great. I emerged elated.

This morning, I woke up sore. And I felt absolutely no better about the looming apocalypse.

Tonight focused on a bargaining ceremony, where everyone wrote what they would offer to restore health to the planet and its people. Some offered fortunes, lifestyle changes, children. And then they burned their bits of paper, since none of that will work, forcing them to know it. Tomorrow night's Collective Depression promises to be as bleak as it sounds, weeping and gnashing of teeth, yes, but also imagine dozens of people lying lethargic on the lawn, admitting they don't really care to move anymore. People will say what they actually think every day, but usually avoid admitting: it all feels really pointless now. All of it. The last day of the contest, people will seek Collective Acceptance. They will meet in small groups to discuss what they will do in the face of the destruction of the planet and a majority, if not all, of the human and animal species on it. How will they live their lives in the face of disaster? It's not here yet, but it is coming. It is close. Paul Kingsnorth, the founder, told me, "There will be no contracts, but there will be commitments made this week. We at The Dark Mountain Project understand the process can't actually happen this rapidly, you can't fully cycle through grief in a matter of days. But we hope that these ceremonies will help people continue to process these events on their own. We want people to still feel joy, still see beauty, amidst letting go of this world." He imagines some people will agree to blow their fortunes on travel, others will seek to reconcile with their kids, others will vow to make a career change. He's excited. "Why not decide to make the time we have left more fulfilling?

I hope we all do that. This weird festival seems like a good way to start.

As the organizers maybe should have predicted, commercial stands sprouted along every edge of the park. Tables with feathered earrings next to tables with souvenir t-shirts next to tables selling a book that chronicled the making of The Aviary. One table was pre-selling a volume of the winning team's photographs and identifications. There were coffee carts and hot dog carts and pretzel carts on every corner. A Dominican food truck from a few blocks away relocated closer, sold platanos maduros, tostones, mofongo, sancocho, red beans and rice. This afternoon, I ordered the combination plate, then pointed to the green soda in a clear glass bottle because why not, and said Gracias. I set the bottle on the ground near my feet and ate one bite of each of the steaming piles of food balanced in one hand. The spices were intense but not overwhelming, my body warmed from the inside out, I looked at the protestors across the street, read their signs and listened to their chants, Money for Education, not Exploitation; Cooperation not Competition. One woman with long hair, bright clothes, not a replica of a Sixties activist, but close, yelled, "PETA, the Animal Liberation Front, Bite Back, Equanimal, the Animal Defense League, and the Animal Liberation Brigade have united to protest this travesty. Animals are not ours to eat, wear, experiment on, use for entertainment, or abuse in any way. It is not right to use these trapped birds for your amusement. We oppose speciesism, and advocate that all human and non-human animals live free from suffering."

I want that too—even while I eat a plate of pork. I saw how little attention they were drawing. I've seen the amazement in the eyes of all the contestants and onlookers.

And this is the moment when I officially am certain that we are not seeking to save anything, anymore, that what we are doing is saying goodbye.

Later tonight, after I turn in this article—let's see what they cut from the draft before it runs tomorrow morning— I'm going to see Ivan Ríos' World Premiere of *Passenger*, the zombie pigeon flick. Eight o'clock at Radio City Music Hall. Live music tonight only by Tool and Radiohead. They're so old! You going? I will never live anywhere but this island. I'll swim away when it sinks.

XXIII.
Ivan, Alastair, Arrow, and Grant

"Do you want to hear your review in the *New York Times*?"

"I don't know, do I?"

"I'll read it first, and then I'll tell you."

Ivan said, "Thank you," and his voice almost broke. It seemed like such an immense kindness. Last night was raucous and affectionate. Their ease together this morning after intensity was startling. And now, Alastair doing this perfect thing.

Alastair read while their Eco steered them to The Aviary. Ivan couldn't tell from the expression on his face if the words were raving or eviscerating. His face was so calm, held so still.

Finally Alastair said, "You definitely want to hear this. It's by Alma Martinez."

"Oh. She's important," Ivan said.

Alastair read aloud:

I was ready for this.

I'm thinking we all were.

I couldn't possibly bear another zombie flick. Dead-eyed flesh-eating people cannot surprise me with their speed or intelligence or their gore.

But alt-Hitchcock de-extinct zombie pigeons? Revenge fantasy meets science-based science fiction? Yes.

I definitely needed something daft, goofy, irreverent, and very spooky. I haven't had this much fun being scared since, well, *The Birds*. Ivan Ríos even styled Grace Shane like a black Tippi Hedren—though his actress is even more gorgeous, and way smarter and stronger. Great update. This is an intelligent film that is never frosty, a brilliant critique of human hubris when we try to mess with Gaia. (The planet, not the graffiti artist, though I don't recommend you mess with her either.)

In art, it's really hard to strike a balance between campy and nefarious, to make me laugh and care. This film does both. The live moody rock music was such a pleasant additional. Dad Rock, no way—Tool and Radiohead still kill. The live sound definitely dominated; both cinema and concert, this wicked film was enhanced by the over-the-top, excessive pounding and wailing. Having Gaga and Estrella on stage together—they aren't on the soundtrack, just a bonus for the premiere—was a teenaged dream come true for me. And man, we thought Fascist 45 would make Rage Against the Machine reunite, and then we thought surely his impeachment would, and then, of course when 47 was elected, the first Muslim female President of color, but no, it took zombie pigeons to get the band back together. They announced their world tour last night, at Radio City Music Hall. The Rockettes are coming with them. Amazing. Ríos made this miracle happen.

Done in pigeon tones, the screen is filled with blues and grays and rosy pinks with splashes of iridescence and flashes of red. Their eyes are red, and yet we still brought them back! What were we thinking? But we will. We will still do this. And it won't turn out like this, but it won't go as we planned either. This film had to be made.

I'm supposed to sandwich the negative critique in here, but I have nothing bad to say about this flick. It's heavy-handed, sure, but that's what makes it so delicious to watch. And there are enough moments, enough delicate camera angles and perfect actor expressions, that I can tell Ríos knows what he's doing—he's a creator, not just clever.

Turns out, in post-postmodern post-apocalyptic flicks, the apocalypse is averted. And that might be the strength of this movie—it's trying to scare some sense into us, it's trying to talk to us about ourselves. We will be our own undoing. But don't expect to be preached to here. All we are are passengers on this planet, and it will go on without us. Yet two women save the day. There is hope for us all. This film is a mind at work, and I can't wait to see what Ríos does next. Might I request you change my mind about vampires, please? Or write *Jurassic Park XII*? No one can do it but you.

Ivan let out his breath and was already smiling.

"Well it doesn't get any better than that," Alastair said. "Wow."

Alastair flipped through a few other pages. "Just for balance, almost everyone else is calling it derivative, not innovative. Trite. Flat. 'You can't just combine genres and call that art.' Others are saying the Po-Po-Apo genre can no longer surprise. That it was obvious theater goers were just there for the show, and they expect seats to be empty tonight."

"That's bad."

"They aren't the *Times*. So other people didn't get the joke. You're making art for the ones that do, right?"

Ivan looked out the window. They were back in his neighborhood. Apparently, tonight this man was sleeping in his bed. His home. "Yes. But if most people are more excited about Rage on tour than the film, if most think I'm a hipster Hitchcock, not the real deal, I'll never get to make my dragon film. Genetically modified hybrid lizards and birds. Like dinosaurs but better."

"That's the new idea?"

"No. There is no new idea."

"Panned and praised. The best art is, love. You'll come up with something else."

"Or I won't."

"Or you won't." Alastair started tying his bowtie.

Who wears a bowtie to an outdoor event? Ivan was in the clothes he'd packed for himself yesterday, but he'd kept the sharkskin belt. When he threaded it through loops this morning, Alastair half-smiled at him. "And what did they say about you?"

"The rags called me fetching in an ascot and tails. They looked me up, learned the flower fabric was my own design. They called me established in London, up-and-coming in the States."

"Does that feel fair to you?"

"That feels grand. They consider us hitched up now. Our careers linked. We'll have to time the breakup to get us attention when we both need it most."

The scowl crossed Ivan's face before he could decide to cover it or not.

Alastair looked at him with raised eyebrows. "Too much sarcasm? Too self-referential? Sorry. We cannot know how long this will last, Ivan. But I figure we might as well keep going. I'm...I'm having a nice time with you. I cannot promise I won't feck up, possibly massively, but I can promise I won't use you to further my career. At least that. Okay? You?"

"I'd keep going. Is that what you're asking?"

"That is what I'm asking."

"Let's see what happens. You're...worth finding out about."

"That's all anyone can say about anyone." When they pulled up to their gate—the Dyckman Street entrance, Gate Four, sponsored by DiFara—both men were smiling.

Ivan thought he was going to live a different version of yesterday all over again, everyone did, and that's what we all want.

People were looking up, so Arrow looked too, but she didn't see anything in the air. People kept looking so she kept searching, but she saw nothing but layers of buildings, tops of trees, dispersed clouds. "Dad?" she asked, but he shook his head. He didn't know either. With so many eyes to the sky, Arrow thought there must be something she couldn't discern. Then she suspected the people didn't expect to see anything, were looking up in disbelief, looking where they wanted something to be but where nothing was.

People had hands on their faces. People had hands on their chests. People had hands folded in front of them, people clutched their own elbows.

Arrow expected ash. Arrow expected flame. An explosion any second. Everyone seemed to have gotten there a bit earlier than she and her father did. She felt unsteady on her feet, as if the earth might start shaking.

They were standing in front of the Nagel Avenue entrance, Gate Two, which led into Leafed Forest, sponsored by Katz's Deli. Arrow had heard they would see Ivory-billed Woodpeckers today, something thought gone but still here. They were waiting to go inside.

"I don't know," her dad said.

No one looked official, so Arrow asked the first person who made eye contact with her, "What?"

The woman's face shifted, she composed it from horrified to ready-to-explain. In a very soft, clear voice the woman said, "Birds are dead. Not all but many. We aren't sure how or why. They opened the gates this morning, and some had fallen out of the trees."

Arrow thought of the net overhead, the fiber that made a false sky. She wondered if any had flown against it, knowing what was happening. She halfway hoped some beaks were sharp enough to pierce through, escape whatever was coming, but she wondered if that was foolish to wish for.

The pair ahead of Ivan and Alastair both had visceral reactions—he clapped his hands to his face, she shuddered. At first Ivan didn't see it. Alastair next to him said, "What?" and then Ivan saw all the bodies. Birds on the ground.

The person behind him walked immediately to one and laid his hands on it, then lifted it, held it to his chest. A bright red bird, no visible wound. He caught Ivan's eye and shook his head, in case there was any doubt. His partner knelt next to him, and he said, "I've never been so close to one."

Alastair stepped forward, and Ivan grabbed his arm. "What if they're sick?" he said into his ear. He didn't want to start a panic. "What if they're contagious?" He didn't want to be breathing.

Someone in another part of the park screamed loudly enough to travel to them, and all the air shifted. The woman who'd seen it first gasped, and without saying anything to her partner she turned and left. She didn't run, but walked with the next-closest pace.

Alastair didn't look afraid, and Ivan didn't know how he looked. Alastair walked up to a black bird on the ground, a raven or a crow, Ivan could never tell the difference, and Alastair pulled out a feather, a long tail plumage, and put it in his inside breast pocket. Ivan would always remember that gesture, the delicate violence of taking something from something not alive, he would always find it a little gruesome, and something he understood. Brown feathers, white feathers, blue feathers—something terrible had happened. Alastair only took one. *It's not the apocalypse*, Ivan said to himself, but this was the closest he'd seen.

Soon a worker came to usher them out. That's when the questions started. The answer to each was, "We don't know yet."

These people from every nation had never had as much in common as this, facing ruination.

Rumors started—it was the protestors, an in-the-park demonstration gone wrong; some contagion had leaked into the filtration system, and all the contestants should get checked as soon as possible for poison in their lungs; the bird flu, the vaccines didn't work. Then everyone started saying it was a man with a gun, a madman who shot as many as he could.

Men and women wearing gas masks, thick uniforms, began to carry birds out on stretchers. Human-sized stretchers, all they had. They carried lumps out on white fabric, covered by sheets. Contest judges stood to the side, examined each, recorded on a sheet of paper, put a sticker with a code on the sheet. Locals gathered to watch alongside the contestants; people who hadn't been in the park to see them when they were alive watched the bodies get carried out. Cameras flashed like heat lightning.

One contestant, dressed in outdoor gear with a thin, tanned face, said, "I can't stand thinking a Gunnison Sage-grouse or Ivory-billed Woodpecker died in there."

"Or a Condor. Or a Blue-throated Macaw. Or a Whooping Crane or an Oriental Stork," the woman next to him answered, identically dressed, equally thin and sunmarked.

"Or a Galápagos Penguin."

"Or a Kiwi."

"You're naming all the big, impressive birds," a man answered, dressed in a black running suit. "It would be just as big of a loss for a Millerbird or a Kirtland's Warbler to die in there."

Another woman said, "What if he killed one of the Snowy Owls we saw just yesterday?"

"The Wilson's Bird-of-paradise."

"That Resplendent Quetzal."

"I finally saw a Lyre-tailed Honeyguide."

"I loved that little Agile Tit-tyrant. He seemed to be following us."

"That Great Gray Owl. He looked right at me."

A woman standing alone started to cry, smeared makeup down her cheek. Arrow wiped at her eyes though they were dry.

A young woman, maybe a teenager, wearing a skirt and sandals and a t-shirt, wild curly hair, started a recitation. She looked ahead at the air. "I can't say it in the Spanish," she said, "but I know the translation."

Erin Stalcup

The Poet Says Goodbye to the Birds, by Pablo Neruda.

A provincial poet and birder, I come and go about
   the world,
unarmed,
just whistle my way along,
submit
to the sun and its certainty,
to the rain's violin voice,
to the wind's cold syllable.

In the course
of past lives
and preterit disinterments, I've been a creature of
   the elements
and keep on being a corpse in the city:
I cannot abide the niche,
prefer woodlands with startled
pigeons, mud, a branch of
chattering parakeets,
the citadel of the condor, captive
of its implacable heights,
the primordial ooze of the ravines adorned with
   slipperworts.

Yes yes yes yes yes yes,
I'm an incorrigible birder,
cannot reform my ways—
though the birds
do not invite me
to the treetops,

Every Living Species

to the ocean
or the sky,
to their conversation, their banquet,
I invite myself,
watch them
without missing a thing:
yellow-rumped siskins,
dark fishing cormorants
or metallic cowbirds,
nightingales,
vibrant hummingbirds,
quail,
eagles native
to the mountains of Chile,
meadowlarks with pure
and bloody breasts,
wrathful condors
and thrushes,
hovering hawks, hanging from the sky,
finches that taught me their trill
nectar birds and foragers,
blue velvet and white birds,
birds crowned by foam
or simply dressed in sand,
pensive birds that question
the earth and peck at its secret
or attack the giant's bark
and lay open the wood's heart
or build with straw, clay, and rain
the fragrant love nest
or join thousands of their kind
forming body to body, wing to wing

a river of unity and movement,
solitary
severe birds among the rocky crags,
ardent, fleeting,
lusty, erotic birds,
inaccessible in the solitude
of snow and mist,
in the hirsute hostility
of windswept wastes,
or gentle gardeners
or robbers
or blue inventors of music
or tacit witnesses of dawn.

A people's poet,
provincial and birder,
I've wandered the world in search of life:
bird by bird I've come to know the earth:
discovered where fire flames aloft:
the expenditure of energy
and my disinterestedness were rewarded,
even though no one paid me for it,
because I received those wings in my soul
and immobility never held me down.

There was applause, muted and saddened. Arrow said, "Thank you," but wasn't sure if the girl heard.

Arrow's father pulled her into a hug. Arrow kept looking over her shoulder, as if the sharpshooter were going to enter the crowd. Arrow, sobbing beyond speech, wanted to say to her father, then Ed, then her mother, that it was horrific they were gone, unfathomable, but she was glad she saw them. Even if she now had to hold this, despair and disbelief and grief, she wouldn't trade it for yesterday, for all that. Arrow felt abandoned by beauty, but it wasn't all gone, it wouldn't all go, it would leave piece by piece but some would stay, *some might last*. Seeing the thing she'd been dreading helped her know it wouldn't happen all at once.

And she decided for her child that he or she should see it. Whatever happened next felt worth it to Arrow. She'd rather be here to see it than not. She hadn't known for sure until now. She knew the worst-case scenarios. Best-case? A child in love with the world, all of it. A child willing to see how we all say goodbye, how we survive. A child willing to see what no other generation yet had—the end of it all. Her father held onto her and kept saying, "I'm sorry. Arrow, I'm just so sorry." She wondered if she'd ever heard him say that before.

Ivan had his arm around Alastair's shoulder. After the nights they'd had together, tenderness that revealed how tender each was, gentleness which showed how sore each was, something they hadn't known they'd needed, seeing that horror hollowed each out all over again and solidified what was about to happen. Standing there, both looking forward, Ivan asked Alastair to move in. "We can get a nicer place if you don't like mine. Just not too nice. Let's stay here until this island is underwater," he said, and Alastair agreed. "Why not move fast?" Alastair said. "Why wait?" They didn't know that day that they would be together until their deaths; no one can see forward to their own demise. The raven feather Alastair had plucked would be the only real one in his collection that he would release in six months, a New York premiere, to wild acclaim. Ivan wouldn't make another film for ten years. Every year his husband would make clothes that baffled and delighted people, and every year he would abandon every idea he had. But all along Ivan and Alastair would push each other to make their best art, to be sillier and more serious, and finally Ivan would have an idea he didn't renounce: a mestizaje of animals, sci-fi fast-forward evolution where monkeys and birds combined, giraffes and elephants, bears and tigers, cats and fish, ridiculous and impossible and hysterical, a film filled with fantastical hybrid creatures better able to adapt to a heating planet than humans, the only ones who couldn't blend. It was funny and tragic and a blockbuster. For the rest of their lives, both men's work would be praised and lambasted for how playful and mournful it was. They would push each other to enhance that, get darker and lighter, both, simultaneously, in the same space. "You're the artist," each would say to the other. "I'm just a hobbyist." Neither agreed.

When Arrow returned home, she made hopeful choices. As soon as she arrived in her hometown, it felt too small for her. Instead of leaving, she decided to expand it herself.

She went to her parents' house for dinner and told her mother she was pregnant. Her father's face was concerned, but her mother's was exuberant. She hugged Arrow and said she was mighty young, but this was the best news. And she knew she'd be a wonderful mother. Arrow needed her mom to think that.

Arrow admitted she hadn't planned to keep it—clearly a thought that hadn't occurred to Siobhan—but she'd changed her mind. Her father cried while they hugged and said he was glad. "I would have understood," he said. "I thought about it, and I understood, and it was your choice, not mine, but I think this will be good for all of us." Siobhan watched with her hands in front of her face.

Arrow talked to them about ways to make her bedroom feel like hers as an adult, not as a child, how to make the spare bedroom a nursery. She said she didn't know how long she'd stay, but she liked the idea of her child growing up around grandparents.

The next day she told Ed. At first, he looked confused, like he didn't know what on earth he was supposed to say, but then it was as if his face cracked open. All delight. Everyone was so happy. He spun her around and around, and Arrow was not small, but sometimes Ed made her feel small, in a good way.

"Let's get married!" he said.

"What?"

He stopped, thought about what he was going to say. That meant a lot to Arrow, that he was trying to make the moment matter, even if off the cuff. "When I first saw you I thought, *That one. That's the one I want.* I think we would make a great family. Arrow, will you marry me?"

Arrow often felt full of dread, but that wasn't the only thing she felt.

Ed said he wanted to take her to the reservation, show her Hopi, have her meet his grandparents and see where he spent time as a child. The mesas on the side of the road looked like fossilized beasts. The rays reflecting were a slightly different timbre, slightly different texture—what shone forth from that stone was heavier than the waves that hit it. The mesas were solid as the mountain Arrow saw nearly every day of her life, as deeply rooted, the earth sculptural yet flat on top as if it wanted to be hospitable as well as monumental. Arrow wondered how far you could see from up there.

His grandparents lived in a trailer at the base of First Mesa, ramshackle on the outside but cozy and comfortable inside. They wore jeans and simple shirts. They had slight accents that felt familiar to Arrow, felt like Arizona. Ed greeted them in Hopi then they all switched to English. Ed was an only child. The lineage stopped here. The grandparents were reserved. They congratulated them. They said they hoped Ed would teach the child Hopi, would bring the child to visit, show him or her where their people were from. "We've always been here," the grandmother said. "Your child can be as Hopi as he or she wants to be," the grandfather said. "Even living in a city." They said they'd always have the trailer to visit, always a home at Hopi. They offered Arrow piki bread, and she loved the intensity of flavor even in such a thin wafer and the grandmother said even boys were making it now, and they would teach the child, if the child wanted to learn. "I grew the corn and ground it myself," she said with a small smile. Blue corn still grew even in the increased heat, and Arrow wondered if it always would. She and Ed bought rings at a roadside stand, made by locals.

Arrow didn't think of the birds the day her child was born, a girl, Whitman Sullivan Talayumptewa, but Grant did. He thought of the bodies that lay on the ground that day and reminded himself that many more bodies still flew on the other side of the fence they'd stood against. He held his granddaughter fourth, after her mother and then her father then his wife, and as his wife handed her over to him, the woman he still loved, very much, he hoped for the best. He said to Arrow that he would help raise this child as best he could for as long as he could. None of them were dry-eyed. Ed's parents held the child next and agreed to help raise her. Whitman, fourth-generation Arizonan on Arrow's side, going back much further on Ed's, and she looked from the moment she was born like exactly half of each of them.

Arrow thought of the birds two years later, when she finally graduated with a degree in education and walked into her classroom. Fifth grade. A cooperative had formed in Flagstaff, education for the future that was to come: the truth about American history early on, truth about environmental destruction, hoping to raise a generation ready to manage all that was ahead. As Arrow turned the door handle, she was submerged in memories of dead birds, fallen bundles of bodies not meant to fall. She shuddered and felt terror, and she walked through the door anyway and wondered if everyone was pushing on through fear. She wondered if their plan would work—tell children the truth, and see what they would do with alarm fully acknowledged. Face the destruction to come. What has always been and will be.

That night a portion of the mountain burned and they all went to watch and mourn, three generations together to see it. The flames were crimson and saffron against cobalt. "It could be worse," they said. Ed was up there fighting it. Her father handed her a beer and Arrow drank it with her daughter on her lap, her mother on one side, mother-in-law on the other. A flock of jays flew overhead, away from the blaze. Steller's. That group can be called a party, or a scold, Arrow knew. Looking at her mountain, full of sorrow at seeing what she has always dreaded, Arrow said, "It

Erin Stalcup

finally happened. Now we don't have to keep waiting for it." Then, "It will recover."

Sunday, September 10th, 2023

Day Three of Canon and Cabela's
Birds of the World
Timed Birding Contest

XXIV.
Interview with "The Wizard"
by Hazel Imafidon
for the *New York Times*

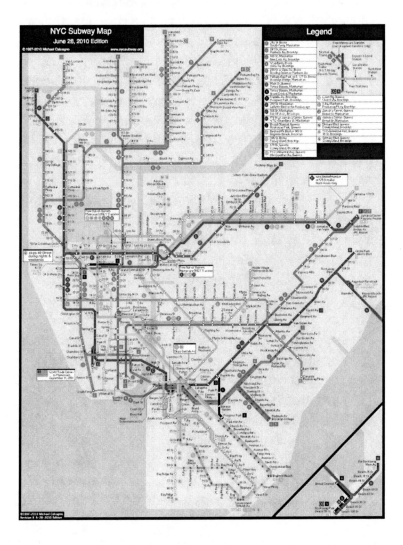

We thought it was the bird flu. We thought maybe science didn't get it right, maybe inoculations that usually take fourteen days can't be made to work in fourteen hours. Maybe the hydrogen-fuel-cell water wasn't as potable as engineers thought. We blamed the protestors: surely one of them got inside, showed us what a bad idea this was after all. Ecoterrorism to somehow save the planet. Then we thought it was a crazed shooter: one guy, one gun, an automatic that fired lots of ammo really quickly. Of course that's how things would get ruined in the United States.

In a city of stop-and-frisk back in full effect we don't think to fear nature. Sure, tides are rising, every summer several die of heat, the winters have been wicked, but this is Manhattan. We fear people—the criminals, and the police. But how did this simulacrum of Mother Nature reach stasis again?

It would be easier if it were a rifle. That tragedy, we've gotten used to. If it's a lone gunman, we get to blame a sicko instead of systemic problems, an individual rather than structural inadequacies. But it turns out the rumors were wrong. It turns out technology is not the solution to the problem technology got us into. Those of you planning to live in pods on Mars—well, maybe it's good we experimented with birds first. And this fact—that our attempts to control an ever-threatening nature failed— that's not a narrative we've told ourselves yet.

I went to go see the person they call The Wizard, to find out what really happened.

"I'm the Systems Analyst for The Aviary," Alice Jameson told me. "That means I track each climate zone, numbers like humidity, percentage of oxygen in the air, toxins, and make adjustments to keep each space at optimal balance for the birds inside. Water purity, amount of snowfall, things like that."

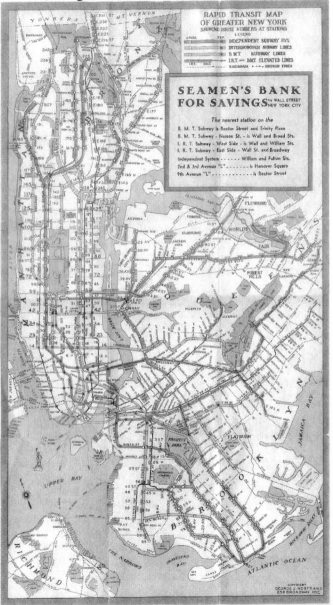

Her office is filled with posters covering every space that isn't a machine or a screen. Old New York City subway line maps, and bird taxonomy charts. I decide not to ask about that first. My recorder is on. Ms. Jameson has agreed to be taped.

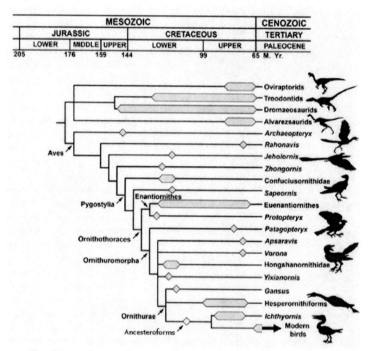

MESOZOIC					CENOZOIC
JURASSIC			CRETACEOUS		TERTIARY
LOWER	MIDDLE	UPPER	LOWER	UPPER	PALEOCENE
205	176	159	144	99	65 M. Yr.

Q: "So what happened?" I ask instead. "What went wrong?"

A: "We didn't calculate something correctly. At first, we thought we'd asphyxiated the birds. For the oxygen level for this combination of people and animals, we'd calculated two thousand humans and just over 110,000 birds, with casual exercise for all—walking, short flights—and we'd originally thought maybe the creatures' respiration was higher than we'd planned. More activity. But I ran that calculation this morning, and that's not the problem. We knew pigeons had started roosting on top of the fiber-optic canopy, and we thought maybe they'd shaded The Aviary too much, but they were removed yesterday, just liked I'd asked, so it wasn't that."

Q: "City pigeons lived on top of this magic cage? And someone had to kill the birds who live here to protect the birds that live here but shouldn't?"

A: "Yes. But that went well. It wasn't any of what we first thought. Turns out, we didn't give them enough food, it seems. We thought they had plenty. Birds can starve to death within hours, we knew that, they need constant influx of nourishment because of their metabolisms. It seems we didn't get those numbers just right for every species."

Q: "So they aren't all gone?"

A: "It seems we lost about three thousand birds. So just under three percent."

Q: "Is that an acceptable margin of error?"

A: "No. When the park is functioning as a museum, maybe. Long term. Per year. That's not ideal, but we can sustain that level of replacement. Twice a year, maybe. Certainly not every other day, like in this case. And not with two thousand contestants watching. Millions all over the globe, if not billions. Losing that many at once. Well. It's been a public relations nightmare. I'm not sure we'll ever recover. Birds are the barometer of the world, the canary on a miner's shoulder as he descends. They're being killed faster in here than they're being killed out there. That was not the plan."

Q: "You're a scientist, right?"

A: "Of course. PhD in engineering, mechanical, structural, and environmental, specialty in robotics and

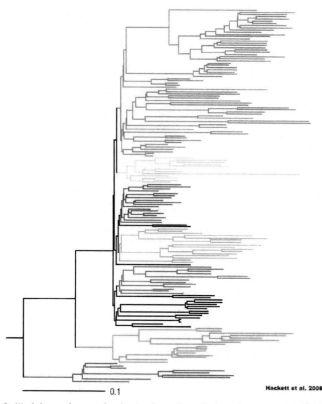

Fig. 3. ML phylogram demonstrating the short internodes at the base of Neoaves and highlighting certain extreme examples of rate variation across avian lineages. Colors are as in Fig. 2. Scale bar indicates substitutions per site. Figure S1 shows the phylogram with taxon names.

0.1

systems analysis, MIT. Bachelor's in ornithology from Yale. It seemed I'd be perfect for this job."

Q: "But you weren't hired for the advertising, damage-control part, right?"

A: "Certainly not. Others are handling that."

Q: "Why are they letting you talk to me?"

A: "They don't know you're here."

Q: "You've already been fired?"

A: "Oh, yes. Rightly so, I should say. This isn't all on my shoulders, but I never should have let this happen."

Q: "So what do you want people to know?"

A: "Maybe this whole thing was a mistake. Maybe we can't be the ones to preserve things. Maybe we really just have to let go of whatever can't save itself."

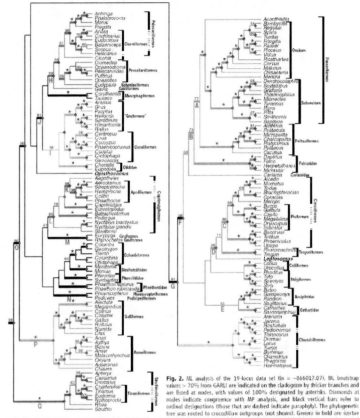

Fig. 2. ML analysis of the 19-locus data set (ln = −866017.07), ML bootstrap values > 70% from GARLI are indicated on the cladogram by thicker branches and are listed at nodes, with values of 100% designated by asterisks. Diamonds at nodes indicate congruence with MP analysis, and black vertical bars refer to ordinal designations (those in bold indicate paraphyly). The phylogenetic tree was rooted to crocodilian outgroups (not shown). Genera in bold are icertae sedis. Branch colors represent major clades supported in this study: land birds (green), charadriiforms (yellow), water birds (blue), core gruiforms and cuckoos (gray), apodiforms and caprimulgiforms (brown), galloanserae (orange), and paleognaths (purple). Large capital letters indicate groups discussed in the text and Fig. 1. Hackett et al. 2008

Q: "That's bleak."

A: "Yes. But we really blew it. And The Aviary hired the best of the best. I mean, if we can't do it, no one can. So maybe we shouldn't. Technology will be part of the solution, but we can't use science to fix nature."

Q: "Are you scared?"

A: "Right now I'm too sad to be scared. Maybe eventually. They say anger is stronger than fear, but I can only be mad at myself at this point."

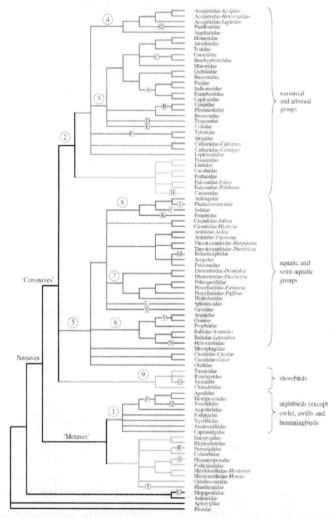

Figure 1. Family-level relationships within Neoaves estimated by Bayesian analysis of five nuclear genes (5007 nucleotide positions). Nodes that received a posterior probability value of less than 95% have been collapsed. Note that the branch lengths are not proportional to the number of nucleotide substitutions along each branch. Neoavian families fall into a few reciprocally monophyletic clades (coloured) that roughly correspond to ecological adaptations of extant taxa. Nodal numbers correspond to clades discussed in the text. Letters in boxes, referring to table 3 in the electronic supplementary material, indicate fossil calibration points. Ericson et al. 2006

Q: "The thought that we are simply highly sentient organisms, no more or less important, meaning no more special, meaning no more blessed, than any other organism on the planet— that thought, does it comfort you?"

A: "We are an invasive species. That does not comfort me. We are the most technologically advanced species. It doesn't seem that will save us. That doesn't comfort me. That the planet, as an ecosystem, won't mourn us any more or less than the loss of wolves or a specific species of butterfly, that makes me feel slightly better."

Q: "Okay. Moving on. What's up with all the posters?"

A: "I like schematics. I like thinking about how things work. How things are arranged. The differences between methodologies. Birds have been more or less then same for centuries, at least. But we classify them differently at different times. The subway tunnels have been more or less the same for decades, we've added and removed a few lines, but how we show how to get from where to where has changed, depending on the renderer. They used the latest tree for

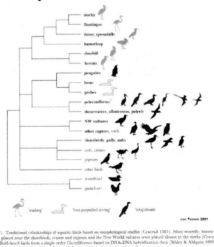

Figure 1. Traditional relationships of aquatic birds based on morphological studies (Cracraft 1981). More recently, herons were instead placed near the shorebirds, cranes and rognons and the New World vultures were placed closer to the storks (Cracraft 1988). Bald-faced birds form a single order Ciconiiformes based on DNA-DNA hybridization data (Sibley & Ahlquist 1990). Pelecaniformes include the pelicans, frigate birds, tropic birds, darters, boobies and cormorants.

the guidebook, the one that uses genome sequencing to decide who's related to whom, not similarities in features. So, we used to think pelagic tropicbirds were related to pelicans and cormorants because they have totipalmate feet, all four toes are webbed, not just three, but turns out, they aren't related at all, any of them. They evolved that kind of webbing separately. So that tree, that tree, and that one are all wrong. And the subway map all the contestants got is the latest, but I think some of the older ones are more stylish. They say the same thing, but they say it better."

Q: "Why keep the wrong ones? The out-of-date ones?"

A: "Beauty. And they'll all be proven wrong eventually. We don't determine how the world is. We just change our ways of describing the world."

Q: "Thank you for talking to me," I said. I had no questions left.

A: "I'm so sorry," she said.

Q: "I am too," I agreed. And I didn't know whether to say it was her fault, or not.

A: "I watched it all," she said. "Through each camera." She pointed to the screens, still turned on, still showing birds acting like birds, flying, scratching, eating, drinking, staring into the air. She showed me a white and gray bird with a black cap that lifted and landed, lifted and landed, like it was looking for something.

Q: "Do they have enough food now?"

A: "Yes. Twice as much as they need. At least. We won't make that mistake again. Arctic Tern," she said, before switching cameras. A green, red, and blue bird looked right into the lens and she said it was a Prince Rusapoli's Turaco. A plain brown bird was a Firewood Gatherer. A tiny spotted thing was a Predicted Antwren.

Q: "Can I see the Ivory-Billed Woodpeckers? Please?"

A: The camera showed one, eating bugs out of a plastic bin, not hunting.

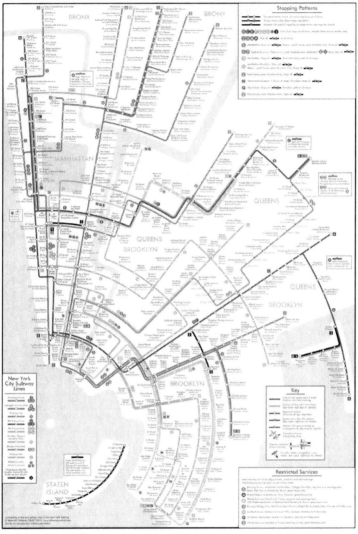

Q: "One?"

A: She nodded. Then she stopped naming, turned on every camera in the park at once so that every huge screen in the small space was a mosaic. We watched empty trees and penguins and eagles and jays and bright things I could never name and plain things I couldn't either. A wing. A beak. An eye. A leg on a branch. How magnificent it almost was, all of them here together. How magnificent it still was. A bird floating on a lake. A flying bird. A feeding bird. A bird making a nest out of sticks and twigs and the wrapped wire handles of lunch sacks and torn pieces of paper.

Acknowledgments

Thank you to all the scientists researching climate change—both the problem, and potential solutions. Thank you to every artist who has made me glad to be alive. Thank you to the readers of earlier drafts of this novel, both for radically improving it, and for also letting it be the strange book I wanted it to be: Courtney Craggett, Andy Briseño, Toni Jensen, and Sidney Thompson. Thank you to Kyle McCord and Nick Courtright for running a rigorous press that also feels like a family, and for all the ways you support your writers and all writers. Thank you to the vast and crucial community of Warren Wilson graduates and faculty who have shaped the ways I think about art and teaching and community itself. Thank you to the NAU students in my novel-writing class (470 spring 2017!) who inspired me to not give up on this book—and thank you to all of my students, for always inspiring me not to give up on humanity. Get better than me, best me. You will. You're going to build a better world.

Justin, you're the best thing that ever happened to me. Thalia, you're the best thing that ever happened to us. I wrote this book for you and with hopes for your future, and I wrote it because I was fortunate to have the mother and father and childhood I had. Thank you for everything you've taught me about land, ponderosas, and family, mom and dad.

About Gold Wake Press

Gold Wake Press, an independent publisher, is curated by Nick Courtright and Kyle McCord. All Gold Wake titles are available at amazon.com, barnesandnoble.com, and via order from your local bookstore. Learn more at goldwake.com.

Available Titles:

Glenn Shaheen's *Carnivalia*
Frances Cannon's *The High and Lows of Shapeshift Ma and Big-Little Frank*
Eileen G'Sell's *Life After Rugby*
Justin Bigos' *Mad River*
Kelly Magee's *The Neighborhood*
Kyle Flak's *I Am Sorry for Everything in the Whole Entire Universe*
David Wojciechowski's *Dreams I Never Told You & Letters I Never Sent*
Keith Montesano's *Housefire Elegies*
Mary Quade's *Local Extinctions*
Adam Crittenden's *Blood Eagle*
Lesley Jenike's *Holy Island*
Mary Buchinger Bodwell's *Aerialist*
Becca J. R. Lachman's *Other Acreage*
Joshua Butts' *New to the Lost Coast*
Tasha Cotter's *Some Churches*
Hannah Stephenson's *In the Kettle, the Shriek*
Nick Courtright's *Let There Be Light*

Kyle McCord's *You Are Indeed an Elk, but This Is Not the Forest You Were Born to Graze*

Kathleen Rooney's *Robinson Alone*

Erin Elizabeth Smith's *The Naming of Strays*

About the Author

Erin Stalcup is also the author of the story collection *And Yet It Moves* (Indiana University Press, 2016). Erin received her MFA from Warren Wilson College's Program for Writers. After teaching in community colleges, large state universities, small liberal arts schools, and prisons in New York, North Carolina, and Texas, Erin now teaches creative writing at her alma mater, Northern Arizona University, in her hometown of Flagstaff. Erin's fiction has appeared in *The Kenyon Review*, *Kenyon Review Online*, *The Sun*, and elsewhere, and her nonfiction about her teaching experiences was listed as a Notable Essay in *Best American Essays 2016*. Erin is currently expanding that essay into a memoir, and editing a book of essays about creative writing pedagogy. Erin cofounded and coedits *Waxwing*: waxwingmag.org. You can read some of her other work at erinstalcup.com.

CPSIA information can be obtained
at www.ICGtesting.com
Printed in the USA
FSOW02n0937230817
37703FS